ONE GOOD MOVE

HAVEN HARBOR SERIES BOOK ONE

LILY MILLER

ABOUT THE BOOK

Let me make one thing clear: I did *not* fly to Miami for a one-night stand. However, I did follow a devastatingly handsome man into a hotel office and do ridiculously filthy things with him on top of a desk. It didn't matter that he worked for a rival company because I had no plans to stick around. Or ever see him again.

But it turns out Grayson Ford is hard to forget. And now, two years later, my one-night stand is suddenly back in my life. Not only is he my shirtless, drop-dead gorgeous new neighbor, but he is also my brother's best friend—which makes me off-limits. Try telling that to Grayson, with his piercing dark eyes and a smirk that gets him whatever he wants. Like me, that night in Miami.

Grayson is very hard to resist, but I moved back home to Reed Point to help my family, not cause more problems.

Our *friendship* works for a little while, but our chemistry is undeniable. It doesn't take long before we both decide that one night wasn't enough. And the more secret nights I spend with him, the more I want a life with him.

I came back to this town to make things right, but my brother will never forgive me if he finds out the truth. I never planned to fall this hard, never mind find love. All I wanted to do was make One Good Move.

Copyright © 2023 by Lily Miller

All rights reserved.

No part of this book may be reproduced in any form or by any electronic or mechanical means, including information storage and retrieval systems, without written permission from the author, except for the use of brief quotations in a book review.

This book is a work of fiction. Names, characters, places and incidents are products of the author's imagination or are used fictitiously. Any resemblance to actual events or locales or persons, living or dead, is entirely coincidental.

One Good Move

Cover photo: Rebecca Crawford, Bare Moments Photography

Cover models: Sami and Alex

Cover design: Kim Wilson, Kiwi Cover Design

Editing: Carolyn De Melo

Publicity: Love Notes PR

PLAYLIST

1. Cover Me Up—Morgan Wallen
2. Blindsided—Kelsea Ballerini
3. World on Fire—Nate Smith
4. Me + All Your Reasons—Morgan Wallen
5. You—Dan + Shay
6. Daylight—Harry Styles
7. Hope That's True—Morgan Wallen
8. Burn It Down—Parker McCollum
9. Psychopath—Morgan Wade
10. Outskirts—Sam Hunt
11. Dangerous—Morgan Wallen
12. Give Me Love—Ed Sheeran
13. In the Woulds—BRELAND, Chase Rice, Lauren Alaina
14. Pick Me Up—Gabby Barrett
15. I'm Yours—Brent Anderson
16. Thinking out Loud—Ed Sheeran
17. Beautiful Crazy—Luke Combs
18. Last Night—Morgan Wallen

19. Can't Break Up Now—Old Dominion, Megan Moroney

*To the girls who love
kissing books,
a happily-ever-after,
and who walk and read at the same time.
This one's for you.
xx*

PROLOGUE

WHAT THE FUCK IS SHE DOING TO ME?

Grayson

Sierra sips back the last drops of her strawberry mojito then licks her lips. "Why is it so hot in here? It's like 3 billion degrees."

"It's definitely hot," I agree, silently reminding myself that we're talking about the club, not Sierra. The light sheen of sweat on my skin has nothing to do with the way she looks in that hot-as-fuck form-fitting dress and everything to do with this muggy Miami night. Definitely.

Sierra twists her long, blonde hair in one hand and lifts it from her neck, holding it there as she fans herself. A few strands fall loose, and I have to stop myself from reaching over and brushing them from her bare shoulder. Instead, I slide an ice-cold glass of water across the table towards her. Tonight has been incredible. It's one of the best nights I've ever had with a woman. Sierra and I have danced. We've talked. We've laughed continuously. And so far, we have managed to ignore this spark that has been kindling between us all night. It's for the best, I remind myself. No need to complicate things.

But still, there's a part of me that is itching to kiss her. And I will, before the night is over. I know myself.

As Sierra sips her water and scans the Miami hotspot, my eyes rake over the fuchsia dress clinging to her body. She's beautiful. Golden-blonde hair, eyes the color of coffee framed by long, dark lashes and a splatter of freckles across the bridge of her nose. Her lips are soft and pillowy, and when she aims her playful grin in my direction, I can feel my heart start to race.

Goosebumps erupt over my skin.

What the fuck is she doing to me?

She's also flirty and easy-going and way too much fun to talk to. I can already see that she's nothing like Layla.

Sierra is the kind of girl you play for keeps. She's not a one-night stand. Lately, one night is about as far as my relationships go. But after tonight, I'm beginning to wonder if it might be time to change that. I know Sierra should be off-limits, but damn do I want to kiss her.

Do I invite her back to my hotel room, or is that too much for a girl I only met three days ago?

And if I do ask her, will she say yes?

I reach across the table, taking her hand. "One more dance." It's not a question. I want her in my arms, and this is the best way to make that happen.

"To this song?" Sierra scrunches up her nose and for the record, it's cute as hell. I laugh and pull her off the stool, noticing the way she fights back a smile. "My friends would never let me live it down if they caught me dancing to *this*."

"Well, luckily for me, they're not here," I grin. "There's a first time for everything." *It's not the only first I'd like to have with her tonight.*

Sierra shakes her head but follows me onto the crowded dance floor. I slip my arms around her waist, then pull her into my chest. Her hands move to the nape of my neck, and I gaze down at her hips squared with mine. The scent of her shampoo fills my nose: coconut and a summer breeze. It is uniquely Sierra. I inhale it in, letting it linger for as long as I can, then dip my face so my mouth is by her ear.

"Change your mind on Santana?" I tease.

She looks up at me with her pretty eyes, pressing her hand against the back of my neck to pull my face closer to hers.

"When pigs fly," she sasses into my ear as we sway to the Latin music pumping through the speakers.

I chuckle and she tips her head back to look at me, staring at me like she's daring me to kiss her. I think about it for a split second but manage to resist, knowing that when I do kiss her perfect pink lips, I won't be able to stop.

So far there is nothing I don't like about Sierra. Besides the obvious—she's ridiculously gorgeous—Sierra is a ray of fucking sunshine. Her laugh is contagious. She's a natural at making small talk. Even though I met her all of 72 hours ago, I feel like I've known her for a lifetime. She isn't a wallflower like some girls. People notice her when she walks into a room—I've seen the stares all weekend.

The song changes but we keep dancing. *Close.* She's so close to me that I'm sure she can feel my cock in my pants pressed against her hip. Our hands keep finding ways to touch each other—mine drifting to the area just above her ass, hers sliding from my pecs to my abs.

The fight in me is gone. I need a quick taste of her, just for a second, and then I'll stop, and I'll keep my mouth to myself for the rest of the night.

Her eyes find mine and she flashes me a devastatingly pretty smile—breezy, relaxed, happy. I soak it in, heart hammering, placing my hand on the curve of her jaw. Then

I bend forward to kiss her. I'm millimeters from her lips when the guy dancing next to us knocks into her. His shoulder collides with Sierra's, and I grab her elbow to stop her from falling.

"I'm so sorry," the six-foot-something guy yells over the music. *Yeah, I am too, buddy.*

Moment lost.

"You okay? Do you want to sit down?" I look around the crowded room, noticing that the table we'd been sitting at is now taken. "Or we could get out of here, walk the beach back to our hotel?"

Sierra shifts her gaze to her feet and then back to me, her cheeks flush. She's sexy as hell. "Fresh air sounds good."

I nod and take her hand, guiding her towards the exit. It's nearly 1 a.m. and when we step outside the clear summer sky is lit by a million twinkling stars above us. In the distance is the sound of waves breaking into shore.

It's quiet when we get back to The Peninsula Hotel, with a few people milling about in the lobby and a few more sitting in the upscale bar just past reception. Sierra's hand is still tightly clasped in mine, where it has been since we walked out of the club. It isn't nearly enough, not when I came so close to kissing her before we were interrupted on the dance floor. I can't help but wonder where we'd be right now if I'd gotten a taste of her.

Fuck it. I need to know what her lips feel like.

I pull her with me and in five long strides we're standing in a hallway, just the two of us. I look down at her and when she giggles and stares back at me with that look in her eyes, pushing her up against the nearest wall feels like the best idea I've ever had.

Framing her face in my hands, I lift her chin, forcing her eyes to lock on mine. They sparkle—a hint that she wants this too. My heart jumps in my chest, and then I lean in and do what I've wanted to do all night. What I've been wanting to do all damn weekend.

I kiss her.

My lips crash into hers and she seals her mouth to mine, kissing me back, her hands clinging to the fabric of my shirt. She wants this just as much as I do.

My tongue swipes along her bottom lip, begging for entry, and she opens for me, sweeping her tongue against mine. She tastes so good, sweet and citrusy like the mojito she was drinking earlier. I. Am. Done. I've been dying for this all night, and now that it's finally happening it's mind-blowing. I've never experienced a kiss like this, and I probably never will again.

She moans when I suck on her tongue and the sound goes straight to my cock, settling between my thighs where every drop of blood in my body has rushed to. God, this kiss is earth-shattering. It's so incredible I almost forgot that we're in public, that anybody could walk by and see us.

I decide to fix that, tearing my mouth away from Sierra's just long enough to pull her towards a door that reads "Employees Only." I get lucky when I turn the knob and the door opens to a small, dimly lit office. I'd rather be laying her out on the bed in my hotel room, but I want her too badly right now to care. I close the door behind us and flick the lock, then back Sierra up against it and kiss her hard.

"Oh God, Grayson. What are we doing?" she asks when my mouth moves to her neck, my hands teasing the hem of her skirt.

"I know exactly what I'm doing, and make no mistake, Sierra, I am very good at it," I reply cockily.

"Prove it," she demands.

Happily.

I clasp the back of her neck with one hand as I push my hips into hers, holding her body tight against mine while I drag her mouth towards my lips. My other hand is on the curve of her hip, that sexy curve that's fucking incredible. I'm going to make her see stars with this kiss—I hope she's fucking ready. I rock into her with my dick as she grips my ass, her fingernails digging into the denim, then my mouth is on hers again. My tongue sweeps skillfully inside, dancing with hers in smooth, soft strokes. She moans the sexiest sound and I fight the urge to haul her legs around my waist and fuck her senseless. Her coconut scent swirls in the air around me, filling my lungs.

Goddamn.

She tastes so good.

More.

I need more.

I run my hand down her hip, not stopping until it's between her legs. Slipping her panties to the side, I tease her opening, slipping my fingers into her, one and then two, hearing her moan. "So wet for me."

Sierra has her head thrown back against the door, her breathing labored and her back arched. I slide her dress up her body, wanting to see more of her, and she raises her arms to help me remove the fuchsia fabric. Her bra and panties go next. Fuck me. Her body is perfect, and all I want is to be inside of it. My cock swells even more, desperate to plunge into her.

"Come here, Grayson," she orders, and I'm only too happy to obey. Her breath hitches when my hand finds her breast, pinching her nipple. "Grayson..."

Removing my hand from her, I quickly undo the top three buttons of my shirt and then peel it over my head. I work my jeans and boxers off next, watching her eyes widen as my cock springs free. She swallows as I take my dick in my hand, fisting my shaft.

"You can have every inch, Sierra. It's all yours if you want it," I tell her. She licks her lips and nods, eyes wide.

Holy fucking hell.

Her perfect pink lips are wet.

She's naked and waiting for me.

Sierra's arms wrap around me as I lift her up, walk across the room and set her ass down on the desk. Her legs lock around my hips and my erection finds her center, aching to be buried inside of her.

I take my time kissing her, her hands tugging at my hair before I line myself up and sink home.

"Oh my God," she murmurs, my cock buried deep. "More."

I ease out slowly, then rock back into her, our bodies sticky with sweat. I do it again, over and over, my hands firmly planted on either side of her on the desk, finding that perfect pace as I whisper filthy things into her ear. The pressure builds at the base of my spine, so intense that every muscle in my body is beginning to tremble.

My body vibrates as she tightens around my dick and cries out my name. I see stars as my own orgasm crashes through me, my cock pressed deep inside of her, her channel pulsing around my length.

"Fuck, Sierra," I curse, my face buried in her neck. My body trembles as I spill inside of her, my chest heaving against hers.

I am wrecked.

Sierra opens her eyes, looking sex-drunk and sated. A small smile tips the corners of her lips and I kiss her, her body still connected to mine.

That was the best sex of my life. I can't help but wonder

what it would be like if we fucked in my bedroom for hours instead of flat against a desk.

Everything in me wants to know.

She breaks the kiss. "Grayson," she whispers. "I'm—"

She stops, clears her throat. She seems nervous now, her expression is hard to read.

I make no move to let her go until she begins to untangle herself from me. I watch her bend down and pick up her clothes, quickly slipping on her panties, her bra, then her dress.

Sierra has thrown on her clothes like the place is on fire. My heart gallops as I get dressed, fumbling with the button on my pants and hopping into my shoes. I catch her by her arm before she has the chance to leave. "Sierra, wait. We should—"

She tenses. "I have to go."

"No, you don't." I face her, taking her hand in mine. "You're not leaving until we talk." Her hair is tousled, her cheeks flush and her soft pink lips are slightly swollen from my kisses. Fuck, that is hot. "Look, if I—"

"It's not you, it's me, Grayson." *Oh, fuck that.* That bullshit isn't going to fly with me.

"That was reckless," she says, finally stopping to look at me. "We didn't even use a condom."

Shit. "Are you—?"

"I'm on the pill. And it's been months since I've been with anyone. I'm good."

I blow out a breath. She's right. What the fuck was I thinking?

"I'm clean too," I reassure her. "Listen, I didn't expect things to go that far. I had a great time with you tonight and—"

She tugs her hand out of mine, then straightens the strap of her dress on her shoulder.

"I had a good time too, but that's all this was, Grayson. A good time. *One* time. Nothing more. Understand?"

"Fuck, Sierra." Her eyes seem to look everywhere in the room except at me. "I'm not asking you to get married and have my babies, but I'm not letting you just storm out of here without talking to me."

The tension between us is practically buzzing. It feels like whiplash, going from what we just did on the desk behind me to... this. Don't get me wrong, I'm not exactly a stranger to random hookups. But tonight with Sierra somehow felt different. For starters, I've never been this fucking turned on by anyone. I've never let myself get so worked up over a woman I barely know.

"Look, if you want to just leave here and not make this a thing... I get it," I tell her. "Even though I really wish that wasn't the case. But at least let me walk you to your room."

Her expression remains guarded, but she finally gives me a small nod. "Fine."

I'm confused as hell, but I'm not going to push her. We slip out of the room and back into the hallway, crossing the nearly-empty lobby to the elevator. We stand together in silence, waiting for the elevator doors to open. I glance at Sierra, trying to read her, but she seems determined to avoid eye contact.

When we reach her door, she stops to dig her key card out of her purse. She opens the door, then pauses and finally looks up at me. "Bye, Grayson. I..." she stops, seeming unsure. "Thanks for a really fun night," she says with a smile.

"I had a great time too."

I lean in and press a kiss to her cheek, and she gives me a small wave before disappearing into her room.

A few minutes later, I'm in my own hotel room, alone, thinking about Sierra. This isn't how I wanted the weekend to end. I had fun with her. For the first time in years, I actually wanted a second date. And now what? I'm supposed to leave Miami pretending I couldn't care less if I ever see her again? I kick myself when I realize I didn't even get her number. I tug my shirt off and toss it on the chair and I'm heading for the shower when I hear a knock.

I haul the door open, hoping I'll find Sierra waiting on the other side.

ONE

THE BIG C WORD.

TWO YEARS LATER.

Grayson

Cracking the tab on my beer, I sit in the Adirondack chair on my porch and look over at the moving truck that's parked outside of the house next door. Sweet old Miss Millie has lived there since I moved in four years ago. We're close, and not just because she's my best friend Jake's grandma. Over the years, she's unofficially adopted me and my friends Holden and Tucker, who rent the place on the other side of me—despite the fact that we are grown men who are capable, for the most part, of looking after ourselves. She regularly feeds us and is always checking in to make sure we're doing okay. Miss Mille is also kick-ass at poker; she gives us boys a run for our money every time. *No joke.*

I take a swig of my Miller Lite, setting the can on the arm of my chair when I spot Holden and Tuck walking across the grass, drinks in hand.

Tuck sighs as he lowers his tall frame into the chair next to mine. "I'm going to miss her, man," he says, nodding in the direction of the movers carrying boxes out of Miss

TWO YEARS LATER.

Millie's front door. "Who would have thought I'd grow so attached to an 80-something-year-old woman?"

"Miss Millie is bad-ass," I say, thinking about how much shit she would give us if we didn't pop over at least once a week to pick up whatever treats she'd bake for us. "I'd hate to be the one checking her into that nursing home—she is going to light them up."

Miss Millie has made no secret of the fact that she's pissed right off that her family is moving her into an assisted living facility. It was Jake and his sister who had to make the decision—they are the only family Millie has left. She doesn't talk about it, but I know she lost her only child, their mother, in a tragic accident many years ago. I tried to ask Jake about it once, not too long after we became friends, but he made it clear the topic of his parents' deaths is off-limits. It was the first and last time I ever brought it up. Millie and I have always kept our conversations light—most of the time we just talk about her favorite team, the Yankees, and whether they can pull it together and win a damn World Series.

Yeah, right. I gave up on that dream a long time ago.

"Yeah, she's pretty pissed," Holden agrees, looking over at Miss Millie's bright yellow house. It's kind of depressing to see the flower beds, once full of colorful blooms, sitting dead and empty. Millie's garden used to be her pride and joy, but eventually ,maintaining it just became too much for her. "You can't blame Jake and his sister, though. Unfortunately for Millie, it was time."

"If we're being honest, it was probably time six months ago," I say. "But I know Jake didn't have the heart to do it."

The situation became more urgent last month when Millie forgot a pot on the stove and it started a small kitchen fire. Not long before that she'd fallen down the stairs—by

CHAPTER ONE

some miracle she didn't break any bones. Her doctor advised that for her own well-being, moving into a nursing home was probably the best decision. It fucking sucks to get old.

"Speaking of... have you seen her around?" Tuck asks, tipping back the last of his drink.

"Millie?" I ask, frowning.

"No, man. The hot granddaughter. Jake's sister," Tuck clarifies with a grin.

"'Hot granddaughter?' Jake would rip your balls off and put them in a blender if he heard you talking about her like that." It's common knowledge how overprotective Jake is when it comes to his younger sister. You can practically hear him growl when he's on the phone with her and she's talking about the date she's about to go on. He can't do much about it, though. Last I heard, his sister was living in Virginia Beach, which is too far away for Jake to chase away any potential boyfriends with a baseball bat. Let's just say that the guys his sister dates are damn lucky Jake lives in another state.

Millie talks about her granddaughter sometimes too, and it's clear she misses her. The three of them sometimes rent a vacation place in Cape May, a few hours away. It's not enough for Millie, who I'm sure would much rather have both of her grandchildren nearby.

"I saw her this morning," Tuck says, apparently still wanting to talk about Jake's sister. "You were too busy riding trails. She's a knockout, Gray. Like a fucking smoke-show. She looks like a sexier, grown-up version of the picture Millie has on her mantel, so there's no mistaking it."

"You've got to be joking. I've seen that picture, idiot, and she's probably about 12 years old in it. She has braces. You should be put in jail for ogling a minor."

TWO YEARS LATER.

"I wasn't ogling her back then, asshole. I'm not some gross perv," Tuck says. "But I do know a hot chick when I see one, and Jake's sister is *hot*. Anyways, I was all ready to go introduce myself this morning but she got into her car and left."

Holden laughs. "Quit dreaming, Tuck. You obviously haven't thought this through."

"And why is that?"

I shake my head, happy to add my two cents. "Because she's Jake's sister. You can't bang her, then ask her to leave the next morning and pretend she never existed. First off, maybe you've forgotten: Balls. In. Blender. Second, Millie is like family, which means her granddaughter is definitely off-limits."

Tucker is a lot like me. He doesn't do relationships either, although according to him, this is the year he's ready for the big C word.

Commitment.

I'm not convinced he's really ready to settle down, but I will admit he's been in a weird mood lately. According to his mom, he just needs to get married and have a couple of kids. I told him a dog might be a better place to start. Baby steps.

As for Holden, he's locked down. He's been seeing the same girl for a few months now and we all like to give him the gears over it. She seems nice enough—an elementary school teacher who surfs in her spare time. She's even been teaching him to ride waves on the weekends.

Tucker and Holden feel more like brothers to me than friends and neighbors. We live on a quiet, dead-end street in Haven Harbor, a sleepy community in the small town of Reed Point. It feels like we have a little slice of paradise all to ourselves here, with just four small houses sitting a stone's throw from the ocean. When the three of us say we will be

CHAPTER ONE

on this little street until the day we die, we're only half-kidding. We've got it too good.

"Man, where's the love? You give me zero credit. Who knows? Maybe she could be the one," Tuck says.

I nearly choke on my beer. "I don't remember the last time you've been on a second date, yet you're sitting here trying to convince us that you're ready to lock it down with Jake's sister?" I raise my brows at him. "You haven't even met her yet. Who's to say you'll even like her?"

"Oh, I'll like her, trust me. There isn't anything not to like." He wiggles his brows.

I chuckle. "Well, I hope you can learn to like living without your balls, because you're absolutely going to lose them if Jake hears you talking about his sister like that."

I settle back in my chair and stare out towards the cove across the street. Tucker, Holden, Jake, and I have spent countless hours here, shooting the shit and staring out at this view. Tucker and Holden were already living next door when I moved in, and they introduced me to Jake, who they met through Miss Millie. We've been like family ever since.

"So, what's going on today? Where's Jake at?" I ask.

"Not a clue," Tucker mutters. "But I'm betting he's with that girl he met at the beach. What the hell is her name again? Emily? No... Elsie?"

"He seems like he's really into her," I say. Jake keeps his business to himself, so the guys and I have had to piece together what he's been up to over the past few weeks.

"I don't know... he sounds stressed every time I talk to him. I think the mystery girl is playing hard to get and it's fucking with him. He's not used to working for it," Tucker points out.

And *that* is why a relationship is not for me. Jake is losing his shit over a girl he's only known for a few weeks.

TWO YEARS LATER.

Sounds fucking terrible. I'll keep on doing what I do best and that's hookups with no strings attached. It's easy, it's fun and they're gone the next morning. You never have to go through the stress of figuring out how to make a relationship work. You never have to introduce them to your family or get into all of the complicated details of your life, past and present.

I wasn't always this way. I did have a girlfriend for over a year, but I learned the hard way that relationships have a shelf life. Sooner or later, the girl will get bored, see something shiny and leave you in her dust. Unfortunately, I know this all too well.

I met Layla shortly after I started college. We instantly hit it off. She was my type—blonde, beautiful smile, a ballet dancer. Oh, and she had a dancer's body that I worshipped every chance I got.

She swept me off my feet. We spent practically every waking minute together. If I wasn't studying or helping my dad at his garage, I was with Layla.

But after a year of dating, I walked in on her with another guy. And if that wasn't enough, the other guy was my best friend from high school. I was heartbroken. I also felt like a tool for not seeing what kind of person she was sooner. I mean, I'm a smart guy—I have a master's in business. That didn't stop me from falling for a girl with no moral compass.

As soon as I caught them in bed together, I dumped her. I later learned that wasn't the first time they'd slept together, it had been going on for a while and I had no clue. Even though several years have passed since then, that ugly feeling of betrayal has stuck with me. I'm not sure I'll ever be able to forget being fucked over by my girlfriend and my best friend.

CHAPTER ONE

I decided right then and there that I would never put myself in a position where I could be let down by another woman. I would never again let my heart be broken.

And I haven't.

"Hey, why are you still here?" Holden suddenly asks Tuck. "Don't you have to be at your sister's house? Isn't it her birthday lunch today?"

Tucker winks. "I'm waiting to introduce myself to Millie's granddaughter."

I laugh. "Yeah, good luck with that."

TWO

MACRAMÉ AND OWLS.

Sierra

"You sure you're going to be okay out here? It's kinda far from town."

"I'll be fine," I holler from the kitchen, opening the refrigerator door.

Grabbing two Diet Cokes, I return to the living room where my brother Jake is sitting on the couch. He's looking at something on his phone, his expression serious. He's been a little quiet all day. I'm not sure if it's because we moved Gran out of her house today and it's weighing on him, or if it's the prospect of me being back in town for the foreseeable future. Or maybe it's something else entirely. He's always been a hard one to read.

I hand him one of the cans. "Thanks, Si," he says, then turns his attention back to his phone. I cock my head at him. I haven't lived in the same city as my brother in four years, and in a way, I feel like I need to get to know him all over again.

"You good, Jake?" I ask. It's not unusual for Jake to be wound tight. He's the definition of Type A. He likes things organized and in their place, and agonizes until everything is perfect. He's also extremely overprotective of me. He always has been, but when our parents died, it got worse. He stepped up as a father figure even though he was only 12 and I was 10 when it happened. He quickly became my fiercest protector, making it known all through high school that if a guy even so much as looked at me he would kick his ass. He told me he didn't trust hormonal teenage boys. Turns out he didn't trust hormonal college guys either.

"You seem like you have something on your mind."

"Nah, I'm good," he says, sliding his phone into his front pocket. "I'm happy to have you back home. I'm just sorry it took Gran falling down the stairs and some other crazy shit to make you come back. I know you were happy in Virginia Beach."

I sigh. I *was* happy. I had a cute apartment not far from the beach, a good job, a few really good friends. On the upside, I was able to transfer my position in the hotel chain I work for to their Reed Point office so at least I'm not out of a job. I'm also now closer to Jake and back in the same zip code as one of my closest friends, Jules. She also works for the Seaside hotel chain—her dad actually owns the company. Jules has earned her position as head of the marketing department, though. She's creative and hard-working and is a big part of why the chain of boutique hotels is a success.

"I was happy there, but I'm happy to be back home too," I say, meaning it. Moving to Virginia Beach was something I needed to do after college. I had to move far enough away to slip out from underneath my big brother's wing and learn how to live on my own. It was a fresh start in a new city where everything didn't remind me of that awful day all those years ago. And it worked. I became a more confident and independent version of myself. Eventually, the nightmares even stopped. But I missed my brother and my grandma a lot. They're the only family I have left.

"You're really going to need to de-clutter this place, unless macramé and owls are your thing," Jake says, looking around Gran's living room. My grandma is obsessed with owls. Ever since we were kids, every time my brother or I saw an owl knick-knack, we insisted on getting it for her. She saved them all, of course, so her home looks like an owl sanctuary at this point and I guess it's our fault.

Now this place is my new home-sweet-home. Moving Gran into an assisted living facility made me realize that time did not stand still when I was away. I had been apart from my family for long enough. So when Jake suggested I move into her small split-level home, it was like the universe had heard my thoughts.

I shake my head. "Gran's been moved out for less than 24 hours and you're already planning a yard sale?"

"Si, don't you want this little guy to find a good and loving home?" Jake asks with mock sincerity, picking up a brightly painted owl bobblehead figurine from its perch on the coffee table.

I laugh. "I guess this place could use a refresh," I say, tossing the year-old copy of *People* magazine I'd been flipping through onto the couch. "I think first I'll box up all of Gran's tchotchkes and then I'm going to paint the walls. Maybe paint the kitchen cabinets too."

"I'll help. I can probably bribe the guys with beer and pizza."

"That's nice of you, but I'll be fine," I say gazing out the front window at my new view of the cove. It's peaceful. "Got any plans today?"

Jake drains the last of his Diet Coke, then pushes up

from the couch. "I'm going to check your dryer to make sure the vents are clear then I'm going to head out. I have somewhere I need to be."

My heart stops in my chest for a moment, the way it always does when I think about the fire. I try to forget about it, moving on to a lighter, safer topic. "So secretive," I tease. "Does she have a name?"

Jake just rolls his eyes. "How about I take you for dinner tonight? We can celebrate your first day back in Reed Point and catch up. My treat."

"Only if it's Cocina Caliente. I think I missed their chicken enchiladas more than I missed you."

Jake cracks a smile, something I wish he would do a little more often. "I doubt that," he says, pretending to scratch his nose with his middle finger.

He's never been any good at talking about his feelings, but he's sweet and supportive and I know without a doubt he would do anything for me. I also know that he's absolutely terrified that he's going to lose me too. Jake has been through a lot in his 28 years. He worked his ass off to take care of me when our parents died, never having less than two jobs from the time he was 16 years old. And then as Gran got older, he took on the responsibility of caring for her too. I may have left Reed Point to give myself some space to breathe, but I also wanted to give my brother a break from feeling like he has to take care of me too.

Jake checks his phone before turning and walking towards the door, where he stops. "If you need anything, my good buddy lives next door in the gray rancher and my other friends live in the house next to his, but you're better to call me first. I'm here for anything you need, Si."

Once he's gone, I pick up the first box I see and carry it to the kitchen counter. I have a lot of work ahead of me, so I may as well get started. I smile as I look around the place. Gran wasn't thrilled at the idea of moving out of this home, but she did seem relieved when we told her that I would be staying here. I promised her I would do my best to make the garden beautiful again. But first, there are a few updates needed inside as well. I love Gran to bits, but owl-themed placemats and pale pink cupboards aren't really my style.

The sun streams in through the kitchen window from the backyard, casting a pretty pattern across the table. I'll have my own garden, a view of the ocean from my bedroom window, neighbour's a short walk away instead of on the other side of my bedroom wall.

It's time to start the next chapter of my life.

THREE

IS THE UNIVERSE FUCKING WITH ME?

G rayson
Pulling up to my house with Morgan Wallen's "Last Night" blasting through the car stereo, I turn down the volume when I notice a white SUV in the driveway at Millie's. The driver's side door is wide open and even though I can't see who's sitting in the car, I *can* see a woman's tanned, toned leg and the hem of a short skirt. I'm guessing it's Millie's granddaughter, and from what I can see, Tuck was right—she looks sexy as fuck.

I debate whether I should just head inside and start the barbecue for dinner or go over and introduce myself. I decide on the latter. It's the neighborly thing to do, I tell myself, pushing my car door open and walking across the lawn in the direction of Millie's place.

"Hey there," I call out when I'm close enough for her to hear me.

The girl pops her head out of the side of the car and then stands, turning to fully face me. My eyes fall on her long blonde hair first, then down to her perfect pink lips. I lift my gaze to see her sliding a pair of large, black sunglasses to the top of her head.

And then her big brown eyes find mine and she freezes.

My breath catches in my throat. You've got to be kidding me. Is the universe fucking with me?

Miss Millie's granddaughter is *Sierra*?

The Sierra from that weekend in Miami. The one I didn't tell a single soul about.

I force a smile. Her eyes dart down to the pavement, while mine stay firmly fixed on her.

"Grayson." Sierra's gaze returns to meet mine, and she lifts her eyebrows just a little. I had forgotten how captivating her eyes are. "What are you doing here?"

"I live here… I mean… there," I say, jerking my thumb towards my house. "What are *you* doing here?"

Surprise flashes across Sierra's face. She looks back at the pavement, to the ocean, anywhere but at me. She's just as beautiful as I remember. I take her in, my heart beating triple time in my chest.

She's wearing a cropped, dark blue top and a floral-patterned miniskirt that shows off her long, lean legs. Her hair is swept back from her face with a thin white headband. It's a little longer than I remember it, falling halfway down her back.

It's been two years since we met at that hotel conference, but that pull I felt towards Sierra is definitely still there. The girl is sexy. I swallow, hoping my thoughts aren't written all over my face.

I can hardly breathe as I watch her remove her sunglasses from the top of her head and put them on the seat of her car. She's in Reed Point. She is Millie's granddaughter. *Oh shit—shit, shit, shit!*

"I… my grandma lives there," she says, motioning over

her shoulder to the yellow house behind her. "I mean, she lived there…"

"Your grandma is Miss Millie?" I ask, the surprise evident in my voice. "I can't believe all this time I never figured out she's your—"

"Wait, you know my gran?" Sierra asks, cutting me off. She fidgets with the ends of her hair, seeming nervous.

"I do. I know her well. We've been neighbours for a while. We're pretty close friends actually," I tell her, tucking my hands in my pockets. "Your grandma is dope."

She smiles softly, and damn if it doesn't get my pulse racing. There's something about the way her eyes crinkle at the corners when she smiles, the dimples that suddenly appear. It's so good to see her again. I'm not used to this fluttery feeling in my chest. The last time I felt like this was in Miami… with her.

I'd be lying if I said I haven't thought about her since that weekend. Sierra isn't a girl you easily forget. Especially after the things we did together on that desk. It was hot and filthy and it's permanently seared into my mind.

Reign it in, Gray. The girl just moved her grandma into a care facility.

But the sight of her standing here, just feet away from me, gets my heart hammering in my chest. I drag my hands through my hair and try to catch my breath.

I've never been able to shake the way she took off that night. It turns my stomach that she just… left. *That* fact is what has always bothered me the most, even two years later. Our time together that weekend, the flirting, the sex—none of it seemed to mean anything to her, even though it meant so much to me. Seeing her again now, feeling the effect she still has on me… I hate that I've kept a place for her in my heart for this long when it seems she couldn't have cared less about me.

I take a deep breath. *Stop dredging up the past*, I tell myself.

"Yeah, she *is* pretty cool," Sierra says with a laugh. I watch her soften at the mention of her grandma, and for a minute I get a glimpse of Sierra's vulnerable side. It's a side of her I've never seen before. She was carefree and spontaneous that weekend we were together in Miami, even wild. "I guess you know she's moved into a care home. I hope you don't think that—"

"Sierra," I interrupt her. "I think you made the right decision. It was time."

Her chocolate-brown eyes settle on me, and I notice the splatter of freckles across her nose, the way her hair is lit up by the late afternoon sun. She's more beautiful than any woman I've ever seen. Her body is a work of art. I could very easily fall for a woman like her. And that is exactly the problem.

Sierra continues to run the ends of her golden hair through her fingers.

"Thank you," she says, and I can hear the emotion in her voice. "It was rough. She didn't want to go and... I'm sorry, I'm rambling. Listen, I should go." She shuts the car door and I watch as she walks to the trunk, popping the hatch open and reaching inside to pull out a large box. She shifts the box to one arm, trying to balance it.

Without thinking, I step towards her. "Let me help you with that."

She looks at me like she's determined to do it herself. "You don't have to help me, Grayson. I can handle it. I'll be fine."

Does she really think I'm going to just stand here and

not help her out? Not a chance. Besides, it's the excuse I need to spend a little more time with her. I'm not ready to leave her yet.

I take the box from Sierra and instead of protesting like I expected her to, she lets me. She grabs another bag from the trunk, then leads the way down the path to Millie's front door.

I can't help but notice the graceful way she moves, the curve of her shoulder blades, her long stride. She opens the door and deposits the bag a few steps into the entryway.

"Thanks. You can just put it here," she says, motioning to the floor. "I'm going to grab another."

I do as I'm told, setting the box on the floor. I pause to gaze around the living room. Everything is exactly as Millie kept it, with just a couple of exceptions: the picture frames that used to be scattered across the mantel and the Lazy Boy chair that Millie liked to sit in while she watched TV are gone.

I've spent a fair bit of time in this house over the years, fixing the odd broken appliance, picking up a delicious meal Millie had made me or sitting in on a poker game with Tuck, Jake and Holden. Even though the place looks mostly the same, it feels a little empty without Millie's larger-than-life presence. Raking my hand through my hair, I blow out a breath as Sierra walks through the door with another box.

"Is that the last one?"

"I think so," Sierra answers, carrying it into the kitchen and setting it on the laminate counter. "But if it isn't, I can get the rest tomorrow."

"How much stuff do you need?" I tease, leaning a shoulder against the pantry door. "It looks like you're moving in."

Sierra blushes. "I am."

LILY MILLER

WELL FUCK ME SIDEWAYS.

Sierra is my new neighbor. She's also my best friend's little sister, I keep reminding myself. The sister I fucked on a desk in a hotel office. Jake is going to murder me. And he'll probably take his time doing it.

She clears her throat, pulling me from my visions of Jake burying my body. "I guess this means we're neighbors."

Neighbors. Under normal circumstances, I'd be happy to learn that the hottest woman I've ever seen in my life is moving in next door. Unfortunately, this particular woman is absolutely off limits.

I guess I could pretend that Miami never happened, pretend that Sierra doesn't cross my mind every single time I catch the scent of a summer breeze. But I've never been any good at pretending.

Sierra is looking at me, her eyes giving away the fact that she's just as unsure about what's happening here as I am.

"Yeah, um... I guess we are neighbors," I echo, scratching my head. "Sierra, is this going to be weird? I mean... you..." I make an awkward hand-flapping gesture between us. "And I... and Miami—"

"It doesn't have to be weird," she insists. "We're adults."

"Adults who have seen each other naked—"

"I know, Grayson. You don't need to remind me. I was there," she says, a blush creeping across her cheeks. I can see that she's flustered, despite her efforts to hide it. She lets out a breath and turns to open the box sitting on the counter. "I don't know if anyone's ever told you this, but it *is* actually possible to act normal around a person after seeing them naked."

"To be fair, though, we did a lot more than just see each

other naked. Am I the only one who remembers what we did in that room?"

Sierra stops and gives me a look that makes it clear I'm an idiot for saying something so stupid out loud.

I shrug. "What? This is a highly unique situation for me. I've never lived next door to a girl I had a hot-as-fuck-night with, so it's going to take a minute for me to adjust."

She rolls her eyes and then turns away from me again. "I'm sure you'll manage," she says, returning to the contents of the box.

I shamelessly watch Sierra as she opens a cabinet door to put away a couple of mugs, noticing the way her tank top rises an inch when she reaches for the shelf. Her blonde hair against her deeply tanned skin. Her long legs. The curve of her hips. It's impossible not to notice Sierra's beauty. My dick stirs in my pants, and I mentally tell it to chill the fuck out, but the big guy isn't getting the memo. I quickly try to adjust myself so that my hard-on isn't pointing directly at her.

How am I going to handle living 30 seconds away from this girl when all I want to do is touch her? But if I have any hopes of keeping my dick attached to my body—which is definitely the goal—I can never touch Sierra again. And therein lies the problem.

"Looks like you've got some work ahead of you," I tell her, realizing I need to put some distance between us. "I should get out of here so you can do your thing."

A quick nod of her head is all I get in acknowledgment as she continues to unwrap glasses from the box. I know that I should turn around and head for the door, but something keeps my feet rooted to the old linoleum floor.

Still leaning against the doorframe, I watch as Sierra's

eyes shift to me, dropping to my pecs for a brief moment before shooting back up to meet my eyes.

Busted. I smirk. I can't help it. Sierra ignores me.

She exhales loudly and rubs the heels of her palms against her eyes. "Listen... Jake doesn't know about us, about what happened in Miami. I would really like to keep it that way."

"Trust me, Sierra, I don't have a death wish. I don't plan on saying a thing to your brother."

She sighs. "Yeah, I don't think he'd take it very well."

"That's putting it mildly," I say, wincing at the thought.

Jake would lose his shit if he found out about me and Sierra. In this case, what he doesn't know won't hurt him—or me. His best friend hooking up with his sister definitely would not fly.

"You know, we never really talked about—" I falter, looking down at my hands. "About that night in Miami."

I haven't seen or spoken to Sierra since I left her at her hotel door that night. I thought about trying to track her down, but after the way she tore out of that office, it kind of felt like she didn't want to be found.

"Grayson, what was there to say? We had fun. I don't think either one of us was looking for something more. End of story," she says firmly. "Now we're going to be neighbors, so let's just forget about what happened that night so that things between us aren't awkward."

I nod. She's right. I wasn't looking for a relationship. All I wanted was a hook-up. For some reason, Sierra just felt like more than that.

"It will only be awkward if we let it be," she tells me, a determined look in her eyes. "We can be friends."

"Friends," I say, my eyes locked on hers. "Well then, I'm next door if you need anything."

When Sierra doesn't say anything more, I turn and walk out her door.

I just got friend-zoned by the one girl I've felt a real connection with.

And she's my new neighbor.

And she's my best friend's sister.

Just my luck.

FOUR

DAMN HIM AGAIN.

Sierra

I take the last item from the box, setting it on my desk with a sense of satisfaction. There's still a ton of unpacking to do at Gran's house, but at least I'm settled into my new Reed Point office.

I linger on the photo of my parents, lightly brushing my fingers over the glass. My dad's arm is around my mom's neck and she's smiling so big her eyes are almost squeezed shut. She's wearing the string of pearls he gave her for their anniversary the year before, the strand that she never took off. He's wearing a T-shirt that reads "*I keep all my dad jokes in a dad-a-base.*" The photo was taken about three weeks before they died. I've lost track of exactly how many days it's been since we lost them. I guess that's proof that I'm doing better, but it also makes me feel incredibly guilty.

A knock at the door wrenches me from my memories. "Come in," I say, just as Jules peeks her head in.

"Hey you! Have time for your new office neighbor?"

"I always have time for you," I say with a grin. "Besides,

you're related to my boss, so I kinda have to say yes. Come here, give me a hug."

"I'm so happy you're here, Sierra," she says, wrapping me in a tight embrace. "It's going to be so much fun working together again!"

I met Jules when I started working for The Seaside. Our friendship wasn't instant—she was the owner's daughter, after all, and I thought it was probably best not to mix business and friendship. But not long after I relocated to Virginia Beach, we spent a long weekend together at a hotel conference in Nashville and we clicked right away. We didn't see each other as much as I would have liked, but knowing Jules would be at the typically boring work conferences that took place a few times a year made me start to actually look forward to them. We would work during the day and party at night. Hard. Jules is easy to be around, and she has the energy of a hundred people tucked into her little-bitty body. It's always a good time when we are together.

"How are Beckett and sweet little Maya girl?" I ask. Jules and her husband Beckett have a 1-year-old daughter who is just about the cutest thing ever. "I can't wait to squish her! Wait until you see what I brought her from Virginia Beach. You might kill me."

"It can't be any worse than the giant, singing shark my dad bought her. Every time I walk in the room, the stupid thing starts shrieking 'Baby Shark' and scares the be-Jesus out of me. I hear it in my nightmares, Sierra. In my nightmares."

"Yikes, that sounds pretty bad."

"It is, but of course she loves the darn thing." She shrugs her shoulders. "What's a mom to do?"

I feel a tiny tug of envy. I'd love a family one day. I have such clear memories of my childhood: eating dinner every night around the kitchen table with my parents and brother, our trip to Disneyland, all the summers we spent camping in a tiny, rickety tent-trailer until my mom finally had enough of the bugs and the dirt. I want all of that again someday.

"So, a quick summary until I have time to really get into the nitty gritty with you," Jules says, rubbing her palms together like she has something juicy to spill. "First, never get caught talking to Carmen at reception when you're in a rush. She will talk your ear off about her granddaughter. She sounds like an angel, but do I really need to hear about the kid's favorite cereal? Love the woman, but it's impossible to get her to stop. Next... if you want privacy, use the washrooms on the second floor. No one ever uses them. And the best place for lunch around here is The Dockside, the new sandwich shop on the corner. Their lobster rolls are ah-flipping-mazing and they come with homemade potato chips. To die for."

"Lobster rolls are gross," I say, sticking out my tongue. "I don't know how you eat those things."

"Excuse me? Don't go shitting all over my favorite sandwich," she teases, looking at me in mock horror.

Jules flops into the chair across from my desk, narrowing her eyes as I fire up my computer and slip on my glasses.

"Are you working already? You literally just got here. You can ease into it, you know," she grins. "You take your job *very* seriously."

"Yes. I take my job at *your* family business very seriously," I tell her with a laugh. I know I've got it good working here at The Seaside. Michael Bennett is a dream boss. He pays me more than generously, gifts me a hefty bonus every Christmas and treats me with the utmost respect.

"Okay, fine," Jules sighs. "But before I go, how is your

grandma doing?"

"Pretty good, I think. I checked on her this morning, but I had to talk to a nurse because she wasn't in her room. She was outside taking an archery class." I shrug. "That's a good sign, right?"

"I don't know," Jules says, eyebrows raised. "I mean, is it smart to offer sharp, pointy weapons to seniors?"

"Yeah, you would think a painting class might be a safer option," I agree. "Not a lot can go wrong there."

"*Well*," Jules begins, sitting up straighter in her chair. "Unless it's one of those naked model art classes where the guy drops the towel and you have to paint his wiener. That could go sideways fast."

I laugh, shaking my head at her. "Great. Now I'm picturing my grandmother staring at some dude's wiener. Thanks for the visual, Jules."

"You're welcome! I need to run, but I wanna pop by your new house soon. How's it going anyways? Is it a little weird living at your grandma's?"

Living at my grandma's house isn't weird. Living next door to the guy I had desk sex with is a bit strange, though.

"So far, so good," I say with a smile, leaving out any mention of Grayson or the fact that I barely got any sleep last night after seeing him again.

"Good. Just let me know when you're free," Jules says with one foot out the door. "I need to take you out for a proper welcome back to Reed Point."

She blows me a kiss and then disappears down the hall.

MY PHONE RINGS as I'm walking outside to grab lunch and when I fish it out of my purse, I'm not surprised to see

Jake's name on the screen.

I debate sending him to voicemail. I've been back in Reed Point for less than 36 hours and my brother is already falling back into his old ways—in other words, he's smothering me. He took me out for dinner last night, called me first thing this morning to make sure I didn't need anything and now he's doing his lunchtime check-in. *Jesus Lord,* he's too much.

But I know he means well, so I answer his call.

"Hey Jake," I say as I dash across the street. "What's up?"

"Hey Si! How's your first day at the new office going?"

"It's going fine. You don't need to worry. I've worked for this company for over four years. I'm just doing it in a different state now."

"I know," he says, sounding distracted. "I'm actually not calling about that. I'm calling to invite you to my house tonight for a cookout. A couple of the guys are coming over and Holden is bringing his girlfriend, Aubrey. She's around your age, I think you'd like her."

It *does* sound like fun. I'm a social butterfly by nature and I've already been missing the circle of friends I left behind in Virginia Beach. But if Jake's having people over, that probably means Grayson will be there, and that could be awkward. Damn him. His piercing dark eyes. His cocky smile. His perfect athletic build. If Grayson wasn't so damn gorgeous, this would be a hell of a lot easier. Damn him again.

It's best that I avoid him. At least until I can figure out a way to be around him without getting goosebumps.

"Sounds nice, Jake. But I think I'll have to take a rain check."

"Are you sure?"

"I'm sure," I say, stepping inside the café that Jules had

recommended to grab lunch. "It's been a busy week, and I still have some unpacking to do."

"Okay. But if you change your mind, the offer still stands."

"Thanks, Jake. I appreciate it." I end the call, then order a clubhouse and take a seat by the window. And try not to think about my handsome new neighbor.

IT'S the middle of the night, but I'm wide awake. Unfortunately, insomnia is something I've gotten used to.

I've had the same dream for years. I'm watching our childhood house go up in flames. The ambulance lights are flashing, and my parents are being taken away. I guess dream isn't the right word—nightmare is a better description. I haven't woken up from one—screaming, heart racing, bed soaked with sweat—since shortly after I moved to Virginia. Now that I'm back home in Reed Point, I'm afraid they will start again.

They're terrifying, and no matter what I used to do to try to stop them, they still came. Jake would wake me up, shaking me, and then lie beside me until I fell back asleep. I don't know if he had the same nightmares after the fire. Jake must have suffered, but he never fell apart, he never lost it in front of me. In some weird way, I wish he had. Bottling up that kind of pain inside is never healthy.

It's also not healthy to keep people at arm's length, but I realize that is what both of us do. It's the reason neither of us have been in a committed, long-term relationship. After losing so much and feeling such intense pain, you never want to risk love again.

Realizing I'm not going to be able to fall back asleep, I

climb out of bed and head to the kitchen. I turn on the kettle, thinking a cup of peppermint tea may help. When it has steeped, I take the steaming mug to my front porch and sit on the porch swing, gazing up at the millions of stars putting on a show in the night sky. Being near the ocean helps. The sound of the waves always soothes me.

The street is eerily quiet, the weather warmer than I remember for early July in Reed Point. I sit in my tank and sleep shorts, rocking the swing back and forth with the tip of my toe. I take a sip from my mug and exhale deeply. Maybe staying at Gran's house is a bad idea. When I decided to move back home, my focus was on Gran and getting her settled, and on transitioning to the new office. I didn't have the time or energy to surf around realtor web pages looking for a place to live. Besides, Reed Point is pricey, so being able to stay here is saving me a lot of money. Money I'm saving for other things.

I relax deeper into the cushions. My eyes betray me, drifting next door to Grayson's house. His truck is parked in the driveway, the house dark except for the soft glow of the porch light. There goes that darn flutter in my stomach. It's the same one I felt in Miami, before it turned into a full body shudder when he was buried deep, pouring himself into me.

My history with Grayson is just that. History. It was one night. Well, technically it was a weekend. One of the best weekends of my life, if I'm honest. Grayson made me feel seen. Beautiful. Wanted. At the club that night, it felt like something may have been happening between us, but I knew as soon as we both finished on top of that desk that sex had never felt like that before. Which is why I needed to go, to put distance between us, to get my head on straight before I started to feel things for him.

But then Grayson wanted to talk. Talk about what? There was no way I was going to stick around to find out. It was supposed to be a one-time thing. Easy. No complications. I never expected that I would feel the way I did. What was that gooey warmth in my chest? I wasn't sure, but I knew it had to be a bad sign.

It was ugly the way I grabbed my things, threw on my clothes and headed straight for the door. Grayson is a good guy, he didn't deserve that. But he was never going to be any more than a one-night stand so the sooner I left, the better.

I didn't let myself google Grayson's name after our weekend in Miami. I told myself nothing good was going to come of seeing that man's chiseled jaw or all-American boy-next-door good looks again. Maybe if I did, I would have pieced it together that he's friends with my brother. I am still not quite over the shock of that. I polished off most of a bottle of wine after dinner with Jake last night, hoping it might help drown the memories of Miami that keep resurfacing. It didn't work.

I take a sip of my tea and try to push these feelings aside, telling myself that I can handle living next door to him. It's exactly what I tried to tell *him* in the kitchen the other day. *Let's forget about what happened between us so things won't be awkward when we see each other.*

I need to take my own advice.

What I really need is to get some sleep, and then I'll forget all about Grayson. He may be my gorgeous new neighbor, but he is also my brother's best friend. And that's all he ever will be. Nothing more. Period.

There's room on Haven Harbor for both of us.

Right?

FIVE

SAUNA-LEVEL HOT

Sierra

Over the past week, I have gone out of my way to make sure I don't run into Grayson. I got used to his schedule pretty quick. Our work hours are basically the same, so I try to leave a half hour before he does and when I come home, I make a beeline for my front door. Do not pass Go. Do not so much as glance towards his house. When I want some fresh air, I now sit on the back porch, hidden behind the tall sycamore trees that are rooted between our backyards. On the weekend, I drove to White Harbor, the big beach in Reed Point, rather than just walk to the beach across the street.

So far, my attempts to avoid Grayson have been a success. Now if only I could find a way to stop thinking about him.

I've been staying up way too late, packing up Gran's things and unpacking my own boxes. I also decided to start painting the living room walls a pale blue. The house is a mess, but I figure it's good to stay busy. By the time I collapse into bed at the end of the day, I'm too exhausted to pay my spinning thoughts much attention.

Scanning the living room, I eye the work that I've done. It's amazing what a fresh coat of paint can do to a place. I'm nowhere near close to getting this place the way I want it, but it's a good start. I still have to tackle the two bathrooms and the kitchen, but Rome wasn't built in a day.

Taking my paint brush and tray to the backyard, I hose them both down and then clean up. I need to get ready for a charity auction that I promised Jules I would attend this evening.

Jules and her husband work for competing hotel chains —Beckett is vice president of The Liberty Hotel Group where Grayson works—and they're co-hosting a baseball game to raise money for cystic fibrosis in a couple of weeks. It's a cause that is close to their hearts as Beckett's younger sister, Bean, lives with the genetic disease.

So, it will be The Seaside versus The Liberty, with the presidents of the two hotel chains acting as head coaches for their respective teams. Tonight they're holding an auction and dinner at the ballpark to kick things off.

I'm pretty sure that means I'll be seeing Grayson. He works for The Liberty, after all, and is close friends with Beckett. The event is guaranteed to be a good time—Jules knows how to throw a party. But I don't know how I'm going to handle being around Grayson without it being awkward. I better figure it out fast.

I throw on a pair of skinny jeans and the company jersey with The Seaside logo on the front, then pull my hair into a quick braid. Before heading out the door, I stop quickly to check my reflection in the mirror and give myself a mental pep talk in preparation for tonight. I've managed to avoid

Grayson for an entire week, but I think my luck is about to run out.

GRAYSON

I'M IMAGINING Sierra in her jersey and a pair of really short athletic shorts when I walk into the ballpark for tonight's big event. My pervy thoughts must be written all over my face because Beckett raises a brow when he walks towards me. "You laughing at your own jokes again, Gray?" he asks, patting me on the back. "I guess that makes one person who finds you funny."

Not true. Everyone thinks I'm funny because I am. "I was telling your mom a few jokes last night when I was—"

"Finish that sentence and I'll make sure you eat your next meal through a straw," he jokes, and we both laugh as we walk towards the field together.

My pulse picks up as I scan the crowd. Sierra is here somewhere.

A whole week has gone by since I've seen her. I'm pretty sure the distance has been intentional on her part.

But that ends tonight. I know Sierra is participating in the fundraiser—I may have glanced at the team list on Beckett's desk this morning, searching for her name. Thankfully I'm looking good, with a fresh haircut and the scruff on my face trimmed nice and neat. I'm wearing a pair of black athletic shorts, a simple, dark-blue T that shows off my biceps and my lucky socks. I do realize it's all for nothing—can't touch Jake's sister with a 10-foot pole and all that bullshit—but I'm still excited to see her.

The late afternoon sun is shining, and the smell of hotdogs and popcorn welcomes us as we approach the tents set up next to the auction tables.

Beckett elbows me as the two of us approach a table. "You put your money on the fishing trip, and I'll put mine on the golf."

I nod. "Divide and conquer, my man," I say, hearing footsteps behind us.

"Hey baby, there you are," Jules says, going up on her toes, giving her husband a kiss before turning to me and pulling me in for a hug. "Hey Gray, good to see you," she says warmly, before adding, "It's a bummer The Seaside is going to slaughter you guys in two weeks."

She hands us each a jersey with The Liberty logo etched across the chest and we slip them on.

"You working for the competition now, Jules?" I tease as she watches us tug our arms through the sleeves.

"When hell freezes over, Ford," she says, calling me by my last name.

While Jules smoothes Beckett's jersey, I take the opportunity to look around again for a glimpse of Sierra.

Sure enough, I spot her standing in the middle of a group of guys. Her boss, Michael Bennett, is by her side. When he moves a little to the left, I can see she's wearing her Seaside jersey and a pair of fitted jeans that are very tight. *She must be trying to kill me in those things.* She's the most beautiful woman on the field, and it's clear that I'm not the only man who thinks so.

I watch the group, noticing the way that one guy she's talking to keeps finding ways to touch her. Another is blatantly staring at her chest. I feel my jaw clench. Why does it piss me off so much?

I would love nothing more than to walk over there and strike up a conversation with Sierra, but I know it would make her feel uncomfortable. So instead, I chat with Jules and Beckett, all the while keeping Sierra in my line of vision.

Several of our colleagues from The Liberty stop to say hello, and I can tell that Beckett appreciates tonight's great turnout. None of us *have to* be here tonight, but we're a tight-knit group at the office and Beckett is a boss we all admire and respect. I know that everyone is happy to show up to support him and his sister. Tonight's cause is a great one, but I have to admit I have an ulterior motive as well. My body has been humming at the chance to see Sierra.

She's been on my mind constantly this week. I've been hoping to run into her, but she's basically been a hermit, leaving the house to go to work and then shutting herself up indoors as soon as she's back home. I've noticed her lights on well past midnight, but she keeps the blinds shut so I'm not sure what's been keeping her up so late. It's obvious she's trying to avoid me, and I understand why, but she can't lock herself away forever.

"I've gotta run, you two," Jules says, flashing a smile at Beckett. "I want to take a few pictures for our socials."

Beckett pulls her against him before she goes, kissing the top of her head and then watching her walk away. A committed relationship isn't really in the cards for me, but if it was, their kind of relationship is what I would hope for.

My gaze then wanders to Sierra again. She's still at the center of her little group of admirers, laughing at something one of them has said. She's only been at the Reed Point office for a week now, but it's clear she's fitting in with everyone effortlessly. I'm not surprised. She has a way with people. She puts you at ease, making you feel like you've known her for years after only being in her presence for 15 minutes. I sigh, frustrated that I'm the only guy here who can't just walk over and talk to her.

Finally, Sierra turns her head in my direction. Her dark brown eyes meet mine and my pulse instantly kicks up 10 notches. My gaze travels to her lips, then down past her shoulders to the length of her legs. I can't help myself. Out of the corner of my eye, I register the fact that Beck is watching me with a smirk on his face.

Sierra pulls her eyes away from me then turns and heads in the opposite direction. It's probably for the best—a work fundraiser is not the best place for an erection.

I'm still watching her walk away when Beckett is in my ear. "I'm pretty sure she's still single," he says in a low voice.

I'm happy to hear it, even though it doesn't make a difference. "That's not the problem," I mumble. "Remember the old lady who lives next door to me, the one who was moved into a care home by her family?"

Beckett looks at me with a confused expression on his face. "Yeah, you've mentioned her. What does she have to do with Sierra?"

"Well, Miss Millie moved out and *she* moved in. Sierra is my new fucking neighbor."

Beckett's eyebrows pinch together. "And..? Isn't that a good thing? Why should that stop you from seeing her?"

"Oh, I haven't got to the best part yet."

"Try me."

"Turns out she's Jake's younger sister."

His brows furrow. "Yeah, I know. How did you not know that?"

I sigh, scratching the scruff on my jaw. "I guess I've been living under a rock. A rock that Jake would use to beat me over the head with if I even touched his sister."

"That's a good point. Shit, man... you *are* fucked."

"You don't think I don't know that already?" I deadpan, kneading the back of my neck.

"Well shit, I better get you a drink."

AN HOUR LATER, I'm standing in the beer garden with Beck. I've made my rounds, talking to everyone I know as well as introducing myself to a few people from The Seaside. Then I polished off a jumbo hotdog from the food tent.

I tip my beer bottle back, taking a good pull. I've lost track of Sierra, and my annoyance at the situation is starting to get the better of me. I tried to make eye contact several times, but she's been avoiding me like it's her full-time job. This is getting ridiculous. We're neighbors, for the love of God. We are going to have to speak at some point. I'm going to eventually see her with Jake, who I saw twice this week, though both times I was too chickenshit to bring up his sister's name. Now I feel like a lying asshole who keeps secrets from his friends.

"How are things going with your dad?" Beck asks, distracting me from my thoughts.

"Seems to be a little better these days."

My dad was badly hurt in an accident at his garage when I was a kid. A car slipped off a lift, pinning his leg underneath and crushing it. He was in and out of the hospital for years with multiple surgeries. Rehabilitation was slow and the pain became too much for him to handle. He eventually became dependant on pain pills. It was tough to see him suffer from the injury, but what might be even worse are all the years he's spent battling addiction since then. He seems to be clean at the moment but I never know if or when he'll slip again.

"I'm glad to hear it. How's your mom?"

"The strongest woman I know." My dad has put her through more shit than any man has a right to, but she's still his biggest supporter. And a damn good mom.

"Beth is top tier, man."

"The best," I say, thinking about how selfless my mom is. It didn't matter what was going on in our lives—whether my dad was off in some treatment facility for the 10th time, or she was having to nurse him back to health after a surgery—she always made time for me and my sister. She never missed a softball game or a dance recital, and there was usually a plate of homemade cookies waiting for us when we got home from school.

On top of all that, she worked a full-time job. She had to. Dad ended up being off work for almost a year, and even after he could return to the garage, he was never the same. He was in constant pain, and more often than not high from the painkillers.

So, I started helping him at the garage. I would answer phones and over time I learned how to do things around the shop because I knew if he got worse, it would all fall on my mom. At night, I would ride my bike down the local trails to clear my head and get away from it all.

And later on I fucked girls. I had meaningless one-night stands because they temporarily numbed the pain and helped me forget about everything else.

I guess old habits die hard.

LILY MILLER

I HEAR Sierra before I see her. The sound of her laughter is unmistakable, and I look up to see her with an arm around Jules' shoulder, mid-selfie. Her legs look a mile long in those jeans, her blonde hair bleached a lighter shade from the sun. I'm torturing myself staring at her, but I can't look away.

Draining the last of my beer, I march in her direction, knowing full well that I shouldn't be anywhere near my best friend's sister. Nothing good can come from this. But I'm hell-bent on doing it anyway. It's the only way I can quench my thirst for this girl. I'm not expecting her to throw her arms around me, but a drink on my front porch together would be nice. There's a very good chance that she'll make up some excuse and run in the other direction like she's been doing all week. Whatever. I'm willing to take the risk. Here goes nothing.

Jules notices me first.

Sierra's eyes follow, then widen.

I seize my chance.

"Ladies," I say to the two of them, looking at Sierra.

Jules looks from me to Sierra, seeming to notice the obvious tension in the air. "Gotta run," she says, then turns and walks away. Subtle. Jules clearly knows about our hookup in Miami, but I'm not sure just how much Sierra has told her.

"Hi." Sierra smiles an irritatingly polite smile. It's a smile that says *we barely know one another*, rather than *I've seen every inch of your body naked.* She clears her throat, which I have noticed she does when she's nervous. "How's it going?"

Why is this so awkward? I've seen plenty of girls I've hooked up with and it never feels like this. Why should it be any different with Sierra?

"I'm good, thanks. How's the new office? All settled in?" I ask, doing my best to make things less... weird.

"All settled. So far, so good." Nope. Still weird.

"And what about the house? How's the unpacking going?"

"Well, aside from the fact that there are boxes everywhere and it looks like a flea market, it's feeling a little more like mine."

"Hey, don't knock flea markets. I once picked up a sweet set of macramé potholders at one of those things."

Sierra looks at me like she's not quite sure whether I'm full of shit or not. I grin back at her. Luckily, I'm not a guy who gives up easily. I've also been told I'm extremely charming and that charm seems to be working because Sierra is smiling at me... and there's the girl I met in Miami. She's slowly making a reappearance. I can sense she's letting her guard down just a bit. Finally. She's also ridiculously hot when she's smiling.

Sauna-level hot.

Maybe that's one of the reasons I'm trying so hard to crack her. Her smile works me up.

I'm grinning as wide as a four-lane highway when I notice Beckett with his arms around Jules, kissing her neck. They're all over each other, madly in love. "It's gross, isn't it?" I joke, nodding to where Beck and Jules are locking lips in a full-on public display. "Someone should tell them to take that back to their bedroom."

"Or remind her that they're on opposite teams and she needs to pick a side."

"Exactly. The winning team," I say, pointing to the Liberty logo splashed across my chest.

She looks like she's fighting the urge to roll her eyes. "I forgot about the competitive streak in you."

"And how would you even know I have a competitive

streak? I'm neither confirming nor denying, for the record," I joke.

"Well for one, Jules told me about game night at her house on her birthday. She said you were all pouty that you lost at Monopoly. Moped about it for days, I hear."

I smirk. "So you two were talking about me. What else did you talk about? About me, specifically."

Her answer comes quickly, her eyes still on me. "I hate to break it to you, but you're not that interesting."

I shoot her a look of disbelief. "Uh-huh. Sure." I smile. "Look, if you were digging for info, all you had to do was ask. The answer is yes, I'm single."

Sierra tilts her head to the side, narrowing her eyes. "Noted," she says, tapping her skull. "And look at that... poof... already forgotten."

I stare back at her, clutching my chest. "Ouch. That was harsh. You're going to make me cry."

"Shut up," she grumbles. Her *you've-got-to-be-kidding-me* face turns to laughter. I might just be getting somewhere with her. "We both know what you really mean by 'single.' I believe that's shorthand for 'playing the field.'"

She's not wrong. Playing the field is what I've always done. Something tells me she's a little afraid of commitment herself, but it doesn't feel like a safe topic for us to discuss, so I decide to move on.

I'd rather be doing what I can to make her smile again. Anything to keep this easy banter going between us. "Just haven't met the right one, I guess." I shrug, digging my hands into my pockets, then flashing her my most charming grin.

"Next you're going to try to sell me a bridge," she scoffs.

"What? You don't think I'm capable of a... relationship?"

She shakes her head. "You can't even say the word."

"Sure, I can. Re-la-tion-ship," I say, dragging the word out into four long syllables. "Maybe it's time."

Looking at Sierra, I almost believe that. Maybe it is time for something more serious. But I quickly back that bus up, remembering she is very off-limits. *Friends, Gray. Just friends.*

And a friend can buy their friend a drink. So, I ask her, "What are you drinking? Can I get you another?"

Sierra tucks a few strands of hair that have slipped out of her braid behind her ear. "No thanks. I'm going to head out soon. I've got some work I need to do at the house."

I'm disappointed, but I'm a glass-half-full type of guy, so I'm going to call tonight a win. We had a good conversation. She didn't bolt when I came over to talk to her and I saw a smile on her face more than once. I half-expected her to climb the fence in an escape attempt when I approached her, so all things considered, I think this went very well.

"Yeah, I've noticed your living room light on pretty late."

"Have you been watching me, Grayson?" She raises a brow mockingly.

I shrug. What's the point of lying? I have been curious about what she's been up to. "I may have looked out my window in your direction a time or two."

She blushes. "I've been painting... among a few other fixer-upper projects. I'm a night owl. I've never been the best sleeper, so I like to get things done late at night." She lowers her eyes, and something tells me there's more to that story. I leave it for now. "Anyways, I'd better go and tackle the mess waiting for me. I'll see you around, Grayson."

"Can I give you a ride home?" The crowd has thinned out, there are only a dozen or so people left enjoying the warm summer night.

"Thanks, but I have my car here. It was good seeing you. Get home safe."

And before I have the chance to say anything more, she's heading for the exit.

But 10 minutes later when I get to the parking lot, I do a double take. Is that Sierra standing next to her SUV? An SUV with a flat tire?

SIX

THE SITUATION SOUTH OF MY BORDER.

Grayson

"Need a hand?" I ask, kneeling to get a closer look at her blown tire.

Sierra ends the call she's on with a huff. "It looks like I ran over a stupid nail. I called my brother to come get me, but he didn't answer. I'm going to call a cab."

She swipes her phone back to life and starts searching for the number.

"Put your phone away, Sierra. I can change your tire for you. You'll be on your way in no time." I stand and round the vehicle, popping her trunk to look for a spare.

"It's not in there," she grimaces. "I might have taken it out to have it repaired a little while ago and then I might not have gotten around to putting it back."

I shake my head and laugh.

"Are you laughing at me?"

Wiping the smile from my face, I slam her trunk shut. "I would never laugh at you—okay, maybe just a little."

I watch her roll her eyes, then fold her arms over her

chest. The gesture makes her tits pop up and I'm a man, so I sneak a peek.

"I'm glad you think it's funny. Go ahead, have a good laugh at my expense." She looks at her SUV with a frown.

"Listen, my dad owns a garage. I'll get this fixed for you tomorrow. But it's staying here for the night, so make sure you lock it up."

"But—"

My eyes narrow at her. "Get in my truck, Sierra. I'm driving you home."

She nods sheepishly. "Okay." Then she smiles the prettiest half-smile that sends a shiver over my skin. The feeling in my stomach is all fluttery. It's some weird shit that I'm not used to. Girls smile at me all the time and I've never felt anything like this before. Not once.

"Thank you, Grayson." She follows me to my truck after locking her Pathfinder, and I open the passenger door for her.

Once she's in, I round the front of the truck and slide into my seat. "You're going to owe me for this," I tease her. "This is really out of my way."

"Just add it to my tab," she groans as I turn up the stereo. 'You' by Dan and Shay floats through the speakers. "I really do appreciate this. I'll give you my Visa number to pay for the repair."

"All good. We'll get it figured out."

Now if I could only get a handle on my overactive libido because everything Sierra does makes me think about sex. My brain is flipping through images of her legs spread wide, ass in the air with her knees sunk into my mattress. I think I might pass out. Having her this close to me and breathing in her intoxicating coconut scent is not helping the situation south of my border. I didn't even think I liked coconuts, but news flash— I definitely do.

I shift a little in my seat, thinking about Jake and the meat grinder he'd put my dick in if he knew the dirty things I wanted to do to his sister. That instantly fixes the half chub in my pants. I exhale.

I roll down the window, the other hand on the steering wheel, trying to act casual. "Have you met Holden or Tucker yet, the neighbors to the left of me?"

"I haven't, no, but I'm sure it's just a matter of time. Jake told me about you guys all living on Haven Harbor. He said the four of you are like brothers."

"Did he also give you an earful about never hanging out with us?" I laugh. "I can only imagine how difficult he's going to make it for the first guy here who tries to date you. Has he always been wound that tight?"

She looks out the window, and I get the sense my question may have been more loaded than I meant it to be. "Jake has the biggest heart," she says. "And to answer your question: yes, he's always been wound that tight."

She reaches for her braid, pulling it over her shoulder, playing with the ends. I shift my eyes back to the road and stay quiet, letting her go on.

"My brother has been through a lot," she begins, no doubt referring to their parents' death. "He was forced to grow up a lot quicker than he should have. He may come across as a bit overprotective, but he means well."

Struggling to find the rights words, and not wanting to muck it up, I say, "Jake is a great friend and I respect the hell out of him. He's one of the best guys I know."

I look over at her and suddenly feel a twinge of guilt. We aren't doing anything wrong, but Jake would probably see it differently. He would probably throw a knee to my dick if he knew about my history with his sister or the filthy things I've been wanting to do to her since seeing her again.

I turn down Haven Harbor with my mind a mess. I don't want this time with Sierra to end. I'm not the guy who asks girls to hang around. I'm down for a good time, we fuck, and it's all over by the next morning. So what the hell is happening to me? Why am I sitting here desperately trying to figure out a way to see this girl again?

Sierra reaches for the door handle as soon as I pull the truck in front of my house. "Thanks for the ride and for taking care of my tire, Grayson." She smiles, and somehow her pretty grin relaxes me. Things between us feel... friendly, and that's what I wanted. *I guess.*

But as she opens the door, I stop her. "Sierra, wait." My hand reaches for her arm, and when I touch her, she shifts in her seat and looks at me cautiously.

"Would you want to sit on the porch one night with me, or go to the beach?" I ask her, stumbling a little over my words. "I mean, as friends. Just friends."

It sounds awkward, like I'm asking her on a date. I'm not, but I still find myself holding my breath and hoping that her answer is yes.

"As friends, Grayson? That's it?"

Not the least bit. That's definitely not *it*. But I can't tell her that.

There's nothing innocent about the things I want to do to her. But I won't because Jake is my friend. I swear.

"Friends. I want to be your friend, Sierra," I say. She looks at me, suspicion in her eyes. "We can do whatever you want. We don't have to go to the beach. I can help you fix up the house instead and you can feed me. It's a win-win."

She sighs. "Grayson, that's all it can be. I'm not looking

to date anyone, and even if I was, it certainly can't be you. We both know why."

It's obvious she's referring to her brother. "Got it. Loud and clear. I promise I'll be good. No trying to date you. No fuzzy feelings. I'll keep my hands to myself. I've got this. So, are you going to let me come over sometime?"

She blows out a breath, shaking her head. "I don't know what I'm going to do with you. You're not going to give up, are you?"

I shrug. "Probably not."

Her eyes narrow in on mine. "Fine, we can hang out."

"You mean it?"

"Don't make this into a bigger deal than it is. I could change my mind."

"You won't." I wink.

She blows out a breath. "So cocky."

Then she slides out of my truck, shutting the door behind her and leaving me sitting in the driver's seat with a stupid smile on my face.

It only takes a moment before I'm already missing her wondering how long I'll have to wait to see her again.

SIERRA

THE MUSCLES in my biceps flex as I push the paddle through the water, feet planted firmly on my board as I glide closer to shore. I tip my face towards the sun and inhale the salty air, enjoying the feel of the wind blowing through my hair.

Predictably, my thoughts drift to Grayson. He's left me alone today, ever since he dropped me off after the ballpark last night. There have been no visits, no driveway encounters, no sightings of him around his house at all. *Not that I've been watching for him.*

Our run-in at the charity event wasn't as painful as I had expected. I did everything I could to steer clear of Grayson, but he found me at the end of the evening. It started out a bit awkward, but thankfully things improved. It's just my luck that I wound up with a flat tire on that night, of all nights. It was sweet of him to give me a ride home, and then offer to take care of my car for me. I have to admit, the drive was actually enjoyable. I had to ignore how my pulse hammered beneath my skin when Grayson had rested his hand on the gear shift just inches away from my thigh. If I'm honest, spending time with him was kind of nice. But it also fried my brain. Being around Grayson makes me feel things.

Digging the paddle into the glassy ocean water, I gain a little momentum, allowing me to glide over the surface for a few beats before I need to start paddling again. My paddleboard has always been an escape. Out here, it's just me and the water.

After our parents died, Jake and I went to live with our grandparents on Haven Harbor. I was still shell-shocked, and on top of that didn't know any other kids in the neighborhood. Jake made a couple of friends and started spending weekends with them at the beach. I would often tag along, promising him that I would stay out of their way. I had this strange attachment to Jake after the fire, I felt anxious any time we weren't together. I felt as though if I could just keep him close, I could make sure he was safe. That fear lived in me for at least a year. Every day I woke up terrified that I could lose him too, so I found any way I could to be with him—and keep an eye on him.

Eventually, I made a few friends at the beach, girls

around my age who were into paddleboarding. We would spend the whole day in the sun, coming home in time for dinner. The girls were from Reed Point— about 30 minutes away from Mayberry, the town where Jake and I grew up— and knew nothing about my past. I liked that they didn't know my story, that they didn't feel sorry for me.

I soon realized that when I was out on the ocean, it was the one time I could stop thinking about how much I missed my parents. I really believe that what I found in paddleboarding ended up saving me.

Carefully, I lower my body down so I'm straddling my board, enjoying the feel of the cold ocean water up to my knees. I hold onto my paddle in front of me, gazing at the view of the cove.

As much as I'd love to stay out here all day, I have a long to-do list waiting for me. I could scrub out the fridge or tackle the wallpaper in the bathroom. I also need to head to town to run a few errands, but I don't have my car back yet. I assume it's at Grayson's dad's shop.

As if he can read my mind, I look up to see Grayson pulling up in front of his house. He gets out of his truck and stands on the street in front of his house for a minute, looking down at his phone. Even from this distance, my heart thuds in my chest at the sight of Grayson Ford. I take the opportunity to stare. He's wearing a pair of shorts, a T-shirt and sneakers. A few strands of blond hair fall over his forehead in that messy-styled way that turns me on. Just the way he's standing there, how he carries himself all confident and cocky, makes me crazy with lust.

Desire rips through me as I watch him walk towards his front door, my heart rate kicking up a notch. It annoys me to no end how drawn I am to him. Grayson has an effect on me unlike any other man I've known.

Once he's inside, I try to wash him from my mind. I've spent way too much time thinking about our conversation last night. Obsessing about how good he looked, the scent of his cologne, the way his eyes held mine longer than they should have. *Friends* don't generally lock eyes like that.

I shake my head, reminding myself why I'm out here in the ocean. To decompress. I look around, taking in the beautiful view. It really is stunning here. I soak it all in, feeling the warmth of the sun on my skin.

This little cove has a secret-spot kind of vibe, even though it's only five minutes from the city. On one side, a bluff rises steeply from the ocean where Haven Harbor comes to an end—a rocky slope of boulders leads down to a shoreline that stretches for around two city blocks on the other side. The beach thins out then, ending at a steep hill that leads to downtown Reed Point. The sand is fine, almost white, and when the tide is high, the beach virtually disappears. I remember visiting my Gran when I was little and asking her where the beach disappeared to. Her answer always the same: The ocean is mysterious, wild, and free. Tides do what tides do. They turn.

A little while later, I'm walking towards home with my board in my arms. There is no one in sight, not even a shorebird on the beach. Grayson disappeared into his house an hour ago and I haven't seen him since.

Until now. I'm 20 feet or so from home when his front door opens, and he steps outside. He starts to head towards the side of the house but stops in his tracks when he notices me staring. He turns and strolls across his front lawn towards me with a smile on his lips.

"Hey! Perfect timing. I wanted to talk to you about your car."

"Okay." The board is heavy in my arms, so I set it and the

paddle down next to my feet. "I looked for you this morning to ask you about it," I say, and dammit, all of a sudden, I feel all fuzzy.

Did it just get 10 degrees hotter outside, or is it just me? I'm warm everywhere. I grab hold of the lapel of the oversized button-up that I threw on over my bikini and fan it away from my body, trying to get some air flow going. I catch Grayson's dark eyes dip down to my chest, staying there for a moment—a long moment—before he tears his gaze away, looking out at the ocean.

I swallow what feels like cotton in my mouth.

"I've got it handled," he says. *What does he have handled? What the heck were we even talking about? I know what I'm imagining handling— Fuck. No, Sierra. Stop thinking about his package.*

His chocolate eyes hold mine as he smirks. He's fearless.

I feel my body flush. Not only is Grayson gorgeous, but he's a huge flirt. He doesn't stop until he gets what he wants. If I'm smart, I should say goodbye now and barricade myself inside my house.

But being around Grayson is fun, and the thing is... I'm lonely. I've been in this house for over a week now by myself and while I know my brother wouldn't want Grayson anywhere near me, I like spending time with him. He makes me feel... tingly. And I like it.

"Your car, Sierra. I've taken care of it. It's at my dad's shop, ready first thing tomorrow morning."

That's right. My car. "Thank you. That's really nice of you and your dad. I appreciate it."

"It's no problem," he says, looking down at my board. "How was your paddle?"

"It was nice, thanks."

"And what are you planning on doing now?"

"I have to get some work done on the house. You?"

"No plans," he says, combing his fingers through his blond hair. Grayson is standing so close to me that I can smell his aftershave. It's dizzying. "How about you let me help you? I'm very good with a paint brush."

His promise from the other night echoes in my mind. *I promise I'll be good. No trying to date you. No fuzzy feelings. I'll keep my hands to myself.* That's when I agreed to be friends.

The corner of his mouth turns up and he flexes his bicep. "I can lift heavy things," he grins, trying to persuade me. *Why does he have to be so ridiculously charming?* "Honestly, Sierra. I have no plans. I'd like to help you."

Friends help each other all the time. We wouldn't be doing anything wrong.

"Okay," I say, before I can find an excuse to turn him down.

His grin turns into a full-blown smile. Charming. Confident. I'm guessing that Grayson doesn't hear the word no very often. Wasting no time, he reaches for my board, and I let him carry it.

"I should warn you, Sierra, in the interest of making this friendship thing work. If we're going to be hanging out, it's probably going to be hard for you not to stare at my muscles." He grins, and grips my board a little tighter, flexing his bicep.

"Friends, Grayson," I say, in my best *behave yourself* voice. "Do I have to remind you that friends don't check each other out?"

"So does that mean I can't tell you how hot you look right now in just a bikini and that shirt?"

This man. What am I going to do with him? Blushing, I say, "No, you cannot."

"Got it. Just checking," he says with a wink.

I roll my eyes, but his words thrum through me. Grayson just called me hot.

And I wouldn't mind hearing him do it again.

MY HEART HAS BEEN THUMPING EVER since Grayson walked into my house. What was I thinking, agreeing to his offer of help? It's not going to be easy having him this close to me looking like... that.

His T-shirt is pulled tight across his shoulders, clinging to his sculpted body. His biceps flex as he tears strips of wallpaper from the bathroom walls.

For the life of me I can't look away. I eye him for another quick moment before he catches me staring. The man is a specimen—an inch or so over 6 feet, carved jaw, smooth olive skin, an athlete's body. If I stand here any longer, I'm going to need a cold shower because all I can think about is getting him out of his clothes.

I groan inwardly. This is going to test every single ounce of my willpower, knowing what he looks like under that T and those shorts, but not being able to touch him.

I need to get to a place where I can be around Grayson and not have the urge to climb him like a tree. I can't lurk in hallways lusting after him like I'm doing right now.

"I got you something cold to drink," I say, stepping into the bathroom with two glasses of iced tea in my hands.

Grayson thanks me, reaching for a glass. He takes a long sip, his Adam's apple bobbing. My attention locks in on the man, mesmerized by him doing something as simple as drinking from a damn glass. I guess if I can't put my hands on him, I can at least look.

He sets the glass on the counter, smiling an appreciative

grin, acting all casual and breezy like being around me is no big deal. He's been this way since he got here. Maybe being friends really is all he wants. It's probably just me who's having these silly fantasies.

Then he lifts the hem of his shirt to wipe his lips, revealing the hard muscles of his abdomen; the grooves and lines of his six-pack above the light blond trail of hair leading into his shorts.

The flutter inside my chest doubles in intensity, then his smooth voice brings me back to my senses. "Have you heard from your brother today?"

I blink. It's a stark reminder of why I need to stop these fantasies. "No. I missed his call while I was out for my paddle."

"Does he know about your car, or that I drove you home from the ballpark?"

My stomach clenches. "No, not yet."

I swallow a gulp of my iced tea, nervous at the thought of telling my brother that I've been spending time with Grayson. It feels like I'm keeping a big secret from Jake, like I'm being dishonest. But I don't want to stop. Something about being around him excites me in a way I haven't felt before.

"If I'm lucky, maybe he'll let me live when he finds out I'm here with you," Grayson jokes.

"Um, I'd say that's wishful thinking on your part."

He laughs, then rubs a hand over his flat stomach. "What time is it? We've been at this for a while."

"You must be hungry," I say apologetically. "Why don't I order us a pizza? Least I can do."

"Pizza sounds great," he says casually. "As long as there's no pineapple. Please tell me you don't put fruit on your pizza."

I laugh. "Why would I do that? People who put pineapple on their pizza are probably serial killers. It's right up there with mint ice cream."

"Right? Who thought it was a good idea to make ice cream taste like toothpaste? It shouldn't be allowed to be sold in stores."

He claps his hands. "Okay, then let's order. I'm starved."

I'm starved too... for so many reasons.

As I google a pizza place around here, I find myself wondering how I thought being friends with Grayson was ever going to work. So far, it isn't easy.

I can do this. I just need to press pause on these thoughts that are making my head spin. Grayson and I can just be friends. Because being around him is too much fun to stop.

SEVEN

YOU CAN GET THAT IMAGE RIGHT OUT OF YOUR HEAD.

G rayson

The pizza Sierra ordered is five-star. So is her company. We cleaned up the mess from the afternoon of work and are now sitting on her back porch eating deep-dish. Somewhere along the way, the topic of conversation moved to go-go dancing, so that's where we're at now.

"Admit it. You're a secret go-go dancer," I say, a smirk taking over my face. "That's what you're doing over here late at night when the blinds are closed."

"Yes, Grayson, that's exactly what I'm doing," she says, shaking her head. "Would you like me to show you?"

Holy shit, I absolutely would.

She must see the surprised expression on my face because her eyes flash a *what-did-I-just-say* look as she playfully bats at my shoulder. "I did not actually mean that, Gray. You can get that image right out of your head."

She called me Gray. I liked it. A lot.

I sit back in my chair, crossing my arms over my chest. Sitting out here with Sierra feels relaxed, even normal. It feels like it did in Miami, before things between us got weird. She looks like she feels the same way, like her guard is down. Finally.

She looks good too, in a faded Rolling Stones T-shirt with a pair of cut-off jean shorts, both splattered with paint. She put her hair up in a ponytail when we got to work on the house. My gaze drops to her neck, a part of her body I am dying to kiss again.

I wonder how many guys have kissed her there since I did in Miami. Is she seeing anyone? Has she ever been in love?

I guarantee that any guy she's ever hooked up with has never devoured her body the way I can. I trace the rim of my glass, pushing all thoughts of Sierra with another man far from my mind.

I know she's off-limits. But fuck, I'd like to worship her body, make her feel better than she ever has. Make her scream. But that can't happen. So instead, I'll be her friend. I'll enjoy nights like this one with her, I'll be the person she turns to when she needs something or someone to talk to.

"So, tell me," I ask her. "How did we both grow up in Reed Point and not know each other?"

She crinkles her brows. "I don't know *everyone* in Reed Point, do you?" she asks over the rim of her wine glass. The almost-empty pizza box has been cast aside and Sierra has poured us each a glass of red. Haven Harbor is so quiet at this time of night that it feels deserted, like it's just Sierra and I and the stars in the sky.

"I might," I tease. "I'm a pretty big deal around here. I'm sure you've heard."

She scoffs. "You're ridiculous. Jake and I didn't actually grow up in Reed Point. We moved here when Jake was 12 and I was 10. We grew up in Mayberry, a little town famous for... wait for it... chili dogs. They have a chili dog eating contest every summer and it's the highlight of the year. Sad I know." She shrugs, staring into my eyes. "Anyways, then we moved to Haven Harbor and I think living here kept us removed from most of the kids our age. We didn't go to White Harbor beach on weekends, we just hung out around here where there's pretty much... no one."

"It's a pretty great place to grow up."

"It was," she says, with a small smile that fades quickly. I watch her start to shrink into herself, but then she changes the topic, switching the focus onto me. "How about you... tell me a little about your family. Any siblings?"

"One sister. She's four years younger than me. Her name is Kyla," I share, reaching for the wine bottle, refilling my glass. "She's going to school to become a physiotherapist."

She nods, absentmindedly tracing a finger around the rim of her wine glass. "So, I guess that means neither of you are taking over the family business?"

"Nope, neither of us have ever wanted my dad's company. Thankfully he seems okay with it. He's never pressured either of us to come work with him."

"Are you and your dad close?"

I shrug, clearing my throat. There is so much I don't want her to know about my dad. There is too much pain there, and enough embarrassment to last a lifetime. If Sierra knew about my dad's addiction, she'd see me differently. I don't want that dark cloud hanging over us.

I take another sip of my wine, stalling. Then I answer her question as simply as I can. "We're not. It's been a long time since I've had much of a relationship with him," I say. "When I was 15, my dad had an accident at his garage. Hurt his leg pretty bad. Needed a whole bunch of surgeries. He was bitter for a long time."

Before the accident, my dad was a great father. He

coached my baseball team, taught my sister and I how to fish and camp and downhill bike. He would tell us every day how much he loved us.

Then it all fell apart. Thank God we had Mom.

Sierra lifts her glass but sets it back down on the table before it touches her lips. "But he's okay now?"

I swallow hard. "He's... better."

"I'm sorry, Grayson. That must have been so hard for you and your family."

I exhale a breath, "It was a long time ago, but he still struggles." This is the part of my life that Sierra never needs to see. If she knew about the addiction my father has struggled with, the erratic behaviour, the anger, she'd probably think twice about wanting a relationship of any kind with me, even a friendship. I come with baggage—a shit load of it. I wouldn't blame anyone for not wanting to take it on.

Especially Sierra who deserves someone who will always be there for her, not someone who might have to drop everything to check his dad into rehab for the 20th time, or work weekends at his dad's garage just to keep the place from shutting down.

I look at her and find understanding in her eyes. Sierra is the type of girl who can make you see your life in a whole new way. She makes you want to be better. But that's not in the cards for us, and it never will be. I need to accept it.

She swallows hard. "How is your mom with it all?"

"Honestly, she's a saint. She's never left his side."

"She loves him," she says quietly, her eyes holding mine. "I bet she's an amazing woman. She raised a good guy."

Her words hit me straight in the chest. I know she didn't mean a whole lot by it, but coming from Sierra, the compliment feels different. I watch as she takes her hair out of the messy ponytail, running a hand through the golden blonde strands. As her hair begins to fall all around her face, I realize I'm curling my hands into fists to stop myself from reaching over to brush it behind her shoulder. This is when I should thank her for having me and go home. Immediately. But I can't bring myself to move.

I've had such a good night with her. We've talked. We've laughed. Best of all— we've been flirty. And there's been this sense of ease that I'm not used to feeling with a woman. I've always been in a hurry to leave. But tonight, I want to stick around.

Which is how I feel whenever I'm around Sierra.

"I have an idea," I say, sitting up in my chair. "Let's go paddling. We both have boards. Plus, I like looking at you in a swimsuit."

She raises her eyebrows, but I can see the beginning of a smile on her lips.

"Right now?"

"Well, I wasn't thinking right now, but sure. I was thinking another day, in the daylight, so I can see you again... in a bathing suit."

She bites her lip, trying really fucking hard not to crack a smile.

"No point trying to hide that smile. I see it." I am aware that I'm flirting with her, but she doesn't seem to mind. "Just admit it, Sierra... you can't resist my charm."

She blushes. "Fine. Maybe I can't resist."

Ah, shit. She actually just admitted it.

"Better watch out... you might fall for me if you're not careful. And when I say *might*, I really mean *will*."

She fights a laugh, stretching her leg out and nudging my shin with her bare foot. But she isn't fast enough, because I snatch her foot in my hand and hold it between my legs, gently massaging her skin.

Sierra stiffens for a second before flexing her foot as my hands work the arch. Her eyes close, a soft sound escaping her lips. The sound goes straight to my groin and I'm suddenly picturing Sierra without clothes on, sprawled out across my bed.

I *can't* think about Sierra naked. What kind of friend would I be?

I will the dirty thoughts about my *friend* from my mind... but there's still a fuzzy feeling in my chest.

I like Sierra. And I want more than friendship.

I stare at her, watching her inhale a deep breath as my fingers move in tiny circles across her foot. When her eyes flutter back open to meet mine, she looks light and carefree. "Thank you, Grayson."

"For what?" I ask, still holding her small foot in my hands.

"For your help today. We got a lot done together. You're a good friend."

I nod. *Friend.* There's that stupid word again. Why am I letting it bother me? No matter what I might want, it's not like there can ever be more between us. I'm not prepared to ruin my friendship with Jake, or drive a wedge between him and Sierra.

I take a deep breath, strengthening my resolve. As long as Sierra and I keep a safe distance from each other, we won't be doing anything wrong.

But I know that even if we keep this strictly platonic, eventually Jake is going to find out that I'm hanging out with his sister. And when that happens, he's not going to be happy.

It's a good thing I have no plans to tell him.

EIGHT

YOU WERE TRYING TO BE NEIGHBORLY, MY ASS.

Sierra

"We've been waiting to meet the girl who Miss Millie has gone on and on about for years."

I can't remember the last time I've been around this many gorgeous men. Do all the hot guys move to Haven Harbor? Is there something in the water here? Tucker and Holden are definitely easy on the eyes.

I was taking a break from working in the garden when I noticed them jogging down the hill on their way back from a morning run. They stopped when they reached my front yard, both shirtless, their carved chests glistening under the sun.

"I guess that would be me," I say, giving a little wave with one hand while holding my mug in the other. "I'm sorry it's taken me this long to introduce myself. I'm Sierra."

"Nothing to be sorry about. It's good to meet you. I'm Holden," says the slightly shorter one must be at least 6 feet. He holds out a hand for me to shake. "Tucker," adds the other guy, flashing a swoon-worthy smile. "We figured we'd give you some time before we came knocking on your door. It seems like you've been pretty busy."

That's an understatement. It's been just over a week since I moved in and I've been going at full steam, getting Gran settled into the nursing home, starting the house renovations, getting used to my new office, trying to spend some time with my brother. There hasn't been a lot of time left over for neighborhood introductions. And then there's the fact that I had been hiding away inside my house, away from Grayson.

Painting. Thinking about my hot neighbor. Unpacking boxes. Thinking about my hot neighbor.

Last night with Grayson was a lot of fun. I'm glad that I'm over trying to avoid him. It had felt so awkward, sneaking around, worrying about what I would say if and when our paths crossed.

"I *have* been busy," I say, taking a sip of my lukewarm tea. "But it's good to finally meet you both. I hear you know my brother."

"Jake is our boy, but you definitely got the looks in the family," Holden jokes. "You seem a lot less serious too. I love Jake, but the guy is about as laid back as airport security."

I chuckle, my shoulders popping up in a shrug. "Yeah, you're sort of right."

"So, how do you like being back in Reed Point?" Tucker asks. "There's no better place than Haven Harbor."

I can hear his love for this secluded street in his voice. I understand why he likes living here so much, but it's more complicated for me. A lot of painful memories live here.

But you can't deny how picturesque the place is, these four little houses with the ocean at their doorsteps. I mean, how many people can say they have a view like this? It's like following a rainbow and finding a pot of gold at the end.

"It really is one of the most beautiful places in the world," I say, looking out at the ocean as it crashes into the rocky cove. Haven Harbor is a magical place to wake up to every day. "I love living by the water. As for Reed Point, I'm a small-town girl through and through, and I'm not sure any small town I've ever visited can hold a candle to this one."

We spend the next 10 minutes talking about Gran and what a spitfire she is. The guys seem to genuinely care about her, which makes me like them even more. I'm surprised when Tucker points out the bright fuchsia petunias I planted between yellow marigolds and snapdragons and tells me that he loves to garden too. He says he's planted a bunch of vegetables in wooden boxes in his backyard and that he used to go to Gran when things weren't growing the way he hoped they would.

"Are you planning on staying here on Haven Harbor then?" Holden asks.

I'm about to tell them that my move here is long-term when my phone buzzes in my pocket. I fully expect it to be my brother, checking in on me like he has every morning since I've been back, but when I see Grayson's name flash across my screen, my heart speeds in my chest. I had given him my phone number before he left my house last night and this is the first time his name has appeared on my screen. I stand in front of my new neighbors with a ridiculously stupid smile on my face.

I swipe the screen to life.

Grayson: You around?

With zero chill, I tell the guys I just need a second to reply to this. Setting my mug down on the grass, I type out a quick response.

> Sierra: Just having my morning cup of tea outside. You?

> Grayson: Picked up your car. On my way to you. See you in 5.

> Sierra: I'll be here.

Another text from him quickly pops up.

> Grayson: We should probably take it out for a drive. Make sure the tire is working right. Maybe grab lunch. Safety first. ;)

I laugh, then shove my phone in my back pocket, apologizing to the guys for the interruption. I ask them about themselves, wanting to get to know my new neighbours—and Jake's closest friends—a bit better. Tucker tells me about his job as a high school teacher and Holden fills me in on his work in web design. The conversation has just moved to my job at The Seaside when I see my white SUV turn down the street, coming to a stop outside Gran's house. Grayson steps out of the driver's side, unfolding his tall frame. His hair is covered by a backwards baseball hat, and a pair of sunglasses shield his eyes. His smile falters when it lands on Holden and Tucker, then he removes his sunglasses, raking his eyes over me. I can feel the appreciation in his stare, making me warm all over. When Grayson's eyes are on you, you feel it in your bones.

"Hey, Sierra." His silky voice lights my skin on fire as he walks towards the three of us.

"Hey." Oh, lord. Time to put on my game face. "I was just introducing myself to your friends."

"You two have already met?" Tucker asks, sounding surprised.

My eyes flicker to Grayson, not sure how I should respond. Shamelessly flirting with the hot neighbor you hooked up with a couple of years ago is all fun and games until other people start asking you questions. This is the problem with keeping secrets.

Something washes over Grayson's face before he thankfully jumps in and answers the question for me. "Yup. Found her with a flat, so I had my dad fix it for her."

Tucker nods, but I can see he still has questions. Grayson hasn't told them about me. Grayson quickly hands me my car keys, changing the subject. "Good as new."

"Thank you." I reach for my keys, taking them from Grayson's hand. He gives me a lopsided grin that sends a wave of heat down my spine. The feeling surprises me and before I can stop myself, I'm thinking back to that night in Miami. He caught me off guard back then as well, and I knew I had to put distance between us. I wasn't going to risk falling for a guy only to have my heart broken, so instead of talking to Grayson, I ran for the door, shutting him out. I knew it wasn't the best move, but at the time my survival instinct kicked in and I just needed to get out of there.

"You coming to Jake's this Friday night?" Holden asks, snapping me out of my thoughts.

I had forgotten all about the invite. My brother called me a couple of days ago to see if I needed anything—the calls and texts were so frequent they were all becoming a blur— and invited me to a barbecue he was having. I told him I'd be there. A night out would be a nice change, I thought.

Now I can feel Grayson watching me out of the corner of my eye, waiting for my response.

"Definitely."

"Good," Tucker says, flicking his T-shirt at Holden's

arm. "I'm gonna run, I need a shower. If you wanna ride with us to Jake's, we have room. It was good meeting you, Sierra."

"I'd better get going too. Glad we finally met," Holden says, before turning his gaze to Grayson. "Gray, I'll call you later." He tilts his head at Grayson with an amused look, then jogs off in the direction of his house, leaving me alone with the man who makes my skin heat.

"Thanks again for taking care of my tire," I tell him.

His smile widens and I find I'm having a difficult time looking directly at him. His blonde hair, his striking brown eyes, golden skin, his chiseled jaw, and that backwards baseball cap. It's a lot to take in all at once.

"Let me pay you." I dig out my phone from my pocket. "I can transfer you the money right now."

He raises an eyebrow before adjusting his ball cap on his head. "Not gonna happen, babe. It's taken care of."

"Wait, no." I put one hand on my hip and narrow my eyes at him. "I want to pay your dad."

"You don't need to. I took care of it. Besides, you agreed to have lunch with me, so that'll make us even."

"I don't remember agreeing to that," I say, crossing my arms over my chest. The gesture makes his eyes dip down for a split second before they travel back up to meet mine.

"I'm pretty sure you did." He grins in that smooth, confident way of his that sets my skin ablaze.

You need to get yourself together, Sierra. You can't have him.

"So, what do you feel like? Tacos? Burgers?" he says with a suggestive wink. "Or maybe we should try the new sushi restaurant on First? I'm easy."

"What *you* are is obnoxious," I tell him, shaking my head. "But sushi sounds good, and I do want to make it up to you for your help with the tire."

"Nah, you owe me nothing. Just let me do this for you. Now about lunch... I'll pick you up at noon. Sound good?"

"Sounds good. And Grayson..."

"Yeah?"

"Thank you," I tell him again. "Really. I appreciate it very much."

"It's nothing, Sierra. I'm just happy I could help you out." His eyes are warm. I take a breath and try to act like the way he's looking at me right now isn't turning my insides to mush. It's not easy acting aloof around Grayson.

As I watch him walk across the lawn to his house, I realize how much lighter I feel when Grayson is around. That dull ache in my chest that has made it hard to breathe since being back in Reed Point seems to fade away whenever he's around. And lately he seems to be around a lot.

I try to take my eyes off him as he gets closer to his house, watching the way he walks with confidence, not to mention his ass in those jeans. I tell myself to go inside and douse myself in cold water, but I stay standing right where I am.

This is the third time in as many days that I'm hanging out with Grayson, and I can feel it getting harder and harder to remember all the reasons why we can't be together. The lines are getting blurry. It's becoming a problem.

Friends is all we can ever be, and I need to remember that.

GRAYSON

I HEAD out to work the next morning, my laptop in one hand and a piece of toast in the other. I'm just about to hop in my truck when I spot Tucker, who is dragging his garbage bin up from the curb wearing only a pair of old sweats and flip flops.

"You look rough as hell," I call to him. "Who was she?"

"I think that's a better question for you." He smirks, parking the bin in his garage. "What's the deal with you and Sierra?"

I shrug, trying to hide my grin. I already can't wait to see her again.

"You're really not going to admit that you have a thing for Jake's sister?" Tucker asks, walking towards me. "It's written all over your face."

I open my truck door and toss my laptop on the passenger seat, trying to hide the smile on my face. "Shouldn't you be dressed for work?" I ask, waving a hand at his attire—or lack thereof.

"I'll get on that when you've answered my question," he presses. "And you might as well tell me the truth. You can't lie worth shit."

"There's nothing going on with me and Sierra. She had a flat tire at that baseball fundraiser we were both at and I helped her with it. That's it."

I take a bite of my toast, hoping he's done with the questions.

"You sure that's all?" he asks, "I mean, I wouldn't blame you if you liked her. The girl is hot. Maybe I should—"

"Tuck." My spine straightens at the comment, annoyance firing up in every part of my body. Sierra is mine. She's off limits.

Tucker laughs. "Look at you, man. You're ready to knock my head off my shoulders just for saying your girl's hot. What did I say? You can't lie worth shit."

"She's not my girl," I insist, though I have to admit I like the way it would sound if she was.

"Yet," he says, backing up with a smirk. "I'll bet you right now that she will be by next week."

I shake my head and slip into my truck, thinking that's one bet I'd be happy to lose.

I'M FEELING UNUSUALLY LAIDBACK for a Monday morning as I pour myself a second cup of coffee in the break room, stirring in two packets of sugar.

My good mood is entirely thanks to the weekend I just spent with Sierra. There has definitely been a breakthrough in our relationship and for the first time, since she moved in two weeks ago, I'm not worried how she'll react the next time I run into her. I know things between us are... okay.

She won't be avoiding me anymore. Conversations won't be awkward. Sierra and I are cool. This is so much better.

After I picked her up yesterday, I took her to a sushi restaurant for lunch. We sipped on green tea and talked about our jobs over a shared meal of spicy tuna rolls, agedashi tofu, and tempura. As we sat together, I could feel Sierra slowly letting go of the *thing* she had been holding against me. It was a relief.

I sat across from her at the small table, mesmerized by her sparkling brown and gold eyes as she told me about her friends in Virginia Beach, the time she broke her leg jumping on a trampoline and all of the Sundays Millie dragged her and Jake to church.

I wanted to kiss her the entire time.

Being around Sierra is like a hit of the best kind of drug; you're always left wanting more. She's like sunshine: warm, bright, and good for the soul.

Smiling, I walk past reception and down the hallway back to my office. I stop at Beck's open door and find him sitting at his desk with his laptop open.

"Hey, Beck. How was your weekend?"

He waves me in, picking up his own coffee mug, taking a sip. "Great. Took Maya to the beach. You should have seen her in the water. Her smile was as big as a slice of watermelon. She's so damn cute," he gushes over his 1-year-old daughter. "How was yours?"

The best weekend I've had in two years.

"Good. Pretty chill," I say instead. "Hung around the house."

He cocks a brow. "You did, did you?" he says with an *I'm-not-buying-it* tone in his voice. "Did you happen to run into your neighbor?"

I stare back at him.

What does he know?

Fuck, I'm in trouble.

Tucker is full of shit about a lot of things, but he's right when he says I am a terrible liar. There's no way I can lie to Beckett.

He sets his mug down on his desk and leans back in his chair with his arms crossed over his chest. I get the feeling he's not done asking questions.

Beck and I have worked together at The Liberty for the better part of four years. He'd mentored me in the beginning, showing me the ropes, offering me advice and guidance. We eventually became friends, hanging out outside of work, and when he became president, our relationship didn't change.

"Sierra? Yeah, I saw her around."

"You more than saw her around." Beckett cocks a brow with a look that says he's caught me red-handed. "Bean saw you walking out of Sushi Box with her yesterday. She asked if you guys are dating. What's up with the two of you?"

Fuck. One of the joys of living in a small town is that everyone knows your business. How did I not see Beck's sister, Bean?

Not that it matters. Sierra and I weren't sneaking around, and there is nothing going on between us that we need to hide.

I scrub my hand over my jaw, stepping further into Beck's office. "We went for lunch. I was trying to be neighborly."

Becks smiles, pivoting in his chair like he knows there's more to my story. "You were trying to be neighborly, my ass. You have a thing for her. Admit it, Gray. I saw the way you were staring at her at the ballpark. I'm sure everyone there saw it. Your eyes were glued to her the entire night."

"It's not like that. We're... friends."

Beckett eyes me for a second. "Have you told Jake about your *friendship* with his sister?"

I shrug the question off like it isn't a big deal. "No."

"I suggest you don't, unless you really enjoy pissing him off."

"I just told you, Beck. We're friends. That's all. He can't be mad at that."

"Oh, he *can* be, and he *will* be," he says, picking up a pen from his desk, twirling it in his fingers. "Look, Gray, Sierra is a nice girl."

"I know that." *Does he think I don't?*

He sighs, narrowing his eyes at me. "Then you know she isn't the kind of girl you fuck around. Just be careful. She's not going to be okay with no-strings."

His words sting, but I try not to let them get to me. He isn't exactly wrong. I'm 27 years old and have never been in a real, committed relationship save for Layla, but that was almost six years ago. Since then, I've had my fair share of hookups, but I haven't so much as thought about another woman since Sierra moved in next door.

I'm hooked on her sweet smile, not to mention the most intoxicating body I've ever laid eyes on. When I'm with her, I don't worry about who her brother is, or all the reasons we can't work together. And when I'm not with her, she's all I've been able to think about. For fuck's sake, I can't count the times I've jacked off in the last two weeks to dirty images of Sierra and all the filthy things I want to do to her.

But as long as I'm not actually touching her, I'm not doing anything wrong.

Jake is just going to have to figure out a way to deal with the fact that I'm hanging out with his sister, because I have no plans of stopping.

"Don't make this bigger than what it is, Beck. She's just moved back to town. I'm only trying to be a friend."

"A friend who will be missing his favorite body part when her brother finds out. Don't say I didn't warn you."

Fuck, I know he's right. But when I think about the way Sierra laughs, and how her eyes light up, I forget all about Jake.

"I'll catch you later. I've got work to do," I say, taking several steps towards the door.

"Catch you later. And Gray—"

I turn in the threshold of his office to face him. "Yeah?"

"If something does happen between you and Sierra, be honest with Jake and tell him before he finds out from someone else."

Beckett stares at me for a long moment, letting his advice sink in, then nods and turns back to his computer screen.

Nothing is happening between Sierra and I, although I'm not denying that I wish there was. After lunch yesterday, I went home to my empty house. I turned on TSN, folded the laundry that I had been ignoring all week and did everything I could think of to stop myself from looking out my front window at the yellow house beside mine. All I wanted was another glimpse of Sierra, even after spending the afternoon with her. That's when I knew that I was screwed. Drowning in Sierra, so deep that I don't want to be saved.

I still don't know what to do about it. All I really know is that being around Sierra feels good. *Like sunshine.*

As I get to my office door, Grant from my team rounds the corner, stopping when he's a few feet away from me. "Heads up... HR scheduled a last-minute meeting at two. The entire team. Check your emails. It just came through."

"On it," I nod. That's strange. I can't think of any reason why HR would be calling us in. "Any idea what it's about?"

"None. Who knows what they're up to?"

"I guess we'll see soon enough."

Grant grimaces, passing by me on the way to his office. My fingers scratch through the stubble on my jaw. Whatever it is, it's not going to ruin my good mood. I'm probably overthinking it. Everything will be fine.

There's still a smile on my face when I take the elevator up to the third floor for the afternoon meeting, but it doesn't stay there for long. Geoff, head of the department, is standing at the front of the room, and the rest of my team are all seated around the boardroom table.

"Hey, everyone," I say, my eyes focused on Geoff as I try to get a feel for the temperature in the room.

"Grayson." Geoff nods to a chair. "Take a seat, we're almost ready to get started."

I slip into the chair beside Grant. "What the fuck is this all about?" he mutters under his breath.

"No idea."

Just then the door opens and all eyes in the room swerve to watch a woman in a black, fitted pantsuit and heels walk into the room. Her hair is pulled tightly back from her face, secured in a sleek ponytail at the base of her neck. She's looking down at the phone in her hand, but when she looks up, her eyes immediately find mine. Then everyone else in the room fades away.

What is she doing here?

Blair. I'm pretty sure I'm remembering that right. Fuck, it is Blair.

It takes a monumental effort to keep my expression even as a large lump forms in my throat.

Blair and I met at a bar two years ago. I was there with some buddies after work, she was there to meet a guy who never showed. I struck up a conversation with her, immediately hitting it off with the pretty blonde. She was pissed that she had been stood up by some guy and wasn't ready to call it a night. We chatted for a while over a couple rounds of drinks, keeping the conversation light. Then we finished the night off at my place, fucking for hours. She never told me what she did for work, and I never asked. We didn't need those types of details for what we wanted out of each other. We both just wanted to get off. The next morning, she left happy.

She doesn't look very happy now.

Blair's eyes jerk away from mine as she sweeps into the room with confidence, stopping next to Geoff, to exchange a few quick, quiet words. He raises his eyebrows at her as if he's asking for her approval. She subtly nods, then they both turn their attention to the rest of us, who are waiting patiently to find out why the hell we were all called here.

Geoff clears his throat. "Sorry about the short notice today but thank you to everyone for coming. The reason we're all here... I'd like you all to meet Blair Winters. She will be replacing Morgan as the new corporate communications officer."

What? He's got to be kidding.

I had no idea they were even interviewing for the position, never mind that they had decided to give the job to Blair of all people. I'm surprised I never once caught wind of this, that Beck didn't mention that Morgan was leaving the company.

Blair steps forward to introduce herself, her slender shoulders pinned back, standing as tall as her five-foot-five frame will allow. She's confident, already in control of the room, and I'm reminded of that night we met at the bar. It had been obvious then she was secure in who she was, boldly holding my gaze when I'd spotted her across the room. But that's not the case today, at least not with me—she hasn't so much as glanced in my direction again.

"It's an honor to be working at The Liberty and I'm excited to get to know each and every one of you. I want you to know, I'm not here to change everything. What the Liberty team has accomplished is impressive. I'm here to work alongside you and make The Liberty even greater."

My heart rate speeds at the thought of seeing her at work every day.

When she's done talking, Geoff explains that she'll be officially starting the position on Monday. He calls the meeting to a close, and the sound of chairs scraping against the laminate floor fills the room as everyone gets up to introduce themselves. It gives me a chance to hang back as I try to decide how I want to approach her.

Too late.

Before I get a chance to say anything, Geoff apologizes to the group, saying he needs to get Blair to legal to finish up some paperwork. I watch as she gathers up her things and follows Geoff out of the boardroom without so much as a backwards glance.

What a fucking disaster. I love my job at The Liberty, but working with Blair could be awkward as hell. I blow out a breath, massaging the back of my neck. Do I tell Beckett about my history with her? Fucking great. It's not even two hours ago that he was comparing me to the town bicycle and now I'm going to prove him right by telling him I slept with our newest hire.

A muscle in my jaw tenses. I tell myself to go back to my office and think before I do something I'll regret, like striding down to Blair's new office to demand that we talk this out. Devise a plan. Get on the same page.

I resist the temptation, annoyed at this unexpected turn of events. This morning the world was my fucking oyster, now it's a cluster fuck of epic proportions.

NINE

I HAVE CHICKS BEGGING FOR MY DICK.

Grayson

It's been five days since I learned about Blair joining The Liberty, but I still haven't said a word to anyone about our past. Not even to Beck. My head has been spinning, and the fact that Blair seems to be actively avoiding me at work isn't helping. I tried to approach her in the lunchroom a couple of days ago, but she walked out as quickly as she had come in when she saw me. I'm starting to wonder if the company is big enough for both Blair and me. Or am I just worrying about nothing?

The one positive in all of this is that the shit storm currently brewing at work *has* helped to take my mind off Sierra for a little while.

It's been days since I last saw her unless you count yesterday morning when I caught a quick glimpse of her as she left for work. I was sitting in my car about to pull out of my driveway when I saw her walk out her door wearing a white button-up blouse, fitted black skirt and a pair of heels that made her legs look five feet long. I'm pretty sure my eyes bugged out of their sockets as I watched her walk to her car, completely entranced by the graceful way she moved.

The lack of contact between us has me wondering if Sierra has retreated back into avoidance mode. *Fuck.* Between the potential disaster at work and Sierra being incommunicado, I can hardly think straight. But at least it's Friday. I'm ready to have a drink or three and forget about all of it for a while.

Right on cue, Tucker crosses the room and hands me a cold beer. I could kiss him. We're at Jake's weekend cookout, and despite my intention to put Sierra out of my mind, I can't help but wonder if I might see her tonight. Will she still show up to her brother's party, knowing that I'll probably be here?

I get an answer to that question when the door opens a few moments later and I look up to see Sierra standing there, just feet away from me. My eyes trace the curves of her body as she walks into the party, taking in her slim waist, full hips, ample tits, and the fitted spaghetti strap dress that hugs her curves. Every single one of them.

My cock swells in my jeans.

I can't keep my eyes off her as she says hi to her brother, Tucker, and Holden. Sierra smiles like there's no place she'd rather be, introducing herself next to Holden's girlfriend, Aubrey, chatting effortlessly as if she's known her for years. I watch as she moves through the room with ease, throwing her arms around Jules when she sees her. Beckett is also a mountain biking addict, so I invited him to join Jake and me on the trails a few times a while ago, and the two of them became quick friends. Jules and Beck are now regulars at Jake's frequent get togethers.

Finally, Sierra turns to me with a gleam in her eyes—or maybe that's just my wishful thinking. I hope that she's as happy to see me as I am to see her. "Best for last," I joke as she walks over to me, trying to ignore my pulse hammering under my skin.

"Do I know you?" she teases back, and I'm so fucking happy things still seem to be okay between us. This is, after all, what I've been most nervous about: feeling normal around her and her brother and our friends. So far, so good. "I don't believe we've met."

I mock pout, then her arms slide around my neck, and I wrap mine around her waist in a hug. "It's good to see you, Grayson."

One second.

Two seconds.

It's just a standard hug, nothing sexual, nothing more than she gave to anyone else at the party, but I soak up every second, loving the feeling of having her in my arms. I haven't been this close to her since that night in Miami; there's no way I'm not savoring this moment.

When we break apart, my skin burns from where her body was just pressed up against mine. I mentally give myself shit for getting so sappy from a simple embrace. I chalk it up to being a touchy-feely guy, but this feels like more of a spark, a high, a buzz inside my chest. And even though we'd just done a round of shots before she got here, I'm positive it's not the alcohol but Sierra that's giving me this buzz.

But before I have a chance to say anything else, Jules grabs Sierra's elbow and pulls her into the kitchen, leaving me wanting more as usual. It's never enough when it comes to Sierra. There's always an audience, always someone around to interrupt us when we're together. It's starting to get frustrating.

"I'm firing up the barbecue," Jake says as he walks past

me on his way to the back deck, clapping my shoulder and knocking me from my thoughts.

An hour later, after we've all filled ourselves on Jake's famous burgers and a buffet of sides and salads, I'm sitting in the house nursing my drink. It's been a nice night—good food, good people, and Jake is always a great host. But I haven't talked to Sierra all night.

Every time I've looked around the party for her, she's been in the middle of a conversation with someone. At dinner we sat on opposite ends of the yard, now we're sitting on opposite sides of the family room.

"It's so good to have you here, Sierra," I hear Jules say as she clinks her glass to the beer bottle Sierra is holding. "I'm still pinching myself that you for real live here. We can do this all the time now, not just on work trips. It's like Thelma got her Louise back."

My eyes are all over Sierra, which is exactly where they've been all night. I wonder what's going on in that pretty head of hers. Has she been thinking about me as much as I'm thinking about her? I hope so. I feel like I'm back in high school, wondering if my crush likes me back. *What is happening to me?*

"Did you forget you have a toddler at home, babe?" Beckett asks, sitting beside her with one hand wrapped around her back, his other on her knee. "I hate to break it to you but it's more like *Full House* than *Thelma and Louise*."

Jules tsks her husband. "Of course I didn't forget about my baby girl. Speaking of, I should check in with my mom and make sure she went down okay. But back to your question: that's what I keep you around for, you're a guaranteed babysitter."

Beckett shakes his head. "It's not babysitting when it's your own child."

"You know what I meant, silly," Jules harrumphs, patting her husband on the stomach and then leaning in for a kiss. A kiss that Beckett deepens.

It's been a year since Maya was born, but I'm still in awe that Beck is a dad. And a damn good one too. The thought of being a parent myself doesn't often cross my mind. Honestly, I have never really thought kids were for me. But seeing one of my best friends so in love with his daughter has opened my eyes to the possibility of one day having a family.

"When is all this PDA going to stop with you two?" Tucker grunts. "It's been two years and we're still being subjected to your gross make-out sessions."

"You're just jealous," Jules says, leaning in close to her husband.

"Jealous? Why would I be jealous? I have chicks begging for my dick," he says with a grin, looking down at his crotch.

"Gross. I think I'm actually going to be sick," Jules says, hiding her face in her hands.

"Yeah, we're all throwing up in our mouths," Holden grumbles. He has Aubrey on his lap. He hasn't been able to stop talking about her, thinking she could be the one. I'm glad he's happy, but if I'm honest, I'm not sure I see it. I've only met her a handful of times, but something tells me she isn't looking for anything serious. She seems to spend most of her time with her girlfriends and doesn't seem to make Holden a priority. But what do I know? I'm hardly an expert on relationships. Maybe the two of them are the real deal.

I push the thought from my mind, sitting back with a smile. I love nights like these when we're all together, having a good time. And after a long week in the office, nothing beats a few drinks with friends. It's even better now that Sierra is here.

And besides having a great night, I suddenly realize I haven't thought about Blair, or what I'm going to say to her when I see her, even once tonight.

I've been too busy watching Sierra. She's currently sitting next to her brother, one long leg crossed over the other. The hem of her dress is riding up her thigh, making me swallow a groan. I can't stop imagining her legs wrapped around my shoulders, my face between her thighs, wondering what she tastes like. And now I'm sporting wood with her brother sitting across from me. *Fucking great.*

But I doubt that he'd notice anyways. Out of the corner of my eye, I see him frown. I glance at Sierra and notice that she sees it too. It reminds me that I've been meaning to check in with him. Jake's always a pretty serious guy, but for the past few weeks he's seemed distracted, worried. He doesn't typically open up and share his feelings. I imagine when you lose both of your parents at such a young age you keep yourself guarded.

"You good, man?" I ask him nonchalantly when I catch his eye.

"Perfect," is his one-word response before he takes a long pull of his beer. I'm not convinced. A few moments of awkward silence pass between us before I decide I need to loosen him up. "Let's do some shots."

"I'll pass, man."

"Why? Come on, Jake."

Sierra's lips tighten into a straight line. She's wondering what's eating at him too.

"I'm gonna finish my beer then I'm hydrating. I've got shit I've gotta do tomorrow," he answers firmly.

"Forget that, man. Let's do a round," Tucker jumps in. "It's Friday night."

Jake is clearly frustrated by our repeated attempts.

There's a vein in his neck threatening to burst, and his knuckles are turning white from the death grip he has on his bottle. "Sorry, can't."

I open my mouth to say something when Holden nudges my knee with his own, causing my drink to slosh and spill onto my lap.

"Shit! Sorry, man," he says quickly.

"Dumbass," I joke, looking down at my pants.

"You fuck-heads better not be spilling your drinks on my couch," Jake growls.

"Don't worry, it's not on your couch. It's all over me," I say, setting my Solo cup on the coffee table. Before I can push up off the couch to go grab a towel, Sierra is leaning towards me, handing me a napkin.

Our eyes catch as I reach for it, and just like that, the sounds of our friends' conversations fade away. "You might need this," she says as I take the napkin from her. There's a pretty blush tinting her cheeks. She sinks back into the couch, never taking her eyes off me.

I watch her as she brings her cup to her lips, sipping from her drink, like she knows that I can't stop staring at her. And she's right. All I want is to wrap her in my arms, to get her alone and run my hands over every inch of her skin, like I did that night in Miami.

Holden nudges my knee with his own, snapping me back to reality. "I told you about the cabin, right?" he asks. "It's all ours for the weekend again. Last one of the summer. You better be coming."

He stands up suddenly and announces it to the room. "Everyone better be coming to The Cape at the end of the month. I've got my uncle's cabin on the water. You're all motherfucking invited."

"—you know I'm there."

"—wouldn't fucking miss it."

"—the bedroom in the basement is mine."

His uncle owns a massive house on the ocean in Cape May, two hours from here. He's offered his place to Holden the past three Labor Day long weekends, and we've all gone up to celebrate the end of summer. It's a weekend I look forward to every year—we grill, drink beers on the dock. It's paradise. The only way it could be better is if Sierra joins us this year.

I glance back in her direction, curious what her response will be. But she's left the couch and is in the dining room, where I can see her already wrapped up in conversation with Tucker. I hear her pretty laugh from across the room. I watch his hand move to her arm, and now I'm clenching my jaw at the sight of Sierra and Tucker together—especially seeing as he's told me he thinks she's hot, which she obviously is.

The way he's looking at her is making me crazy. Tuck is one of my closest friends. I've seen him flirt like this with dozens, if not hundreds, of girls. I grind my molars together, trying to stay calm as I watch my best friend put the moves on Sierra. *My* Sierra. I know him too well. He fucking likes her.

I tear my eyes away, try to focus instead on the conversations going on around me. But I can't stop myself from glancing back in their direction every few seconds. When Tucker's hand lingers a little too long on her shoulder, I practically jump out of my seat and run into the dining room.

Sierra's eyes connect with mine for a moment as Tuck claps my shoulder in a bro-hug. "Ford, I was just telling Sierra about Labor Day weekend, trying to convince her to come."

I relax a little. Maybe I misread things. Hopefully I have nothing to worry about, but I still don't like seeing her with someone else. *What is wrong with me? I've never felt this possessive over a girl in my life.*

"I'll be there," I chime in. "That's all the convincing she should need." The comment earns me a laugh from Sierra, and I like being the one responsible for her pretty smile. "But seriously, you should come. It will be fun."

"It sounds like it."

"So, you'll come?" Fuck, I sound eager.

"It's a definite maybe."

"Aw, she's coming," Tuck says, putting his arm around her shoulder, pulling her into his side." My spine stiffens. There he goes fucking touching her again. Sierra smiles, then unravels herself from his big arm. My spine loosens.

"Tuck, did you forget the nachos in the oven?" Jake hollers from the couch.

"Shit, sorry. I'll grab 'em," Tuck says before taking a long swig of his beer.

"I'll get them," Sierra says, waving him off. "I need to get another drink anyways."

I follow her across the kitchen, not bothering to hide it from Jake or anyone else here. I'm done with playing it cool. I'm not waiting another second. I need to get Sierra alone.

She grabs the oven mitt from the counter and removes the pan of nachos from the oven unaware that I've followed her. I watch her open the cupboard where Jake keeps his drinking glasses. She startles when I tug on the end of her ponytail, turning around to find me only inches away from her. Her breath hitches. Sierra blushes, then drops her eyes to the floor.

Her coconut scent fills the air around us. Man, she smells incredible.

"Grayson," she whispers.

I know I'm too close to her. I know there's a chance someone will walk in here and see us, but I can't step away. Her doe eyes that have been finding mine all night, her scent. *That fucking scent.* Her playful smile. *Fuck, that smile.* It's all more than I can take.

I've spent all night having to watch her talk to every guy in the room but me. Now that it's just the two of us in the kitchen, I want a minute alone with her. I want a lot more than that—it would be so easy to close the distance between us and kiss her right now. It would also cost me my balls if Jake caught us. Right now, I can't seem to care.

"You look beautiful, Sierra," I breathe, looking down at her. "You're making it real hard to just be *friends.*"

The corners of her lips tip up in a small smile as she looks around the room, no doubt making sure we're alone. The Sierra everyone else here knows is the most outgoing person in the room. The one cracking jokes, making everyone around her laugh. This vulnerable side to her is so different from the one she shows the rest of the world.

My eyes drop down to her mouth. Does she want me to kiss her as badly as I want to fuse my mouth to hers?

Fuck, what the hell am I thinking?

She holds my gaze and takes a step back, so her ass rests against the edge of the counter. "Thank you, but this is a bad idea. We shouldn't be alone in here."

"Why? Because you're scared if you're alone with me, you'll remember everything about that night we spent together in Miami?"

"No," she says in barely a whisper, trying to hide the fact that she's just as turned on as I am.

I allow my eyes to take in every inch of her. They wander down her body to her legs before slowly climbing back up again. Her expression changes. I can tell by the way she straightens her spine, squares her hips with mine. This is the Sierra I met in Miami. She makes no move to turn away or stop me—even though we both know I'm enjoying the view. She just stands there, confidently, until my eyes reach hers.

"I think about it, Sierra. All the fucking time. I know you do too."

Her eyes shut briefly as she inhales and then they're back on mine again. "Grayson... I can't think when you're this close to me. And we're not alone, remember? Someone will see us."

I know I'm crossing a line right now. I know what I'm doing is stupid, reckless. But I can't fucking stop. Being this close to her, wanting her this badly, wondering if she wants the same things too, has pushed me past my breaking point. I want a repeat with Sierra. I want one more night.

This feels like it might be the right moment to take my chance. I lean into her, my hands on either side of her on the kitchen counter.

She sucks her bottom lip under her teeth before slowly releasing it, her hands flying to my chest to apply the gentlest amount of pressure. But they don't make a move to push me away. I wait for her to tell me to stop, but surprisingly, she allows me to cage her in. Her shallow breathing tells me that she likes me this close to her.

Sierra's tiny hands are still flat against my chest, eyes fixed somewhere on my mouth, her pink lips parted. We're only an inch away from each other now.

"What would happen if I kissed you right now?" I murmur, so close to her lips.

She swallows, and her hand grips the cotton of my T-shirt. My heart pounds like a drum in my chest, fast and steady, making me feel alive.

"You shouldn't, Gray," she whispers softly.

"That's what I thought too, until now. But I'm tired of feeling this way. I'm over it. I'm into you." I groan. "I think about you all the time and I think you think about me too, so, why are we fighting something that we both want?"

A small sigh escapes her. "You're not thinking clearly—"

"I am," I insist, interrupting her. I may be intoxicated by Sierra's proximity, but there's no doubt in my mind. "I know what I want... and what I want is you."

"Gray—"

Her eyes glimmer with heat, fixed on mine. She looks nervous, but slowly that look in her eyes is replaced with the same need I feel. She wants this. My heart tightens.

She tugs me closer by my T-shirt, until my lips are only a breath away from hers.

"Sierra, are you coming with those nachos?" Jake hollers from the other room.

Sierra blinks at the sound of her brother's voice, then pushes me away. Spell broken.

Instantly I feel shattered, my heart sinking to my stomach. "I'll get 'em. You stay here," I say.

I let out a deep exhale and then give her a cheeky grin as I lean in and kiss her forehead. Reaching to the counter beside her, I quickly grab the oven mitt and still-warm pan of nachos and make a beeline for the living room before she has a chance to get mad at me.

Dropping into the sofa, I mentally give my head a shake. I was seconds away from kissing Sierra with her brother in the next room.

TEN

BARE CHESTED. GRAY SWEATS. BARE FEET.

Sierra

It's the night of Jake's cookout, and despite the fact that it's 3 a.m. I'm wide awake.

I was torn from sleep the same way I always am—short of breath, heart racing. And it doesn't matter that it has almost been 16 years since I was carried out of the house that went up in flames—I still feel scared and alone and filled with sheer panic.

I sit up in bed, pajamas soaked, my mind still re-playing the images from that night like a reel. It's pretty clear I'm not falling back to sleep anytime soon. Taking a deep breath, I flip the covers off and slip out of bed, knowing it will be at least an hour before I'll feel relaxed enough to crawl back into bed.

This is how the nightmares work. They keep me up, unable to stop my mind from spinning in a million different directions, down terrifying paths of what ifs.

I change into a tank and sweat shorts then grab a glass of water from the kitchen, carrying it to the swing on the front porch. I only lasted two weeks back in Reed Point before the nightmares returned. It didn't take long.

I tuck my legs underneath me and watch the waves roll slowly into shore, concentrating on taking deep, even breaths. My gaze then drifts to the porch light I left on and the one firefly chaotically dancing under its glare.

My mind drifts back to tonight's get together at Jake's house. After tidying up the kitchen, I said goodbye around midnight, just after Holden and Aubrey left. Grayson had just cracked open another beer when I left, with Jake of course walking me to the door making sure I got to my car safely.

My brother made me promise to message him when I got home, and also called me to make sure I locked the front door as I pulled my car down the drive. Same old Jake, clearly falling back into his overprotective ways.

Will it always be this way between us? When I'm 40 years old with three kids, will my brother still be checking in on me with a million warnings and reminders? I'm sure he'd freak the fuck out if he knew I was outside on my porch, in the middle of the night, all alone. I won't be telling him.

But a few minutes later, I'm not all alone.

The street is dark, save for my porch light and the soft glow of the moonlight streaming over the ocean, but not so dark that I don't notice the movement coming from Grayson's porch.

I sit up straighter on the swing when his front door swings shut and he pads out into the night air. I can only see a shadow of him, but I can feel his eyes on me.

"Sierra, what the hell are you doing out here all alone at this time of night?" he calls, concern in his voice.

Oh great, I'm getting it from Grayson too. I'm a grown woman, I don't need a chaperone to sit on my own porch. I am perfectly capable of taking care of myself. Why does that seem so difficult for these guys to understand?

"Relax, Grayson," I say. "I'm barely five feet from my front door. What is the worst that could happen?"

"I can rattle off a list," he says, scrubbing his hand through his blonde hair. "You shouldn't be out here by yourself, Sierra."

I frown. "I can take care of myself, Grayson." I already have to deal with one man who treats me like a child, I won't deal with another.

Thankfully he is smart enough to stop the chastising, "Okay," he says, raising his hands in a gesture of surrender. "I haven't seen you out here before. You okay?"

I cock my head at him. "You say that like you're often out here in the middle of the night."

He shrugs. "I'm not the best sleeper. I like it out here in the summer. The night air feels good."

I pause, surprised that he feels the same way I do. On nights like this when I can't sleep, sitting outside is the only thing that seems to help. "I know what you mean. I'm not always the best sleeper either but I've been finding this spot on my porch makes me feel a little better."

Grayson is quiet for a second, like he's deep in thought. His eyes find mine, holding my gaze. I sit still, soaking up every second of his eyes on me, until he asks, "Want some company?"

"Sure." My answer is honest, easy, but still, it feels like hundreds of butterflies have been let loose in my stomach. Jake's kitchen flashes through my mind, remembering the feeling of having Grayson so close to me, and how badly I wanted him to kiss me. I wasn't sure what would have happened if my brother hadn't interrupted us from the living room. With Grayson Ford only inches from me, his eyes searing into mine, no one could blame me if I gave in.

Grayson walks across the lawn to my place, a silhouette in the dark. As he gets closer to the glow of my porch light, I suddenly notice what he's wearing. Or what he's *not* wearing.

Bare chested. Gray sweats. Bare feet.

My mouth waters.

My libido short-circuits.

His sweats are slung dangerously low on his hips, the V in his abdomen taunting me with a fine dusting of hair that disappears into the waistband of his joggers.

My eyes remain there, following his happy trail to the imprint of him behind the thin cotton fabric, something illicit immediately heating my core. I tear my eyes away, fighting to hold onto a shred of self-control. When it comes to Grayson Ford, I don't have much of it.

"Couldn't sleep?" I ask him as he climbs the three steps to my porch and takes a seat beside me. I take a drink of my water then set the glass down on the porch.

I don't hate the idea of him coming over. Not when he's looking like that, his joggers leaving nothing to the imagination, his abs flexing every time he moves. I slide over on the porch swing to make space for him.

"Nah. You?" he says, reaching for my bare foot, massaging the arch just like he did the last time he was here on my porch.

"Something like that," I say evasively. I sigh at the feel of his touch. Between the glow of the moon, the sound of the waves and Grayson's warm hands on my skin, I feel my body starting to relax.

Grayson gives me a look but continues to rub tiny circles over my foot. It makes me wonder if he knows my story.

Given how guarded my brother can be, I doubt he would have told his friends about what happened to our parents.

It's not an easy story to tell.

"I'm assuming you don't know... about my parents." I clear my throat.

"I know you and Jake lost your mom and dad, but that's all."

I take my time with what I tell him next. He's patient, still, as I gather up the strength I always need to talk about my parents. "They died in a fire."

For a second, Grayson's face goes white, eyes widening as he sucks in a short breath. But then I recognize a different emotion—not shock or pity, but more like an acknowledgment of the loss I suffered.

Compassion.

It feels like the expression of someone who is here to listen. And some part of me really wants to share my story.

"Your house that you grew up in?" he asks gently.

I nod. "We lived in a split-level home on a quiet street, and it was the middle of the night. My dad woke me up, screaming at me from the side of my bed. Said there was a fire somewhere in the house and we needed to get out." I look down at my hands because it's easier than looking back at Grayson.

"My mom went to get Jake in his room, but none of us knew at the time that he wasn't there. He had snuck out of the house to go bike riding with a friend." I swallow as Grayson stops rubbing my foot, inches across the bench, and reaches for my hand, holding it in his.

My chest aches remembering that night, the smell of fire, burning wood, the sound of sirens, my parents...

Every second of it is etched into my memory, as clear as the night it happened.

"There was already so much smoke filling the hallway when my dad got me to the front door. Even at 10 years old, I knew that we needed to get out of there. But my dad went back in to find my mom and Jake."

I bite my lip, watching Grayson's thumb trace tiny circles over the top of my hand. I can tell by the way he lowers his head that I don't need to tell him any more about that night.

"And your grandparents took you in," he says quietly.

I nod. "Jake and I moved here to Haven Harbor the next day."

It wasn't easy for my grandparents for all the obvious reasons, having to raise two young kids while grieving themselves. Jake went off the rails, plagued with guilt for having snuck out of the house. I never blamed him for our parents' deaths, but he blamed himself. He took it all on, and sometimes it would overwhelm him, and he would scream and cry and throw things, but my grandparents were somehow always able to calm him down.

Grayson gently squeezes my hand in his, pulling me from my memories. I can feel him watching the profile of my face as if he wishes he could say or do something that would make it all go away. I can feel how much he cares about me.

"How about you, Grayson? Why are you outside tonight instead of asleep in your bed?"

His brows pinch together like he's holding a secret too, but then he smirks at me like the smart-ass he sometimes is. "Why would I want to be in bed when I can be out here with you?"

I laugh despite myself, shaking my head.

"What?" he asks. "You don't believe me?"

"No, I don't. Not for a second," I say, a shiver rolling up my spine.

"You look cold," he says. "Come here."

And so he moves closer, tucking me into his side, his arm behind me over the back of the cushion. I look down at my bare thigh pressed against the gray fleece of his joggers, feel the warmth of his bare chest through my thin T-shirt. I allow my eyes to rake over his abs, to appreciate the way the grooves and valleys of his muscles shine under the soft glow of the porch light. He is all chiseled perfection, with the perfect amount of body hair that makes him look like a man.

And I ache to run my fingers over him. I want to trace a finger over every line and valley, then run my fingers further down the trail of hair that disappears into his sweats.

He squeezes me so I'm even closer to him. To anyone on the outside looking in, it would seem like we are a couple, enjoying each other on a warm summer night. The truth is so much more complicated.

But I have to admit, this feels so good.

We fall silent for a short while as his foot rocks us gently back and forth, the sound of the waves in the distance crashing against the rocks. Eventually Grayson breaks the silence.

"I haven't been able to stop thinking about you since the moment you showed up here on Haven," he says softly.

I draw in a shaky breath.

Grayson, on the other hand, is solid as a rock, not moving, waiting for me to say something. I sit up, turning to face him, and I can see from the unwavering look in his eye that he wants me to give in to him. To give in to the attraction that is always there between us, floating in the air, lying at the surface. And I want to.

But we can't.

We are forbidden.

We would upset someone who means a lot to both of us.

I find the strength to pull my hand from his and stand, pointing a finger from me to him. "You know why this can't happen."

I take a step towards the house, but one is all I get before Grayson grabs my hand, then stands and pulls me closer into him. My skin blazes where his fingertips touch me, one hand on my forearm, the other on my hip. I drop my eyes to the ground, knowing if I take one look at his bare chest so close to mine, all bets are off. I won't stand a chance.

"Look at me, Sierra," he says, his voice thick like honey. The gold and green flecks in his brown eyes stare back at me. "I'm tired of fighting this between us. I've never wanted anything more in my life and I think you want this too."

"It doesn't matter what I want, Grayson..." I inhale sharply as his hand cups the side of my jaw, my eyes momentarily closing at the feel of his hands on me in a possessive way. I keep them closed, savoring the way I feel when his thumb traces my bottom lip, then the edge of my jaw to my ear, like he's studying every inch of me.

"We can't be together," I manage, my voice powerless, weak.

"I don't care."

"My brother will."

Both of his hands grip my jaw, tilting my chin and forcing my eyes to meet his. His expression is heated, intense. It's the same look he gave me earlier in Jake's kitchen. A rush of heat floats down my spine, and a blip in my heart rate follows when he says...

"*We* both want this, sunshine, and that's all that I care about."

Sunshine.

His voice is rough and husky, but then he whispers my name like a plea, and I am done.

Grayson's lips part, and I close my eyes, ignoring every voice inside my head that warns me not to do this. And I surrender, wanting his lips on mine almost as badly as I want my next breath. Another rush of heat covers my whole body this time as I wait for his lips to seal to mine.

He leans in, his mouth so close that the slightest move by either of us would give us the relief we both need. I ache everywhere.

It feels intoxicating.

My adrenaline surges.

I'm powerless to fight this any longer.

All the air rushes out of my lungs when his lips brush lightly over mine. I want to taste him again. It's been so long, and for a little while I did remember how he tasted— like lime and sugar —but after a few months, that memory faded. What I never forgot was the way his mouth felt sealed to mine. His lips, soft but demanding, making me forget about every other kiss before and every one that would come after. Grayson ruined me for anyone else.

I am so close to feeling that way again.

And then it happens.

His mouth captures mine in a possessive kiss, his tongue sweeping against mine in soft, lazy strokes.

Grayson is kissing me. He. Is. Kissing. Me.

He tastes so good. Exactly like I remember. Fresh, like mint, and hope, and all male. His lips are warm, soft and he's taking this kiss, not asking me for it. I whimper into his mouth as he moves his hand to the nape of my neck, powerful and controlling as I give myself over to him.

Grayson's fingers curl around the back of my neck, holding me tight against him, his hips square with mine, his hard-on pressed between us. I let out a gasp that I have no control over when his tongue runs a line down the column of my throat, and I rise to my tiptoes, allowing him better access. Red flags wave in my head, warning me that this is Jake's best friend who is unraveling me with every kiss. Grayson Ford, my neighbor, the one man I've felt anything for other than lust. The one man I have been trying to forget for the past two years.

But I ignore every warning and run my hands over his bare skin, wrap my arms around his body.

"I wanted to touch you all night," he says, whispering against my skin, his fingers tugging at my hair at the base of my neck. He kisses me again, his other hand slipping under my tank top, warm and strong against my back. "I couldn't stand watching you with him. I fucking hated it."

"Who?" I breathe against his chest.

He drops his mouth to my jaw, kissing me there, then lower down the column of my neck, making me moan. "Tuck. He was touching you. It should be my hands that are all over you. Mine, Sierra. You should be mine."

His admission should have infuriated me. I'm not his. I'm not anybody's. But still a shiver rolls down my spine. His cocky, over-possessive claim that I should belong to him turns me on, and when his mouth moves back to mine in a punishing kiss—my body aches.

I vibrate under his touch as he kisses me and then nips my bottom lip with his teeth, then kisses me again. Time stands still—it's just Grayson and I under the late July moon.

Suddenly my mind kicks in and the realization of what this would do to my brother hits me like a ton of bricks, my heart hammering behind my ribcage loud and heavy. I can't betray my brother. Not after everything he has done for me.

I tear my mouth away, pushing out of Grayson's hold on me. Then I take a few steps back until my back hits the siding of the house.

Grayson's lips are swollen, and I'm sure mine are too. I swipe away the hair that has fallen into my face, tug the hem of my tank down to cover my exposed skin. "Grayson, that shouldn't have happened. That can't happen again." My fingertips cover my lips, wiping away the wetness from Grayson's greedy kisses.

"Sierra." His eyes search mine. "It's okay. Breathe. We didn't do anything wrong."

"Tell that to Jake," I say, every breath I take feeling like I just ran 20 miles. Feeling like I've just betrayed my brother, one of the most important people to me on this earth. "He will flip if he ever finds out."

"He doesn't need to know."

I've never lied to my brother. We've been through too much—heartache, loss, grief—to keep secrets from one another. What am I supposed to do now?

I just stand here, waiting for the solution to come, feeling more confused than ever. This was the problem with having our lives intertwined with one another's, how living this close to Grayson would be a constant temptation. And now, after that kiss, I know it's only going to make things harder. This kiss could drive a wedge in between Jake and I, and my relationship with my brother is far too important for me to allow that to happen.

"We'll figure it, okay?" Grayson says.

"How?"

"I don't know, yet. But we will."

"Okay," I say, battling the urge inside of me to kiss him again, wanting to do so much more. Instead, I allow myself one last, long look before I go inside. The way he's standing with his blond hair a mess, his eyes hopeful, makes it hard for me to think. "It's late, I need to get some sleep. You need to get some sleep too."

Grayson eyes me like he can see right through me and my need to put some distance between us. "Goodnight, Sierra," he sighs.

"Goodnight, Gray."

I walk inside as quickly as I can before I can talk myself out of leaving and start kissing him again instead.

Secrets have a way of getting out. I know I need to tell Jake about Grayson and me, and soon, before he finds out from someone else.

ELEVEN

THAT SHUT HER UP REAL QUICK.

Grayson

Sweat covers my forehead as I finish up replacing the drain plug, tightening it until it's snug. Tossing the torque wrench to the side, I towel off my face before the sweat runs into my eyes. It's hot as balls in the grease pit at my dad's garage.

My mom called me last week to talk about things. When I asked how my dad was, she told me that his leg was stopping him from working. The arthritis in his knee had flared up. I know she would never outright ask, so I offered to go help out on my next day off.

Once I've finished the oil change, I strip off my overalls and then head upstairs, where I find my dad at the coffee bar. He finishes pouring cream into his coffee and then takes a hefty gulp.

"Come on, Gray," he says, nodding in the direction of his office. "Let's talk in there."

I'm silent as I follow him out of the inspection bay, watching him limp, his breathing labored. He moves behind his desk and lowers himself into his chair with a grunt.

"Thanks for the help today. I tell your mother all the time not to bug you, but you know how she is. She's a fixer."

I take the seat across from my dad hesitantly, stifling a yawn, wishing that I'd poured myself a cup of coffee too. My dad and I never do this. We don't... talk. I'd rather be anywhere but here right now. I turn into a dick when I'm around my dad at the best of times, but today I'm too tired to even hold a rational conversation. But I'm here for my mom because I know it will make her happy if I spend some time with him.

I didn't get much sleep last night, tossing and turning after that kiss on Sierra's porch. I know that we crossed a line, that things won't be the same between us. If that wasn't enough to keep me up all night, I still have to figure out how to handle the situation with Blair at work. I can't let this drag on any longer, I'm going to have to find a way to talk to her tomorrow at the office. I just need to figure out what I'm going to say.

My dad winces as he stretches his legs out with noticeable effort. I look at him from across the desk, noticing the physical similarities between us even though in all other ways we're worlds apart. His blond hair is a shade darker than mine, his shoulders not quite as wide, but we have the same dark eyes, the same coloring, the same Roman nose.

I can't even remember the last time I was in a room alone with my dad. I know it has been a long time. And I know it upsets my mom that we're not closer, that I don't make more of an effort. She says he's doing better. He's off the pills. *I promise you, Gray, he's so much better. He's changed. He's not the same person.* That's what she said to me the last time we talked. The thing is, I've heard all that many times before, and all those times ended with me feeling let down.

"Gray—" my dad interrupts my thoughts.

"What?" I ask, scrubbing my hands over my face, running on probably four hours sleep. Once I left Sierra's porch it took me forever to calm down enough to fall back to sleep.

"Late night? You look tired."

I fight the urge to roll my eyes. He's one to talk. He always looks tired. Strung out. High, because he usually is. I sigh. This is me being a dick.

"Yeah, late night. But I'm fine. I can stay and help with whatever you need."

"Well, there's an oil change that needs to be done on the F150 if you don't mind. I'll be able to take it from there."

"I got it covered," I answer, pushing my chair back, ready to be done with this conversation.

"Wait—" he says. "How are you, son?"

My chest tightens hearing him call me *son*. He would always call me that when I was a kid. Back when things were good between us. Now, though, it feels forced, unnatural.

"I'm fine."

"You just seem... tense. Are you sure there's nothing you want to talk about? Is something going on at work?"

My dad and I don't talk. Ever. So I'm confused why he seems to want to start now.

"Everything's fine at work."

"You seeing anyone?"

"No."

My answer feels like a lie, even though it's not. I'm not seeing anyone, but my relationship with Sierra feels like *something* to me. An uncomfortable feeling settles in the pit of my stomach. I don't know how to navigate any of this.

"Maybe you should. You know, think about something other than work. Meet somebody special, focus on a relationship rather than the hotel. You used to date... had that girlfriend back in college, and you seemed happy then. You haven't brought anyone home since."

This time I do roll my eyes. It just proves how little he knows about me. I wasn't happy then. The only good that came out of dating Layla was that it taught me that relationships aren't for me.

"I'm fine, Dad. I don't need a relationship. I have a normal amount of stress in my life. The same as anyone else."

I don't have the energy to argue with him about this, I have enough on my mind as it is. Things with Sierra are confusing as hell, the Blair drama at work needs to be resolved. And now my dad feels like he knows me well enough to start offering fatherly advice? We barely even talk, so I'm not sure why he's so convinced he knows what I need in my life. Sure, I'm interested in Sierra, but getting into a full-blown relationship hasn't been on my radar for a very long time. My dad has no clue what I need.

I scrub my hand over the back of my neck with a heavy sigh, willing this conversation to end. Apparently, my dad misses my telepathic memo.

"Listen, Grayson—" he says, trying again.

I quickly cut him off. He hasn't earned the right to put his two cents in when it comes to my happiness and how I choose to live my life. "I need to get back to work. Say hi to mom. I'll let myself out when I'm done."

He just nods, frowning slightly, then he slips on his reading glasses and starts flipping through a stack of invoices on his desk. I'm relieved this conversation is over, but as I walk back to the car lift, I can't seem to quiet the tiny voice in my head that wonders if my dad is right.

Maybe I *do* need Sierra.

But I can't have her.

LILY MILLER

Ever.

SIERRA

MORGAN WALLEN SINGS "COVER ME UP" through the speaker in my kitchen as I strip the hardware from the kitchen cabinets. The brass pulls were on trend in 1960, therefor they have to go. Once I get the handles off, my plan is to paint the cabinets white, then switch out the pulls for black ones. Then I need to change out the countertop. If my career at The Seaside doesn't work out, I'm sure I could get a job in home renovations at this point.

Earlier in the day, I had visited Gran at her nursing home. I found her in the common room playing cards, and she made me wait while she won three more hands before we could finally go outside for a walk around the grounds. When I suggested she put on a sweater she threatened to put me on her not approved visitors list if I didn't stop bossing her around.

"Do it and I'll stop sneaking in Kit Kat bars for you," I replied. That shut her up real quick.

With that settled, we found a bench in the shade where we sat while Gran updated me on the nursing home gossip. Her neighbor John refuses to accept the fact that his hearing is going, so he turns his TV volume up so high that she can hear every word through the wall. Her favorite nurse, Isabel, the one who washes and blow-dries her hair on Fridays, has a new boyfriend who she talks about constantly.

"But just between us," Gran told me, lowering her voice a bit. "I'm just not sure it's going to last."

Once I was all caught up on the lives of Gran's neighbors

and nurses, she turned her attention to *my* new neighbors at Haven Harbor. She seemed very curious to know how I was getting along with Grayson, Tucker and Holden.

"Are those boys looking out for you?" she asked, a concerned expression on her face. Once I had assured her that they'd been very welcoming—I tried to will myself not to blush when I thought of just how *welcoming* Grayson has been—she smiled and gave my hand a squeeze.

"So then," she said with a glint in her eyes. "Which one do you think is the cutest?"

Grayson, obviously. But there was no way I was going to admit to that, no matter how much she pressed. And she did press. Gran had a ton of questions about the guys. It was clear that she missed them, which gave me the idea to have her over for dinner and invite the three guys, and of course Jake too. Her face lit up when I suggested it and before I left, I promised her I would put plans in place for the evening very soon.

I'm still singing along to the radio in my kitchen when my phone chimes on the counter. I set down my screwdriver and check the screen.

> Grayson: Need a hand over there?

I smile. I haven't seen him since we kissed on my front porch a week ago, but we've texted here and there. We've both steered clear of the big topics—that kiss, where that kiss could have led, the many ways my brother would torture Gray if he found out about it—and instead kept things light and easy.

It's been exactly what I've needed. A little space to give me time to think, but enough contact to reassure me that things between us are okay.

> Sierra: You bored, Gray?

> Grayson: That obvious?

I smile, shaking my head.

> Sierra: I'm replacing knobs on the kitchen cabinets, so if you're looking for something to cure your boredom, I'm not much help.

> Grayson: If you're wearing those cut-off shorts, I wouldn't be bored.

I shake my head and smile some more.

> Sierra: I hate to disappoint but I'm not wearing my jean shorts.

> Grayson: Tell me what you're wearing. (purple devil emoji)

My cheeks heat.

> Sierra: Again, not too exciting... athletic shorts and a tank and my hair is a mess.

> Grayson: Good God, Sierra. Do you have any idea what that image does to me?

> Sierra: It doesn't take much with you, does it?

> Grayson: Not when it comes to you.

He ends the text with a fireworks emoji. The heat in my cheeks deepens. The texts he's been sending me all week have gotten flirtier and flirtier, making it hard for me to remember why we shouldn't be texting in the first place. Whatever this *thing* is that has developed between the two of us... I have to admit it's a lot of fun. I also have to remember that I shouldn't be encouraging any type of relationship with Grayson, secret or otherwise.

I sigh, sending one last text before setting my phone down and getting back to work.

> Sierra: I better get back to it. Night, Gray.

Fifteen minutes later there's a knock on my door and when I open it, Grayson is standing on my porch in a light blue T-shirt that clings to his hard chest, a pair of board shorts hung low on his hips and flipflops. His hair is a tousled mess, like he's just woken up from a nap. I stare at him, my heart dipping in my chest.

"Grayson," I say, wondering if he can tell my pulse is thumping like a bass drum. Bright orange and pink rays from the setting sun cast a warm glow across half of his body, doing nothing to lessen how gorgeous he looks.

"Hey, beautiful."

Exhale... that feels good, hearing him call me beautiful. I realize how happy I am to see him.

I watch his eyes dip lower, my body heating under his gaze as it roams to my lips, down to my tank, then to my legs. He shakes his head, smile wide. "Geez, Sierra, if I knew you looked like that, I would have been here a long time ago."

This man.

"Seriously, Grayson, you are ridiculous." I look down at myself, suddenly self-conscious of the old, worn-out tank I'm wearing and the fact that my hair is in desperate need of a wash. I brush a few loose strands from my face in a feeble attempt to make myself look more presentable. But if I look like a disaster, Grayson doesn't seem to notice. He smiles, lighthearted and playful like he always is.

"No more renos tonight," he announces, taking the screwdriver I'm still holding and setting it down on the entry table.

"What? Why?"

"I've missed you, Sierra."

My heart squeezes in my chest. His words don't come as a complete shock—that night on my porch it was pretty clear Grayson wanted to take things further— but I *am* surprised it feels this good to hear him say it. I have spent way too many hours this week thinking about Grayson, and now that he's standing in front of me, I know exactly what I want.

A repeat of that kiss.

My God, it was a great kiss. I am positive I've never been kissed like that before, and every fiber of my being wants to feel that way again. His eyes search mine. "I want to take you somewhere."

"Oh really? Where are we going, Grayson?"

I'm not sure why I even bother asking. The way he's looking at me right now, I think I would go with him just about anywhere. But he doesn't need to know that. I cock my head at him, eyes narrowed.

He smirks as if to say *can't you just work with me here?* "We're going paddle boarding, like we talked about."

"Right now?"

"Right now. And don't bother arguing, Sierra, because I know you want to come with me."

I rest my hands on my hips. "Is that so?"

His brown eyes glimmer under the evening sun. "It is. You've missed me just as much as I've missed you."

"What makes you think that?" I ask, even as a shiver passes over my skin.

"I can't be the only one who's been thinking about that kiss all week," he says, looking at me with a sudden intensity. "At least, I really hope I'm not."

Before I can answer, he grins again and nods toward the beach. "It's a perfect night. The water is calm, there's barely a breeze. So, what do you say, Sierra? You down for this?"

Of course I'm down to spend the evening with Grayson.

There's a boyish hope in his eyes that hits me square in my chest again, and I wonder if it will always be like this. How can Grayson Ford get me to do just about anything? I feel like putty in his hands.

"I'm down. Give me a minute." I leave him at my door, heading to my bedroom to change into a clean top and shorts and pull my hair into a ponytail. I throw a sweatshirt on and return to my door, where Grayson is still waiting.

"Ready," I say, slipping into slides and following him outside.

"I'll grab your board," he says, jogging over to my garage, where my paddleboard is leaning against the wall. He tucks it under his strong arm like it weighs nothing, smiling like he's just won a bet. And I am a goner. Going out with him tonight alone is a very bad idea, but that doesn't stop me from following him out to the front yard.

Grayson picks up his own board from where he's left it on the grass, and I notice him cast a quick glance towards Tucker and Holden's house. Following his gaze, I blow out a sigh of relief when I see that both of their cars are missing from the driveway. There isn't a doubt in my mind that if they were around to see Grayson and I together, it would only be a matter of time before my brother would hear about it. And I am definitely not ready to deal with Jake.

I blink, forcing away all thoughts of my brother. Grayson is busy shoving his flip-flops into his backpack and I take the opportunity to ogle his insanely perfect biceps, the fine blond arm hair against his tan skin, the way his T-shirt stretches over the broad muscles of his back.

"I can take off my shirt if you'd like?" he asks with a smirk on his face. "I like it when your eyes are on me."

I'm so busted, but the funny thing is I don't even care. "Maybe I like looking at you, Gray."

"We can skip this whole paddleboarding thing," he says, throwing a thumb towards his house. "And we can watch Netflix and chill."

A laugh bursts from my lips. "You never fail to amaze me."

"You like me, sunshine, admit it. The sooner you accept it, the quicker we can have a repeat of that kiss you can't stop thinking about."

"Sunshine?"

"What? You don't like it?"

"That's not what I said. I'm just curious why you call me that."

"You're like sunshine, Sierra. You make me feel all warm, and I want you on my skin all damn day."

Ohmygod. "You are too much."

"And you're obsessed with my *too much*."

We both laugh, and I feel butterflies flutter in my stomach.

Grayson casts his eyes towards the beach, tucking his board under his arm. "So, are we doing this?" he asks with a smile, and it's then that I realize that I haven't taken my eyes off him.

TWELVE

MY CONSCIENCE HAS LEFT THE BUILDING.

Grayson

The sky is ablaze in pinks and blues as we walk down to the beach with our paddleboards. We stop where the sand meets the ocean, both of us taking a moment to look out at the water and breathe in the salt air. I take in this view every single day, but it never gets old. I doubt it ever will. And being here with Sierra only makes it better.

We're the only ones here—not all that surprising, seeing as it's 9 p.m. The beach emptied out a while ago, and I couldn't be happier that Sierra and I have this stretch of sand to ourselves.

We set down our boards and I take off my backpack and drop it in the sand. The further we get from the porch lights of Haven Harbor, the quieter it feels. We're met with a gentle, cool breeze as we sink our feet deeper into the sand.

Sierra lifts her sweatshirt over her head and stuffs it in her bag, then looks back out to sea, a smile playing across her lips. I take her in. Her hair is starting to curl around her face thanks to the salty air. She's wearing a white sports bra and a pair of running shorts—it's not the bathing suit that I was secretly hoping for, but she looks beautiful, her tanned, smooth skin glowing golden in the sun.

"You ready?" I ask before she can catch me staring. I'm anxious to get out there with her.

"Let's do this."

We carry our boards into the shallow water. I watch Sierra stop to tighten the ponytail at the top of her head, then push her board further into the water, squealing when the cold ocean water hits her legs. She kneels in the center of her board, wrapping the leash around her ankle. I can't take my eyes off her.

Sierra looks over her shoulder at me with a grin and I reach to give her board a little push. She pushes off the board effortlessly until she's standing tall, her stance easy but solid. She's completely in her element.

Wading into the water, I hop up onto my board and quickly find my balance, eager to catch up to her. I follow her out towards the horizon and away from the lights of Haven Harbor. We spend the next half hour paddling side by side, a comfortable silence between us. Eventually we both drop down so we're straddling our boards and then we just float, the breeze a few degrees cooler now. Sierra wraps her arms around her middle for warmth.

The orange ball in the sky is inches away from disappearing, but despite the darkening sky Sierra seems in no rush to head back.

"Ever paddle this late?" I ask, my feet gliding back and forth underneath me, my body acclimatising to the cold water.

"When I was younger, but I haven't been out at night for a while," she says, turning to face me, smiling as she brushes a strand of golden hair from her face. She takes my breath away when she smiles. It's fucking contagious when her face lights up, and I can't help but mirror it. Whenever I make Sierra happy, it feels like my heart physically swells in my chest making me want to do it as often as I can.

"Jake and I used to drive Gran to drink when we paddled at night. She would stand in the front window, arms crossed over her chest, and watch us the whole time we were out. Her rule always was she needed to be able to see us and if we couldn't see her, we had gone too far."

"Did you do it? I mean, stick to her rules?"

She shakes her head. "I did, but not Jake. He would paddle behind the bluff and Gran used to get so mad at him," she says gazing out at the steep bank to the right of us, a flash of sadness in her eyes.

A knot forms in my throat, and I swallow it down as I watch Sierra get lost in the memory. I hate that she carries so much pain after losing both of her parents. I hate that she has trouble sleeping, that she's haunted by the memories of that horrible night. I would do anything to be able to fix it, to help her, but instead it is all out of my control. But I feel a deep urge inside of me to protect her, to be someone she can turn to.

Sierra lifts her chin and when her eyes land on me, I am frozen where I sit. Mesmerized.

Her hair is windblown, strands falling loose from the ponytail she'd twisted on top of her head. Her cheeks are tinted pink, her skin luminous with the splatter of freckles across her nose under the twilight sky.

"It's so peaceful at night," she says, her stomach muscles flexing and straining as she glides her leg through the water. "I'm really happy you asked me to come out here with you. I needed this."

"I'm glad I did too," I tell her, opting for an easy response instead of telling her how I really feel in this moment.

Instead of telling her that I want to be consumed by her. I'm feral for this girl.

Fuck it, a voice in my head urges. So, I try again, this time telling her the truth. "You know, Sierra... I meant what I said back at your house tonight."

A crease forms between her brows. "Meant what?"

"That I missed you." I swallow. "I had to see you tonight."

I'm close enough to her to see the shiver that rolls over her skin. I'm not sure if it's from the breeze or my words, but her nipples are stiff under her white sports bra and fuck, I want to rip off her top, suck each peak into my mouth and then worship the rest of her body. Then her chocolate eyes lock with mine and it's devastating. The way she's looking at me with such curiosity and wonder awakens a need inside of me, a craving that roars to life. I need to feel her.

"Come sit with me. I'll keep you warm," I tell her, patting the board between my parted thighs.

She doesn't question it. She doesn't worry how she's going to make it from her board to mine, she just moves, sliding her paddle under one of the straps of her board so it doesn't float away, un-Velcroing the leash from her ankle, then carefully moving to her knees. Taking the leash, I tether her board to my own to prevent it from floating away and then spread my legs as wide as I can. My hands grip both of her thighs to keep her steady as she crosses over to my board and then she slowly sits down in front of me, her back to my front, legs straddling my board. Exactly where I want her.

Sierra lets out a long breath, then leans back into me as my hands snake around her waist. Holding her tight, I inhale her scent, appreciating the way her body feels molded to mine. I inhale the scent of her hair, enjoying the feel of the soft strands against my neck. With her ass so close to my groin, my cock starts to respond. I silently tell my dick to take it easy.

"This feels good, Sierra," I say, tightening my arms around her waist. "You feel good."

"I like being in your arms too, Gray. I like it a lot." She nestles further back into me, resting her arms on top of mine.

I kiss the top of her head, closing my eyes for just a moment, wanting to freeze this moment in time. The hesitancy I've felt from Sierra since I ran into her in front of her grandma's house that first day is gone. Maybe it was our kiss the other night that finally broke down the walls she'd built up. Maybe she's just decided to stop fighting this pull between us.

Over the past week I've given Sierra some time and space to wrap her head around the kiss on her front porch, hoping she would accept that it's impossible to ignore this thing simmering between us. Tonight, it feels like she's ready for me to push a little further.

"Have you thought about that kiss the other night as much as I have?" I ask.

She hesitates before answering. "Grayson, can I ask you a question?"

"Anything," I say into her hair.

"Was the kiss a big mistake?" she asks softly. "I mean... I don't want to ruin your friendship with my brother. And what about—"

"I don't want to talk about Jake. I only want to talk about us," I say, my voice firm. "You felt that kiss, Sierra. I know you did. I know it was just as incredible for you as it was for me. So why the hell are we fighting this?"

Her chest rises and falls as she inhales a deep breath. I'm

positive she wants what I want, she's just too scared to admit it. That kiss on her porch last week was the kind of kiss some people wait their whole lives for.

When she cranes her neck to look back at me, my hands instinctively move to her waist and I carefully turn her around on my board to face me, my hands moving to her hips. She's now straddling the board facing me, her eyes on my mouth, her bottom lip caught beneath her teeth.

"Gray—"

Before she has time to finish the sentence, I lean forward and seal my lips to hers. My body melts into hers and the lump in my throat dissolves.

She opens for me, allowing my tongue to sweep inside. Her lips are cool from the ocean air and the kiss tastes like salt. I'm drunk on the taste of her, almost forgetting that we're balancing on a paddle board. When the board teeters from side to side, we both laugh quietly into the kiss, smiling against each other's mouths. I grip the edges of the SUP with my thighs while I plant both of my hands flat on the surface between us to keep us from flipping.

But it doesn't stop us from taking the kiss further. I take control, deepening the kiss, and when a soft whimper escapes her throat, I groan, my cock so painfully hard that not even the cold water around us can settle it down.

When the board rocks a little more, her hands fly to where mine are placed between us, covering them without breaking the kiss. It's sensual, hot—it feels like everything I've ever needed and not close to being enough all at the same time. The kiss is me showing Sierra how much I fucking want her. How much I need her.

When we both come up for air, she looks towards Haven Harbor.

"We're too far out. Nobody can see us," I say, reading her mind. "It's okay. I promise, Sierra."

She shifts her gaze to me, and I can't stop myself from leaning towards her, kissing her forehead. I allow my lips to linger there for a moment before pulling back and when I do, my stomach twists at the sight of her. Her eyes are glossed over.

"You were right, Gray," she murmurs.

"Right about what?" I ask, her hands still resting on top of mine.

Her eyes dip down to our hands before shifting back to meet mine, her lip trapped again under her teeth as if she's deep in thought. "I think about Miami too. All the time."

Her confession is enough to knock the wind out of me. God, just thinking of Sierra remembering our night together in her mind—and often— makes my pulse beat double time under my skin.

"What we did in Miami was so hot."

She blushes. "And it probably shouldn't happen again."

Even now, two years later, I remember how good it felt to have her pushed up against the wall, how she allowed me to take control and how I ached everywhere when I pushed myself inside of her.

"Fuck yeah, it should," I say, flipping my palms over to interlace her fingers with mine. "Do you remember how good my dick felt inside of you? How good it felt when I fucked you on that desk?"

"Grayson... I..." she breathes, shuddering at my words. "I remember every single thing about that night. How could I ever forget? And that's the problem—"

"How can that be a problem? I don't understand what you're saying, Sierra."

"What if this is more than just one night? What if it isn't

enough? What if I want more?"

"Then I'll give you more, sunshine girl. I'll give you whatever you want."

My heart rate speeds up, chest aching as I take a moment to soak Sierra in. I take her face in my hands, leaning in closer to her, my lips hovering over hers. Her lips part as my hand moves up to the spot behind her ear. The soft brush of my fingertips sends a shiver over her skin.

Her eyes close and I inhale a long, deep breath, gathering up strength.

"Gray," she murmurs. "My brother is your best friend. Neither of us want a relationship. This is a terrible idea. It's a disaster waiting to happen."

"Or it's the best fucking decision we'll both ever make." My thumb draws a line over the edge of her jaw. "I know you want me as bad as I want you. Having sex with you was fucking amazing."

"Gray?" she breathes, the sound of my name thick with need.

"Yeah, sunshine? What do you want?"

She is all I've wanted for weeks now.

She leans forward to kiss me and my tongue sweeps into her mouth to taste her. I savor this perfect moment—the two of us out on the ocean under the jet-black sky. She breaks the kiss. We both exhale before she leans back to look me in the eyes.

"I want you to take me back to your house."

SIERRA

I MUST BE out of my mind.

My conscience has left the building, my brain is fried, my willpower is at zero. Did I really just tell Grayson I want to go home with him?

But what woman would fault me? I spent the last two hours out on the water, under the moonlit sky, pressed up against the most beautiful man I've ever laid eyes on while he kissed the ever-living hell out of me. So, when he asked me what I want, I told him. And now here we are, standing on his doorstep.

I recognize that this is probably an enormous mistake, but the truth is... I don't care. I want Grayson Ford too badly to care about the consequences and the repercussions. I can deal with the fall-out tomorrow. For now, I want this man to ruin me. Wreck me in the most carnal of ways. Make me feel like I did in Miami—forbidden, sexy. Mark me as his for one, secret, steamy night.

Grayson's house is dark, the only light coming from a lamp on a side table in the living room. My eyes haven't even had time to adjust before Grayson closes the door behind us and immediately cages me in. His hands grip either side of my face as he walks me backwards into the house with a look in his eyes that tells me I'm going to remember this night for the rest of my life.

And then he kisses me.

His arms wrap around my waist in a sudden embrace and then he sweeps me off my feet, both of his palms gripping my ass until my legs wrap around his hips. My arms fly up to his neck, holding onto him tightly as he continues to kiss me breathless.

He has me halfway down the hall to his bedroom when a wave of guilt washes over me, winding itself around every bone in my body. It feels like a betrayal, like this is too big a risk to take. But then Grayson kisses me again and it forces any doubt out of my mind. We're not hurting anyone, I tell myself. I deserve to be happy, and being here with Grayson makes me deliriously happy.

The truth is, I don't think I could stop even if I wanted to. God, this is a kiss. Grayson Ford knows exactly how to kiss a woman. A rush of dopamine and oxytocin surges through my system like the perfect cocktail, making me dizzy. My heart beats at a fevered pace as I melt further into his touch. His lips have barely left mine since we walked through his door and he's still ravishing me with his mouth as he blindly walks us into his bedroom.

He lets go of one of my ass cheeks to flick on the bedroom light, then sits down on the edge of his bed, bringing me with him so that I'm settled onto his lap. Sinking down onto him, I straddle his waist, feeling his cock hard between us. I can't fight the urge to ease this ache between my thighs any longer, so I roll my hips over his length. Grayson groans in appreciation. Knowing that he's just as turned on as I am only revs up my libido more.

Then his mouth leaves mine, kissing a line down the center of my throat before he whispers against my skin, "I haven't stopped thinking about how good you felt fucking my cock." He looks at me, eyes dark, every girl's fantasy.

I have his shirt fisted in one hand while the other one snakes around his neck. Grayson grabs the elastic of my sports bra and pushes the material up, then massages my bare breast. It's rough, unexpected, and I love how possessive he is with me. He pinches a nipple, making it stiffen, and a whimper escapes my mouth at the feel of him flicking and tugging the sensitive pink peak between his fingertips. That feeling only intensifies when he rips my bra over my head and sucks my nipple into his mouth. My head falls back, the sensation of his tongue licking and swirling, over and over again sending a shockwave to my core. My hands fly to his hair, holding his face against my chest, wanting more as I grind myself over the hard ridge in his shorts.

"Feel good?" he asks, looking up at me with a smile, my breast still against his mouth.

"So good," I rasp, gripping the short blond strands as he moves to my other one, paying it the same intense attention. And when he takes the taut peak between his teeth, biting gently, I pant in bliss.

"I fucking love how responsive you are, but I'm just getting started," he says when his lips pop off my nipple.

"Lie on the bed," he commands.

The heat in his voice sends a shiver down my spine, and I do as he says. I watch as Grayson grabs the hem of his T, pulling the fabric over his head. I'm unprepared, practically drooling at the sight of him—firm pecs with a light dusting of chest hair, abs that rival any professional athlete's, and a V of muscle that leads down to the waistband of his shorts like it's pointing to buried treasure. I inch backwards on my ass towards the headboard, never taking my eyes off him.

Once his shirt is on the floor, Grayson kneels on the bed and crawls between my thighs until he's hovering over me, then dips his face to mine for a slow, lingering kiss. It's soft and searching, the kind of kiss that breaks open your heart. I suddenly understand why some kisses are described as earth-shattering, because that is what this feels like. Like I'll never be the same.

And I want more. I want to breathe him in, taste him, inhale him—all I want is Grayson.

My fingers grip his hair, holding him against my lips. The stubble on his face rubs against my skin and I find myself wondering how it would feel rubbing against my thighs as he tastes me.

When he breaks the kiss to lick a path down my throat, I think I'm about to get my wish, but instead he explores my collarbones, licking and sucking. I tip my head back to give him better access as he nips at my neck. When his mouth trails lower, past my chest to my bellybutton, he looks up at me with heat in his eyes.

"I'm going to bury my face between your thighs," he growls. "Because that's what I've wanted to do since that night your legs were wrapped around me, and I came so fucking deep inside of you."

I can't speak but manage to nod as he roughly drags my athletic shorts down my legs onto the floor. His eyes dip down to my lace thong, the only scrap of fabric left on my body. He swallows, his Adam's apple bobbing in his throat. "Fucking killing me, sunshine," he says, slowly brushing the pad of his thumb along the center of me where I ache.

"Are you wet for me, Sierra?"

I nod, sucking in a breath, desperate for him to touch me again, for the friction I desperately need to ease the ache that's thick between my legs. When I whimper, he seals his mouth over mine and I open for him, my arms snaking around his neck, pulling him closer while his tongue teases mine. His body sinks into me, his weight pressing over top of me like a luxurious blanket. He hikes my leg up so that he can grind his hard-on into me. I want his clothes gone. I want him inside of me. I want to feel every inch of him.

He kisses me while he continues to grind his erection into my drenched panties and I groan at how good it feels, pushing my pelvis up into the hardness behind his board shorts, craving more.

"So eager," he teases against my mouth. "You want my cock, Sierra?"

"Oh, God...fuck... yes." I've never felt anything like this

before. This primal need to have him all over me, in me, is all I can think about.

Pushing up on his hands, he presses wet kisses down my sternum until he's on his knees again between my thighs. One finger teases the length of me over my lace thong and when his finger slips under the material, teasing my entrance, I grip the sheets in desperation.

"Drenched for me," he growls as I prop myself up on my elbows, watching him hook his fingers into my panties, silently begging him to rip them off me and devour me with his tongue like I'm his last meal.

"Touch me," I beg. "Put your mouth on me, Gray."

And when Grayson pulls my pale pink lace panties over my hips and down my legs to the floor, white-hot heat rolls over every surface of my body, setting my skin on fire. He kisses a path back up towards my center, his mouth slowly gliding up the inside of my leg. My core aches in anticipation when his face meets the connection of my thighs.

Everything inside me pulses, aches, takes flight when he pushes a finger inside of me and then buries his face between my legs, exactly where I want him most. My head falls back for a moment, but then I return my gaze to meet his and he looks me in the eye as he flattens his tongue along my seam. His tongue swirls over my most sensitive spot, licking and sucking in long, smooth strokes as my legs shake on either side of his head.

He's unrelenting, the way his tongue fucks me, devours me, sucks me. I finally have to fall back against the mattress, chest heaving as my climax climbs closer and closer.

There are no words to describe what this man can do with his tongue. I'm hanging on for dear life, fighting the orgasm that is threatening to push me over the edge. But it feels so good. So good that I never want it to end. I try not to give in, but when he adds a second finger, I'm powerless to stop the orgasm that washes over me. I shudder, crying out his name as I arch my back while he continues to lick and suck until I squeeze my thighs together, forcing him to stop.

He wipes his smile with the back of his hand, grinning as he crawls up my body, his blond hair a mess. "Good girl, sunshine," he says, kissing my lips so I taste myself, then my jaw and the tip of my nose, as my sated body sinks into the comforter. "Now you're going to be a really good girl and come all over my cock," he tells me, his gaze darkening.

My heart races. I've never been this turned on by anyone in my life.

"Strip for me," I tell him, dizzy at the thought of him naked in front of me.

He smirks and begins to crawl off the bed; I sit up to enjoy the view. Then his boxer briefs hit the ground, and Grayson's long, hard, beautiful dick springs free. I'm speechless as I watch him at the edge of the bed, completely naked, stroking his cock in his hand. I might even be drooling. Grayson is huge and judging from the smug grin on his face he's well aware.

I lean back against the pillow, and he moves towards me, crawling over the bed, pushing my legs apart, his dick brushing against my entrance.

I realize I've been holding my breath since his briefs hit the floor, remembering how sore I was the day after we had sex in Miami. I've had sex with many guys in my lifetime and not once had I ever felt sore—now I know why. That night in the hotel office everything had happened so fast, I didn't really get a chance to see Grayson naked. He must notice my apprehension when he kisses me gently. "Don't be nervous. We already know I'm going to fit."

He reaches for his nightstand, to pull out a foil packet

from the drawer and I watch him tear it open with his teeth. Once he's suited up and ready, he lines himself up with my entrance, his brown eyes dark with lust. His eyes sear into mine as he slides his hardness over the length of my slick opening, his thick, hard erection creating the perfect amount of pressure there—enough to ease the pulse that is once again beating a heavy rhythm after the mind-shattering release he gave me not even five minutes ago.

"Feel good?" he asks, with a satisfied grin.

"You know it feels good. My God, Grayson. I want you now. Please."

"No need to beg," he says. "I'm going to give you every inch."

Then his smug expression fades as he pushes inside of me—slowly, inch by inch like he promised—giving me time to stretch for him. There's a burn, followed by the feeling of being full. My eyes squeeze shut, my skin tingles, every muscle in my body begins to unravel.

"I'm only half-way," he says, his body stilling, his gaze moving from where our bodies are joined up to my eyes. He drops his forehead to mine, then kisses me there. "You okay, sunshine?"

"More than okay. Keep going."

And he does, until he's all the way inside of me, his arms planted into the mattress on either side of my body. I feel gloriously full, my body having adjusted to his size. We both moan at the feeling and then we're panting and groaning as his hips start to find a rhythm, rocking back and forth, my hands gripping his thighs.

My body comes alive. My hands move to his biceps, his shoulders, anywhere I can reach. I can't stop touching him. I feel unravelled, desperate. No man should have this much power over me.

It feels nothing like our first time in Miami, where he fucked me hard and fast, and it was all over before I even had a chance to realize he wasn't wearing a condom. Tonight, Grayson is taking his time, slow and thoughtful, drawing out every bit of pleasure. When I think he's going to speed up, he slows down instead, as if he's fighting for control of his orgasm.

"Fuck," he breathes. "I love the way you feel. I've never... you... fuck, Sierra... I love fucking you." He kisses me, then a devilish grin comes over his face. "I'm going to fuck you harder, Sierra. Fast and hard. You ready?"

"Gray." My breath hitches. "Take me. God, I want you to take me." My body feels like an inferno, I'm on the verge of erupting as his hardness sinks into me so deep that I lose my breath.

He picks up the pace, driving into me, the intensity of his stare making my toes curl. It's all so overwhelming, so surreal, that I look down at us in awe, watching him disappear inside of my body, a second orgasm just seconds away. Stroke after stroke, each drive of his hips sends a fierce pleasure to that spot between my thighs, my climax threatening.

"Fuck, Sierra," he breathes, his teeth clenched. "I want you to come for me, baby. I need you to come again."

And that's all it takes.

I. Am. Done.

My orgasm crashes through me, pulse after pulse, until I'm broken in pieces. My body is trembling as my head falls back into the pillow, the bedsheets gripped tightly in my fists.

Grayson follows right after, jaw slack, eyes squeezed shut as he pours into me, filling the condom.

I am wrecked. Wholly and fully wrecked.

I've only ever been ruined like this one other time and

that was with Grayson. Never in my life have I felt like this with anyone else. When I open my eyes and see that smug smile that he wears like a loaded gun, I suck in a breath.

He's so beautiful it's crazy. His skin glistens with a light sheen of sweat, his hair a mess from my hands. I'm still coming down from that high when Grayson collapses on top of me, his erection still buried inside of me.

"I remembered a condom this time," he laughs against my neck before his mouth sucks on my skin. "Speaking of," he says, kissing my mouth. "I should take care of that."

While Grayson is in the bathroom, I drag myself from his bed and start gathering my clothes. I'm about to pull my panties on and get dressed when he walks back into the room. He meets me at the end of the bed, still nude. The sight of him naked, his cock soft, is mouth-watering. He slips his hands over my hips, lips pressed against my hair.

"Not happening," he whispers as his hands trail lower, cupping my ass and pressing his body into mine. "You're not going anywhere this time."

"Get back in bed. I'm a cuddler, sunshine. I want to wrap myself around you like a blanket until you're hot and sweaty and can't take it anymore."

I laugh, shaking my head as he walks us to the edge of the mattress, lifts the duvet and guides me back into his bed. Then his big body envelops me, and I breathe in his scent. The room smells like sex and Grayson's cologne.

"I didn't have to argue with you this time," he says, running the tips of his fingers over my arm.

I smile into the soft chest hairs across his pecs. "After making me come twice, it's the least I can do."

He kisses the top of my head. "We're just getting started, sunshine girl. It's only the beginning."

THIRTEEN

SUCH A GOOD GIRL FOR ME.

G rayson

Monday morning came too soon, but there wasn't a cell in my body that felt the least bit tired.

I strolled into the office at 8 a.m. for a meeting with Beckett before going over a pricing strategy and sales forecast that my team and I will be presenting next week. According to Beckett, The Liberty is inching closer to being named the leading global boutique hotel company, beating out its rival, The Seaside. We have never held the title—for over 10 years that honor has belonged to The Seaside and the Bennetts. But this year we are hot on their heels.

The day we *do* gain hold of the top spot, Beck has promised us all a vacation, first class at a pricey Italian villa —*Lifestyles of the Rich and Famous* shit. It's going to happen, and I can't wait to be sitting in a cabana sipping an Aperol Spritz and puffing on an Arturo Fuente with Beckett.

But before any of that can happen, I need to talk to Blair.

When I walked out of my morning meeting with Beckett, Blair was on her way in. She was trying to act like she didn't recognize me, but I could tell from the hitch in her

ONE GOOD MOVE

breath and the way she swallowed it down that it was all an act. I wasn't going to chase her down, but we sure as hell need to talk.

And now's my chance. I take the stairs up to her office on the third floor and knock on her door. "Come in," she calls, clearly not realizing that it's me who's waiting. I open the door slowly, peaking my head in.

Blair is sitting behind her desk, her focus glued to whatever it is on her computer screen. "Hello Blair," I say, and at the sound of my voice she looks up, removing her thick-rimmed, tortoise shell glasses and setting them on her desk.

"I can't say I haven't been expecting you," she says, nodding her head to the seat across from her. Closing the door to her office for privacy, I stride across the room and sink into the leather chair.

"I thought we should talk."

As I sit across from her, I find myself wondering how I was ever intimate with the woman. I fucked her in my bed all those months ago, but right now I feel zero attraction. No fluttery thing in my chest. Nothing even remotely close to how I feel about Sierra.

She smells like coffee and some expensive designer perfume. It's not at all like I remembered, and nothing like Sierra's intoxicating, beachy scent.

"Talking sounds good," Blair agrees, fixing me with a smile as she taps her manicured nails against her desk. "I'm glad you stopped by, Grayson. I know this is uncomfortable, but it really doesn't have to be. I was actually pleased to see you at The Liberty. I think we could work well together."

She's looking at me like I'm a deer and she's the mountain lion and it puts me immediately on edge.

"You don't have to look so worried. I'm not planning on telling Beckett or anyone else," Blair says, assessing me from her side of the desk. "You can relax, our little secret is safe with me."

"Okay," I say. "So... I guess that's it then. We can leave the past in the past and move forward as colleagues."

"Right. Colleagues," Blair repeats, sweeping her hair over her shoulder, her eyes still on me. "But Grayson, there *is* one small favour you can do for me."

My stomach twists. It seems like Blair is not going to make this easy after all. "What kind of favor?"

"There is a dinner I've been invited to. Some of the most influential people in Reed Point are going to be there, and I'll be the new face in town. You know how boring these events can be without the right company."

"I guess," I mutter, wondering where the hell she is going with this.

She leans back in her chair, crossing one leg over the other. "I'd like you to be my date, Grayson."

Her date? Is this woman for real? I'm trying really hard to keep my cool, but this feels a lot like blackmail to me.

"Your *date*?" I ask incredulously. "That doesn't seem like a good idea, Blair. We work for the same company. It wouldn't exactly look professional for us to go on a date."

Never mind the fact that I'd rather set myself on fire than date this woman.

"It's not a *real* date, Grayson. It's just a favor. One night. Besides, no one else from The Liberty will be there, so they won't know a thing about it. Unless you decide to tell them. But I'm pretty positive you know how to keep a secret," she says with a smirk.

"Look, Blair, this doesn't feel right to me."

"Don't overthink it. Beckett actually suggested it. He thought it would help if you were there to make some introductions for me," she counters. "Do you really want to have to explain to the boss why escorting me to an industry event makes you uncomfortable? Besides, it'll be fun. I promise."

My hand squeezes the arm of my chair. *Fun*? I seriously doubt that.

"Sorry, Blair," I clip. "Not interested."

There is nothing more to say. Nothing remotely nice, anyways. I look at her, waiting, pissed right off.

"It's Saturday night, September 3rd. I'm sure you'll have a change of heart," she says, slipping on her glasses and turning back towards her computer screen.

I can't get out of this office, and away from her, fast enough. But as I stand and turn to leave, I notice Blair grinning, like she's won. My skin crawls.

I stride down the stairs to my office, still shaking my head in disbelief. Someone needs to remind the head of our HR department about the strict no-fraternization policy around here.

I PULL INTO MY DRIVEWAY, trying to erase today's shit show at the office from my brain. Shifting the truck into park, I look up to see Sierra stepping out of her car and it turns out that's all I need to make all thoughts of Blair instantly vanish. Sierra is wearing a fitted pencil skirt that highlights every curve, and a pair of sky-high heels that remind me of a runway model. *Damn*. I've gotten so used to seeing her in weekend mode—athletic shorts, T-shirts, her hair swept back into a ponytail. Don't get me wrong, she looks hotter than hell in all of it. But when I see her in her business clothes, my blood runs hot. I turn feral for her, forgetting all about the bullshit at the office.

I'm completely fucking gone for this girl. I haul ass to

turn off the engine and slide out of my car in time to talk to her before she heads inside. "Sierra, hey."

She turns around, her gaze taking in my tailored suit and white dress shirt. She likes what she sees. "Hey, Gray." I notice that her smile doesn't quite reach her eyes though. *Fuck.* Is she regretting last night? I'm sure as hell not.

I can still hear the quiet moans that fell from her lips, can still feel the way her slick, warm channel hugged my dick. It was the best sex of my life. And I actually *liked* the cuddling afterwards, having Sierra in my bed. I didn't want to let her go. Present tense—I *don't* want to let her go. She eventually fell asleep in my arms, but when I woke up halfway through the night she was gone, and I missed her. After that kiss on her porch the other night I was pretty sure that one night with Sierra wouldn't be enough. Now I know that's true. There is no going back after Sierra.

She has to know what last night meant to me. She has to know she's mine. I need to make her see that I would do anything for her, that I want her, that I've never felt this way about anyone else.

Sierra stands at her doorway, frozen, eyes on me. So, I go to her, walking across the lawn to where she stands. I hold her gaze, images of last night playing through my head.

My God, the way she makes me feel.

"Hey," I say again stupidly, my brain powering down at just the sight of her. "How was your day?"

"Good."

I take a step closer but stop when she flinches. "Sierra—"

"I'm sorry. I'm nervous."

"I can see that. Wanna tell me why?"

She anxiously smooths her hands over her skirt as she casts a glance towards Tucker and Holden's place. Both of their cars are parked out front, but there's no sight of them at the moment. "Maybe... can we talk inside?"

"Good idea."

Dammit to hell, we're officially hiding from our friends.

I follow her inside, closing the front door behind us. Dropping her purse on a table in the entryway, she heads to the kitchen, where she pours us both a glass of iced tea.

"Ready to tell me what's eating at you?"

She looks up at me, her fingertips grazing the edge of the glass in a circle. "I feel bad," she sighs.

"What do you feel bad about?"

"I hate that I'm keeping a secret from my brother, it feels wrong. But I'm just not ready to tell him about..." Sierra motions a hand between us, letting her voice trail off.

"I don't want to lie to him either, but I also don't want to stop, Sierra. I like you a lot," I say, taking a couple of steps towards her. "I'm not particularly keen on the idea of drinking my food through a straw, but if it's important to you that Jake knows about us, then I'll be a man and have that conversation. I'll do whatever I need to do to keep seeing you."

"No. Not yet." She bites her bottom lip, and I can't help but wonder if the real reason she doesn't want to tell Jake is that she's not convinced that things between us are real. I'm sure my feelings are written all over my face, but is it possible that Sierra still thinks this is just a game to me? How do I make her see that with her, for the first time, I'm playing for keeps?

She drops her head, rubbing one hand over her eyes. "I'm not ready to tell him, Gray. But what does that mean? What happens now?"

My fingers itch to touch her skin. Things between us are

different now. I'm not willing to go back to the way it was before.

"Whatever we want to happen. This can be our secret."

Her warm brown eyes search mine, and then she reaches out and pulls me closer to her. "I know what I want."

"And what's that?" I ask, voice low and gravelly, as I pin her against the counter with my hips. "I want you to tell me exactly what you want, Sierra, so there's no way I misunderstand you, because I'm seconds away from reminding you how hard I can make you come."

I skim a finger along the waistband of her skirt and her palms reach for my hips. I swallow, my eyes glued to hers, hoping that she wants the same thing I do. She's mine, dammit to hell. She has to know she's mine.

"I don't want to stop what we're doing, Grayson."

I inch my finger down past her waist and across her hip. She shivers and all I can think about is that Sierra Matthews is mine. "You want me just as much as I want you, don't you, sunshine?"

"Shut up, Gray and kiss me."

I pull her into me and seal my mouth to hers. One sweep of my tongue against hers and she melts in my arms, the softest sigh escaping from her throat. The sound shoots right to my cock making it harden behind the zipper of my dress pants.

Sierra rises up on her toes, her hands searching my chest, my neck and up to my jaw where they scrape through my stubble. I give her what she wants, my tongue dancing with hers as I push her up against the quartz, my hard dick firm against her hip. Then I move my mouth to the shell of her ear, sucking on her tiny lobe. "You get me so hard, sunshine. Feel what you do to me?"

She reaches down to my cock, palming me over my suit pants. "Yes," she says, making me groan against her neck.

Behind us, the living room blinds are open, giving a perfect view to anyone who happens to be walking by. Reluctantly, I break the kiss, and as soon as I do, she laces her hand in mine and pulls me down the hall to her bedroom.

I wasn't expecting this when I drove down Haven Harbor today after work, but fuck am I happy it's happening.

The moment we reach her bedroom, Sierra lifts her top over her head and then unclasps her bra, letting it drop to the floor. Her hair is pulled tight into a knot at the base of her neck, and while it turns me on seeing how proper she looks, what I really want is to see it spilling out all over her gorgeous tits.

"Turn around," I demand, smiling when she does exactly what I say. Then I inch closer, sucking on the back of her neck while I slowly unzip her from her skirt. I turn my attention to her hair next, pulling the pins out, one by one, as I kiss her neck until her golden strands fall loose into a waterfall down her back. The scent of her coconut shampoo wafts in the air around us as I comb my hands through her blonde waves. Then I turn her around to face me and she surprises me by dropping to her knees.

It takes her a second before she works the buckle of my belt open, then unzips my pants and pushes them down to my ankles. I can't stop staring at the sight before me. Sierra on her knees for me, her hair wild, in nothing but a black lace thong is enough to destroy me. She shatters me.

I shudder when her fingers skim the waistband of my briefs, dipping inside to grip my erection. I groan at the feel of her hand wrapped around my shaft, and a small grin spreads across her face. My cock swells at the thought of Sierra's sweet lips wrapped around it.

"Pull out my cock, Sierra. I want to fuck your pretty face with it."

I unbutton my dress shirt and slip it off, watching her eyes darken with eagerness as she licks her lips and pulls my dick out of my briefs. Then she sucks me to the back of her throat, and I swear my vision goes black.

"Fuck, Sierra. You look so fucking beautiful on your knees for me." Her warm mouth takes me over and over while her hand fists the base of my cock.

She licks me, sucks me, takes me in as far as she can go, tongue swirling as I hold her in place, my fingers tangled in her hair, tugging at the roots. Sierra's mouth is ecstasy—warm, wet, tight. Her tongue runs paths back and forth along my shaft then over the tip.

"Shit, yes," I rasp. "So fucking good. Such a good girl for me." She swallows as much of me as she can before taking a breath and then doing it all over again. She works me faster, deeper until a shiver of heat jets up my spine. "Make me come, Sierra."

Her brown eyes connect with mine and she smiles with me still in her mouth. This girl fucking ruins me. I'm on the verge of spilling down her throat but before I do, I change my mind. I pull her mouth off me and tell her to get on the bed.

She doesn't hesitate, crawling over her light blue duvet, settling on a mound of pillows with her feet flat on the mattress.

"Take them off," I say roughly, watching her from the foot of the bed as she slips the lace down her legs. "Now spread your legs. Let me see you."

I pause, taking her in. Blonde hair fanned out over the

pillows, perfect tits that I can't wait to suck into my mouth and a body that was meant for me. And all I can think about when I look at her is *mine.*

I need Sierra to be mine.

The caveman inside of my brain doesn't want any other man to ever have the right to touch her. She is flawless and I'm going to make sure when I fuck her now that she knows that.

"Grayson," she pleads as I fist my shaft in my hand, stroking it a few times at the sight of Sierra naked and spread out on her bed for me. "Please."

I kneel on the bed as I continue to stroke myself. "What do you want, baby? Do you want me to fuck you?"

"God, yes," she says, her voice raspy, full of need.

I let go of my cock so that I don't spill too soon, then I move further onto the bed, skimming my hand up her thigh.

"Sierra, I don't have a condom. I wasn't exactly expecting this."

She swallows hard. "We don't need one. I trust you and I'm on protection."

"Are you sure?"

She huffs out a breath. "Dammit, Grayson, kiss me and bury your dick between my legs, right now."

I laugh and then, wasting no more time, climb between her legs and crawl over her body until my mouth is just millimeters from hers. "Is this where you want me?" I tease her, skimming the head of my dick over her slit. "Right here, sunshine?"

"Yes," she gasps as I repeat the motion. Sierra is so damn responsive to my dirty talk it only makes me want to tease her more.

"That was so hot, Sierra. Your little mouth wrapped around my shaft while I fucked your face."

I position myself between her legs and swiftly sink into her in one long thrust. The frustration on her face is instantly replaced with pleasure, her fingernails sinking into my forearms, and *fuck*, she feels so good. I'm not going to last much longer.

"My God, Gray," she hisses, reaching for my hips and holding me tight against her pelvis. "You feel amazing. You feel so good like this."

"Say it again, baby. Say my name again."

She moans as I rock into her, finding the spot that makes her see stars. "Gray."

Fuck, I love the sound of my name on her lips.

I pull out and push back in a few more times, watching her tits bounce underneath me, then lean down and finally suck one breast into my mouth. She arches her back, pushing her chest into me as I pump into her in a perfect rhythm.

I want to be as deep inside of her as I can, so deep she feels me in her stomach, so I pull out of her, and lie on my back. "Get on top. I want you to ride me."

Her lips are swollen from my kisses, and she has a purple mark on her chest from my mouth, another on her neck. If I had my way, she'd have them all over her body, marking her as mine.

She slings one leg over my body, straddles my waist and positions herself over me. Then I grip her by her hips and watch her sink down on my cock until she's fully seated... and groan.

She stills for a second, eyes locked on mine before she slowly begins to grind against me, buried so deep it's hard to know where she begins, and I end. Her hands are planted firmly on each of my pecs, my name falling from her lips in a whisper. Needing more, my fingers grip the skin of her hips hard as I lift her up off me then drop her back down, again and again, until we're both panting. It must be what paradise feels like.

"You gonna come for me, sunshine?" I'm spiraling. I'm so close to that feeling we're both chasing, teetering on the edge, trying to hold on, but I need to get her there first. I reach up and lightly grip her neck, my hand putting pressure on her throat as she's quivering in pleasure, euphoria. I tighten my hold around her neck and with one more rock of my hips, she's coming undone, lips parted, cheeks flush. It's one of the most beautiful things I've ever seen. I feel her body clench around me, and I can't hold off a second longer before I'm exploding into her, my world rocked. I let go of her neck then crash my lips to hers in a hungry kiss, so fucking overcome with emotion for this girl.

Breathless, we both collapse on the bed, looking up at the ceiling, until I haul Sierra overtop of me, lifeless and out of breath.

"I love it when you're bossy with me," she teases.

I laugh. "I know. And I love being the one to boss you around in bed. I can't wait to do that again," I say out of breath, pushing the strands of hair from her face so I can see her pretty eyes.

She looks up at me from where her head is lying against my chest, one brow raised. "Me too."

We both smile and then she buries her head back on my chest as I stroke my fingertips down the length of her arm. We lie like that for a while, time ticking slowly by. Eventually, I stir, dragging myself out of her bed and then scooping Sierra up in my arms.

"Where are you taking me?" she squeals, wrapping her arms around my neck.

"What? You all of a sudden don't trust me?"

She rolls her eyes. "I think I just proved that I trust you."

I let her down once we're in her bathroom, where I start a hot shower and pull her under the spray with me, my hands all over her. Eventually, we towel off and while Sierra is getting dressed, I order us take-out.

I meet her in the kitchen, where she pours me a glass of water. "I ordered us Thai," I tell her. "I hope that's okay?"

A sweet smile paints her face. "It's more than okay, Grayson. Thank you."

An hour later, full, and happy, I clear the empty containers away and then guide Sierra into the living room with me. I pull her onto the couch between my legs, leaning back so that she's resting her back against my chest. She sighs, sinking into me as I trail a finger up and down her bare arm.

My mind wanders to Jake. He's one of my best friends. He's talked me through some really tough times with my dad, never judging me or my family. It doesn't sit well with me that I'm sneaking around with his little sister. I really don't want to push Sierra on this, but I can't ignore the sinking feeling that the longer we keep this from Jake, the worse the fallout will be.

As if she can hear my inner dialogue, Sierra shifts in my arms to look at me, a crease between her brows as if she's worried about something too.

"Hey, what's up? You might as well tell me so I don't have to sit here and try to guess. I'm a man. I'll guess the wrong thing every single time."

Sierra laughs. "You make an excellent point," she says, untangling her body from mine and pulling herself up to sit cross-legged on the couch beside me. "Just nervous about how my brother will take the news when he finds out," she admits, an anxious look in her eyes.

"I know," I tell her. "But we'll worry about that when we need to. For now, you can pick my place or yours, but we're sleeping together tonight. And don't even think about arguing with me. It's not a question, Sierra, it's a demand."

She smiles and nods in agreement as she takes my hand in hers, but I can see she's still spinning thoughts around in her head.

"It's just... I hate change and everything is changing," she tells me.

"Change can make things better," I say gently, kissing the top of her hair. "Just promise me you won't have a change of heart in the morning."

Sierra peers at me from beneath thick lashes, then leans in for a kiss. "I'm staying, Grayson. I'm not going anywhere."

FOURTEEN

THIS IS THE DAY I FUCKING DIE.

Grayson

For all of our worrying about talking to Jake, we've yet to actually do it. Sierra and I are still sneaking around, keeping our relationship a secret from her brother.

We've spent every night together, either at her house or at mine, and every morning I wake her up with my hard-on pressed against her ass, followed by a morning round and a cup of her favorite peppermint tea after we've showered. Together. Because I can't seem to get enough of Sierra Matthews. Ever.

It's not just the mind-blowing sex that has me hooked on her. Every minute I spend with Sierra leaves me grinning like an idiot. We spent one night painting her kitchen cupboards, then ordered in pizza and ate on her back patio, her head against my chest as we watched the stars slowly paint the sky. Another night she came home with a basket full of apples she had picked from a farm just outside of Reed Point, her cheeks flush with excitement as she told me she was about to make me the best pie I've ever tasted. I sat at the counter chopping apples while she rolled out the pie crust she'd made from scratch, draping it over the pie dish so perfectly that it was like watching one of those cooking shows on TV.

And she was right about it being the most delicious pie I've ever had. The girl can bake. Add that to her many talents. It was un-fucking-believable, so good that I brought a slice to work with me the next day for lunch. I had to lie to Beckett when he asked me where I bought it. I'm fucked if he actually goes to The Dockside and tries to order a damn slice.

Tonight is the first night in a week that Sierra and I aren't having dinner together. Instead, I'm sitting at a bar table at Cocina Caliente with Jake, Holden, and Tucker. We're eating tacos, drinking Coronas, and shooting the shit, but I'd rather be on the couch watching a movie with Sierra.

I'd rather be doing just about anything with Sierra.

I don't have a clue what's going to happen between us. Whatever it is, I know that it's probably going to cost me my friendship with Jake. That should be enough to stop me from seeing her, but there's no way I can. I'm simply powerless.

Holden orders another round of beers for the table before checking his phone for the third time in the past 10 minutes, no doubt hoping for a text from Aubrey. The guy is whipped, trading guys' nights for time alone with his girlfriend. It's made sneaking around with Sierra a lot easier because he's rarely ever home anymore, spending most nights at Aubrey's place. A month ago, I would have been calling him out for choosing a woman over his bros, but I'd be a hypocrite now if I bitched at him about it. It seems I'm just as whipped as he is.

Our server approaches our table with a bucket of beer, taking our empties with her. When she's gone, Tucker addresses the elephant at the table.

"You gonna keep your face in that phone all night?" He nods at Holden before taking a pull of his beer.

Holden looks up from his phone. "Aubrey is out with some friends. They're at Catch 21. Just checking in to see how her night is."

"Is she checking on you too or is it just you who needs hourly updates?" Tuck fires back.

I look over at Jake, but he seems to have missed the entire conversation, his gaze on the TV above the bar playing Yankees highlights. He snaps to attention at the mention of his sister's name, though.

"Sierra has your grandma's house looking good," Tucker says, changing the subject. "She's got a green thumb. The flowers she planted out front look great."

"Yeah, she likes that shit. Always has," Jake says, and I feel tension immediately take root in my shoulders. If Jake knew that his sister is *the girl* I've been sneaking around with for the last four weeks he'd definitely lose it. And then he'd probably bury me alive.

"I saw you leaving her house the other day," Holden says, looking over at me. My stomach drops, and I look at Holden, then to the bar, then to Tucker, who is shooting his housemate a look that says *are you insane, her brother is right there*. I look anywhere but at Jake. "So, how's she doing with her reno?" Holden asks me.

"I'm not sure, you'd have to ask her. Maybe Jake knows," I say, busy trying to act fucking normal, like my dick was not shoved all the way down his sister's throat last night.

"You were at my sister's house?" Jake asks, eyes narrowed directly at me. "What the fuck were you doing at Sierra's?"

This is the day I fucking die.

"I lent her my power drill," I say with a shrug, praying I don't sound as nervous as I feel. "I ran into her taking her garbage out and she mentioned she needed one, so I found mine in the garage and dropped it off for her." One lie turns into another, and then another, until I've spun a completely bogus story without an ounce of truth to it. It feels terrible. I feel like shit for lying to my friends.

"Is that it?" Jake asks with a pissed off look on his face. "Because you know my sister is off-limits, right?"

My hands fly up like two stop signs. Like I didn't just fuck his sister with my tongue yesterday. "Right. Off limits." *Another lie.* "Got it."

"I hate to be the one to break it to you, but your sister is a grown woman," Tuck says between bites of his taco. "She can date whoever she wants, man. Would it really be so bad if she wanted to date one of us?"

Holden and I both visibly wince. He's going to get punched in the throat for that comment.

"Try it and see," Jake says, his voice taking on a menacing note. "I'll smash your brains in."

"Okay, okay," Tuck says, leaning back in his bar stool. "Take a chill pill. I'm just saying that she's going to date someone eventually, Jake, and there are far worse dudes out there than us."

"Are you shitting me right now? I know your track record, you, and Gray. You would fuck her and never talk to her again. You think I'd be okay with that?"

My stomach coils. I can't blame him for thinking the way that he does. It's true that I don't do commitment, and neither does Tuck. But Sierra is different. I would never do that to her. And I wouldn't put Jake through it either. I wouldn't shit all over four years of friendship just to get off.

But I can't expect him to believe that when he knows my history with women. I rub the back of my neck, trying to ease away the tension. I knew this is how Jake would react, so why am I still so bothered by it?

"Besides, she has big goals, and she doesn't need a relationship right now to get in her way. She doesn't need the distraction."

"Is she going back to school for something?" Holden asks cautiously.

"She wants to open her own bakery," Jake says, and I try not to let my surprise register on my face. I don't know what I expected him to say, but it wasn't that. She's never said a thing to me about owning a bakery.

"A bakery?" Tucker asks, sounding equally puzzled. "Why does she want to do that?"

"It doesn't matter, she just does. Anyways, that's just one reason she doesn't need a guy screwing her around. She has a lot going on with The Seaside, my Gran, a new house in a new city."

"I get all that but getting into a relationship— or not— is up to her. You don't get a say," Tuck says, trying yet again to make his point.

"She's not looking for a relationship. Trust me. She's so busy we barely have time to get together these days. I was going to stop by last night to help her out at the house, but she said she had too much work to catch up on," Jake says before stuffing his mouth with a bite of his taco.

I almost spit out my drink. *You haven't seen her because she's been too busy riding my cock while she screams my name.* I busy myself straightening the cutlery next to my plate, going out of my way to avoid eye contact with Jake.

When it feels safe, I sneak a sideways glance at him. He's

wiping his mouth with a napkin, a sour expression on his face. He tosses the napkin on his empty plate then takes a swig of his beer.

"Don't even think about my sister," he says. "I promise you... I'll make sure you won't be able to walk. Or talk."

"Message received," Tuck says. "Loud and clear."

I sit in complete silence, my life flashing before my eyes. I have absolutely no desire for broken bones, but I also know that even the prospect of a full body cast won't stop me from seeing Sierra.

Despite Jake's threats of bodily harm, I can't get his mention of Sierra's dream of opening a bakery out of my head. My curiosity is definitely piqued. The girl can absolutely bake, but she has a good job working for an incredibly successful company. Would she be willing to give that up?

If Sierra was on my mind before, she's all I can think about after the conversation we just had. While the guys continue talking, I go to the bathroom and pull out my phone because I apparently have no restraint.

> Grayson: Miss me?

> Sierra: I'm re-watching The Last of Us so I have Pedro Pascal to keep me company. No complaints here. ;)

> Grayson: Pedro who? Can he make you come like I can? Answer is no. And I'm the only man who gets to keep you company. I'm trying to wrap this up. Be in my bed when I get home.

> Sierra: Maybe I'll be tired. Pedro can really wear a girl out.

> Grayson: I'm positive you're not too tired. Gonna make you come so hard when I get home.
>
> Sierra: I'll try my best to wait up… can't make any promises.
>
> Grayson: Sierra, if you're not in my bed when I get home, I swear I will knock down your door and carry you across the lawn to my house.

I slip my phone back in my pocket before I take this text exchange any further then return to the table. I'm already pushing it by texting Sierra while Jake's sitting in the same restaurant as me. The device vibrates against my hip, but I resist the urge to check it, reminding myself of the shit storm that will follow if the guys catch on. I heat at the thought of what could be on that text though. Sierra is becoming bolder, more daring when it comes to dirty talk and sexting. My phone burns a hole in my pocket while I hurry to down my beer and get home to her.

"You good, man?" Tucker asks, making my head whip over in his direction. I'm wound so tightly, the fear of getting caught with Sierra has me in a vice grip. But his question is directed at Jake, who looks up from his phone with a frown.

"It's my sister. Why the hell isn't she answering my texts?"

My heart might beat right out of my chest it's pounding so hard. I breathe in, trying to steady myself. I do my best to act normal, to say what I would say if I wasn't fucking his little sister. Thankfully, Tuck steps in before I have a chance to respond.

"You just finished saying she's busy, right? Relax and let

the girl settle in," Tucker says. "Speaking of girls... what's happening with that girl you met at the beach?"

Jake tenses. "Complicated."

"Does it need to be?" Holden asks, after a moment.

"It just is," Jake grunts, then takes a long pull of his Corona.

"How old is her kid?" I ask. "A girl, right?"

"She's seven."

He's barely forming complete sentences, which isn't like him. Sure, Jake can be on the quieter side; he tends to be a bit more serious and lost in thought than the rest of us, not comfortable being the center of attention. But he's usually better with conversation, especially when it's just the four of us. The way he's been acting lately though, something feels off with him.

The waitress reaches across the table to remove our empty plates, and Jake asks for the bill.

It breaks the tension of the moment, and Tucker and Holden quickly get caught up in an argument about the Yankees' latest loss. Jake looks to be happy to have the attention off him, so I leave him be. *For now.* I'll circle back to this conversation again another day.

After we pay the bill, I say goodnight to the guys and head out to the parking lot. I'm barely out the door before I dig my phone from my back pocket like it's on fire to check the last message from Sierra. I swipe the screen to life.

> Sierra: I might just stay where I am then and let you come get me. A riled up Grayson is so much fun.

Oh shit! This woman knows how to push my buttons. She's going to pay for that in the filthiest way.

Twenty minutes later, I'm kicking off my shoes in my front entrance, pulling my shirt off over my head and praying like hell Sierra's sprawled out on top of my bed, preferably in her birthday suit, when I stride down the hallway to my bedroom, my voice teasing, "You better be in my bed naked, so help me God."

"Hi," she says, when I push open the door. "Took you long enough."

Fuck me.

She's curled up under my covers, her arms stretched over her head, and as far as I can tell she isn't wearing a thing.

I stumble out of my pants, then my briefs as Sierra giggles. My cock is ecstatic to see her, giving her the one-eyed salute.

"Someone's eager to see me."

"He's more than eager, he's ready to fuck you into oblivion," I say, peeling the covers back and crawling in next to her. She's naked, like I hoped. She turns onto her side to face me and because I'm hard as a rock and aching for her, I pull her body against me tightly.

Sierra smiles and rolls herself onto my chest, pressing the lightest kiss to my lips. I pull back slightly to look at her, my eyes locking on hers, and I realize in this moment that she is the only girl on this planet for me. The only girl I've ever felt like I can't live without.

So, I start from the beginning, from the first time we met.

"You rocked me in Miami, sunshine, right from the start. Besides being the hottest thing I had ever laid eyes on, you were funny and intelligent and you made everyone around you happier just by being in the room. And the more I've gotten to know you, the more I see how amazing you really are. You're sweet to your grandma, a loyal sister, a pretty impressive home renovator and you're also incredible as fuck in bed."

Sierra's cute smile turns into a laugh. I slip my hand over the curve of her waist, where soft skin meets my fingertips.

"I'm serious, baby. I want you all to myself. I don't wanna just fuck, I want a relationship."

She shifts her weight a bit, propping herself on an elbow to look at me. "How can you be so sure? No offense, Gray, but commitment isn't really your thing."

"People can change, Sierra."

She nods, her expression thoughtful. "I didn't mean it like that. I know people can change—"

"Then you understand that meeting you has changed me. We have incredible chemistry. I like being around you. I get this stupid, happy feeling when I'm with you. You make me laugh and I drive you crazy with my insanely good looks," I add with a grin, teasing her. "We're good together, sunshine. Admit it. We make each other really happy."

Somehow in the last month Sierra has become the first person I think about in the morning and the person I can't stop thinking about at night when I'm trying to get some sleep. She's always on my mind, whether I'm at work, or out with the guys. Our flirty texts have become the best parts of my day, apart from those moments when we can actually be together.

She lifts a hand to my forehead, lightly brushing her fingers through my hair. "You do make me incredibly happy, Gray."

I haul her on top of me and kiss her, widening my legs so she settles in between them. "Now that that's out of the way, can I shove my tongue down your throat? I've been fucking dying to kiss you."

Then I roll her onto her back, wrapping her legs around my waist, and show her exactly why she's mine.

FIFTEEN

BE A GOOD GIRL, SUNSHINE.

S ierra
"This is so much better than microwave popcorn."

"Literally anything is better than microwave popcorn," Jules answers flatly, watching me toss a kernel in the air and try to catch it in my mouth.

"You look like a seal," she laughs, tossing a piece in my direction.

We're sitting in the dugout assigned to The Seaside waiting for the charity baseball game to start.

Grayson is on the other side of the diamond with Beckett, who's holding 1-year-old Maya in his arms. Jules' dad, Michael Bennett, is there too, the four of them posing together for the photographer hired to capture images of the day. I watch Grayson reach for Maya, and she goes happily into his arms. I can't look away. He looks hotter than hell in black athletic shorts, his red and white Liberty jersey, and a backwards baseball hat—and I didn't think it was possible, but the fact that he's holding a toddler makes him even more attractive.

How am I supposed to process this image without my ovaries exploding?

Good god. I am toast.

I've been trying all day to take my eyes off him, but he isn't making it easy. And it only gets more difficult when his eyes find mine, his smile slipping as his gaze washes over me. I try not to combust under the heat of his stare, the look in his eyes so intense that I know he's struggling too. It feels impossible being so close but not being able to touch each other.

But we're still keeping things under wraps, so stealing glances at each other is all we can do.

He smiles at me softly before he's pulled into a conversation. I force myself to tear my eyes away from him and try to catch my breath. I'm coming down from the high of Grayson's smoldering looks when Jules smacks the side of my thigh.

"What the hell was that all about?" she asks, raising her chin to where Grayson is standing on the field.

"What?" I shrug, feigning ignorance.

"You know exactly what I'm talking about," Jules argues. "Grayson just eye fucked the hell out of you. Don't even try to deny it. What is going on with you two? You better tell me everything."

My cheeks heat until I'm positive they're the color of tomatoes. "There's nothing to tell."

"Bullshit there isn't. I'm not buying that for a second. He just looked at you like Beckett looked at me when we were hiding our relationship from my brothers," she shoots back. "Maybe I should go over there and ask him myself." She makes a move to stand up from the bench and my hand flies to her arm, pulling her back down beside me.

I sigh. "Fine... but you can't tell a single soul. I'm serious,

Jules. We don't want it getting back to Jake before I have a chance to talk to him myself."

Jules arches a brow, rubbing her palms together. "Ooh, this is so good. A secret relationship. Forbidden love. So much fun. Now spill."

If anyone knows about forbidden relationships, it's Jules. She and Beckett snuck around for weeks before telling her family that they were together, afraid of how they would take Jules dating a rival from their family business' top competitor. I feel safe trusting her with this secret, knowing that she's been in a similar position.

I tell her how I tried to stay away when I first found out that Grayson was my neighbor—how I tried so badly not to fall for him, but his persistence won out. Then, with a tingle in my chest, I tell her about the night on my porch when he kissed me, about the night he showed up at my door to take me paddle boarding.

She listens with undivided attention as I tell her about all the nights and mornings we've spent sneaking around. When I finish, she takes a deep breath then flings her arms around me and squeals. "This is so exciting! He's a great guy, Sierra. I can't believe this. I am so happy for you."

My eyes float over to Grayson. "This has to stay between us, okay? I don't know what we are yet or where this is going to go. I'm scared, Jules. Neither one of us wanted a relationship before this thing between us started. How do I know this isn't going to blow up in my face?"

My throat tightens. I'm terrified of getting hurt by Grayson, of letting myself fall for him only to lose him and end up with a broken heart. But the alternative of living without him in my life just doesn't feel like an option. I've never wanted to hand my heart over to another person before. It feels scary and wonderful all at the same time.

Jules sighs, squeezing my arm. "There are no guarantees when you fall for someone. That's what makes it feel so good," she says, shifting to face me on the bench. "It's a leap that you need to decide to make and it's scary, but if you never take the jump you'll never know if he's the one for you."

My heart is in my throat as I stare at him across the field where he's tossing a baseball around with Beckett. "I'm scared to death."

"I get that, Sierra, I really do—but don't push him away before you give him a fair shot. You deserve to be happy. You deserve that great big love," she says. "And if things don't work out and you fall apart, then I'll be there to help you pick up the pieces."

I lean into her shoulder just as we're called out onto the field to start the game. Jules and I line up on our side of the diamond facing The Liberty team.

The stands are full of spectators—Jake, Tucker, Holden and Aubrey included—as we sing the national anthem. Then Beckett makes a moving speech about his sister Bean, who stands next to him, that makes me blink back tears.

When Beckett has finished speaking, Mr. Bennett takes the microphone to say a few words. I try to focus on his speech, but I can't stop myself from stealing glances at Grayson.

He looks so good it hurts.

Suddenly his eyes lock on mine, lighting up when I flash him a smile.

He winks.

I blush.

He doesn't look away.

My heart squeezes in my chest.

It's all too much. His eyes sear a hole right through me

with my brother in the stands less than 100 feet away, our friends scattered throughout the ballpark. It feels like a million eyes are on us but neither of us seems able to look away.

Grayson licks his bottom lip, shaking his head. I swallow, unable to control the heat crawling up my spine. Before I combust, I force myself to rip my eyes off him.

Suddenly the speeches are over and someone yells, "Let's play ball!"

Three hours later, The Liberty has beaten The Seaside 8-5. I barely survived watching the sexy way Grayson cracked the ball out of the park, how his muscles flexed as he ran the bases. We snuck glances at each other the entire time, my temperature rising with each passing minute on the clock, and by the time the game was over all I wanted to do was drag him home and devour him.

"Killing me all day long, sunshine," Grayson says in a low voice. "I hate not being able to touch you."

I shiver and turn around to see him smirking behind me. "I can't suffer for much longer, Sierra. I need to kiss you."

I vibrate with the need to kiss him too, but there is no way I'm going to give into that feeling here, with Jake talking to Beckett and Holden just feet away from us.

"Meet me over there in five minutes." He motions towards the dugout, already backing away.

"Gray—"

"Be a good girl, sunshine," he says. "Five minutes."

Then he's walking away while my heart beats triple time in my chest. *Is he crazy?*

This is such a bad idea. But my traitorous feet follow him anyway.

When I turn the corner of the batter's box, he's on me in seconds, pushing me against the wall behind the dugout, my back hitting the cold cement as one of his hands cradles the back of my head. I know this is way too risky, but I can't put up any resistance. I want him too badly.

"You didn't really think I could go all day without getting my lips on yours," he growls, his lips finding the edge of my jaw.

I whimper under his touch, losing the fight to regain control of my senses. "Gray..." I breathe. "Aren't you worried someone will see us?"

"Nope," he answers, not backing off. "I need you too bad right now. This'll be quick."

Then his lips trail a path over my jaw, to my mouth. I open for him as his tongue greedily pushes inside, letting him kiss me despite the consequences of getting caught. I'm not sure how he's getting me to go along with this. I'm not ready for anyone to know what we're doing, especially when *I* don't even know what we're doing. What I do know, though, is that Grayson has this incredible power over me. He takes control and is somehow able to coax me into doing anything, like he owns my body.

Grayson is bold, he takes what he wants, and it's clear how much he wants me right now. I want him the same way —I want him to keep kissing me, to ease the pulse between my thighs. I bite my bottom lip to stop the whimper that threatens to escape when his mouth kisses a path down my neck, one hand sliding up my bare skin under my jersey, the other hand tangled in my hair. We're being too careless, but there is nothing I can do to stop it.

After moving back to my mouth and sucking on my bottom lip, Grayson pulls back, his eyes flashing quickly to the corner of the dugout. What the hell are we thinking? We could have easily been caught.

"We'll finish this tonight, sunshine," he says, tugging his

hand through his hair, motioning for me to go first. I pat my hair down and walk past him towards the field, but he grabs my waist and pulls my back into his chest.

"I mean it, Sierra. I'm going to feed you my cock tonight before I fuck you senseless," he whispers in my ear before loosening his grasp on me.

Damn him and his filthy mouth. I inhale a deep breath and round the corner of the dugout to make my way to the field, trying to gather my wits, praying that no one saw us.

That's when I run face first into a hard chest.

GRAYSON

"SHIT! SORRY, SIERRA."

My heart freezes when I hear Tucker's voice as I round the corner. Tuck is staring down at Sierra with wide eyes that only grow wider when he looks over her shoulder and spots me with my hand on my mouth, wiping away Sierra's lip gloss. Neither Sierra nor I say a word to Tuck, but it's clear that he knows exactly what we were doing. It's written all over his face.

He smirks at me and opens his mouth to say something, but I cut him off before he has the chance. "This stays between us, Tuck. I mean it."

"Holy fuck," he says, shaking his head, looking from me to Sierra with a pleased grin on his face. "You two are... holy shit... Jake is going to lose his mind. Gray, it's been nice knowing you, man. You are going to be murdered for this."

"Keep your voice down," I warn. "We'll talk about this tomorrow. Got it? And no one is going to die." I'm not sure if I'm trying to convince him or me.

"Fine, but seriously. This is awesome. I'm so down for this. You've got my blessing—"

"We don't need your blessing," I tell him, shaking my head. "But thanks."

"Tucker, look... I'd like to be the one to tell my brother, and I know it's a lot to ask but please just don't say anything to him about this," Sierra pleads, a crease marring her forehead.

Tucker nods. "Lock and key, Sierra," he promises, miming turning a key at his lips and then tossing it away. "I won't say a thing. Besides, I like Gray too much to watch your brother chop off his dick. Your secret is safe with me."

"I'm going to head back," Sierra says, her worried gaze moving to me. "We'll talk later." She slips past me towards the crowd of people, a look of uncertainty painted across her face.

When she's far enough away, I look at Tuck with a warning in my eyes.

He beats me to it. "I told you... I'm not going to say a thing. But are you sure you know what you're doing?"

"I've never been more sure, man. I couldn't stop seeing her if I tried."

"When are you going to tell him?" he asks, obviously referring to Jake.

"I don't know. I haven't gotten that far yet." I chew the inside of my cheek.

"Not my sink, not my dishes," he says with a shrug, but I can see the concern in his expression. "I'm heading back to the beer garden. See you there?"

I tell him I'll be there soon. For now, I need a minute to get my head around what just happened. I was reckless, fooling around with Sierra in public like that. It's bad enough that Tuck found us, but it very easily could have been Jake. It's a sobering reminder that we need to be more careful.

On the drive home, I'm antsy. Sierra avoided me for the rest of the afternoon, and it felt like we were right back to where we were all those weeks ago. I can't help but wonder if she's having doubts after what went down with Tucker today.

Will I check my phone to find a text from her saying that we need to stop, that none of this is worth it? That would kill me. If the uneasy look on her face this afternoon is any indication, I'm probably minutes away from having my heart ripped out of my chest.

When I get home I'm anxious, pacing the floors, peeping out of the window to see if I can catch sight of Sierra. The uncertainty is killing me. Before I hop in the shower, I send her a quick test.

> Stay at my house tonight, sunshine. The door is unlocked.

I step into the shower and let the scalding hot water spray over my muscles. Once I've dried off and changed into a pair of sweats, I check my phone, hoping for a response from Sierra.

My heart leaps in my chest when I see a message waiting for me, but then plummets when I see it's from Blair.

> Blair: Hi Grayson. Sorry to message you after hours, but I'm in a time crunch and I'm looking for a copy of the most recent sales forecast from your team.

Fuck me. Blair is the last person I want to think about right now. I debate just ignoring her, but I'm afraid she'll keep bothering me if I do.

> Grayson: I emailed a copy to your assistant this morning, he should have it.

> Blair: You're a lifesaver. By the way, Max Collins will be at the Travel Forward Gala on the 23rd, this could be a good chance for us to get some time in with him. You'll be there?

The thought of attending that event with Blair makes me want to stick pins in my eyeballs, but I really don't want to have to explain to Beckett why I refused to go. I have enough to deal with as it is. And I've been trying to pitch to Collins' company for months. That contract would be huge—maybe even enough to push The Liberty past The Seaside. I groan at the thought of giving Blair the satisfaction of giving her the answer she wants. Instead, I avoid answering at all.

> Grayson: Not sure, I've got a packed schedule.

As soon as I hit send, I toss my phone on the counter. I rake my hands over my face. The gala is still a few weeks away. I'm going to need a very stiff drink or three if I'm going to get through that evening.

My phone buzzes, vibrating against the counter. *Leave me the fuck alone, Blair.*

But when I pick up my phone to silence it, I find a text reply from Sierra.

> Sierra: I'm on my way in 5.

And that is enough to make me forget all about Blair and the gala from hell.

I blow out a breath I didn't realize I had been holding,

immediately feeling a weight lift from my shoulders. I spend the next 10 minutes waiting on pins and needles for her to walk through my door and when she finally does, my heart skips a beat. Her hair is wet, hanging in loose waves framing her face, she's wearing shorts and a T-shirt, her long, toned legs setting my pulse racing. She slips inside quickly, like walking through my door is wrong. It shouldn't feel this way, but now it does, and I hate it.

"I feel bad. Are we supposed to feel bad?" she asks as she walks into the living room and flops onto my couch. She pulls her legs underneath her, wrapping her arms tightly around them. I sit on the couch next to her, pulling her against me.

"It's okay to feel bad," I answer. "I get it. But we're really not doing anything wrong. It's okay to want to be together, Sierra. We aren't breaking any rules. And we're certainly not hurting anyone."

A frown crosses her beautiful face. "We're sneaking around, Gray. We're lying to our friends, to my brother."

"Yeah, we are, but we aren't intentionally trying to hurt anyone. But Sierra, now that Tucker knows, we're going to have to tell Jake soon."

"I'm scared of his reaction... for both of us."

"He will get over it. And as for him being mad at me... I'll deal with it. Things will be okay."

She shifts away from me just slightly, dropping her eyes to the floor. It's like she can't look at me. *Fuck.* Sierra blows out a breath and rests her chin on her knees.

"What is it, sunshine?" I give her a minute before reaching out and running my hands through her damp hair. "Do you want to keep doing this? If it's upsetting you too much, we can stop."

We can't stop. There's no way I can.

My heart is racing in my chest. I've put it out there and already I want to take it back.

She unfolds her legs, shifting her body to face mine. She looks tense, guarded. "Is that what you want, Gray? To end things?" she asks softly.

"Not even a bit," I say honestly, reaching for her hand. "I want the opposite. I want more. I want you to be my girlfriend. I want to take you on dates. Real dates where we aren't hiding, like a restaurant or the grocery store—"

Sierra laughs. "The grocery store isn't a date, Gray."

"I don't know," I tell her with a sheepish grin. "I haven't done this in a long time, and I might not be very good at it. But I want to be with you. I mean... if that's what you want too?"

She's silent for all of three seconds, but it's three seconds too long for me. Then, finally, she says, "I want it all."

"You do? Like for real?" I want to scream, high-five someone, pump my fist in the air. "So, can I call you my girlfriend? I really want that stupid label if it's okay with you?"

"It's okay with me."

A smile lights up her whole damn face. I lean towards her, and she does the same and we meet in the middle but before I kiss her, I ask her one more question.

"Are you sure? I want you to be sure because I'm 100 percent in this with you."

She closes the distance between us, sealing a kiss to my lips. A kiss that feels like a promise. "I am positive." She kisses me again. "Can you be patient for just a little while longer? I promise to tell my brother. I just need to think about *how* to tell him and find the right time to do it."

My hands frame the sides of her face. "We can tell him together if you want, or I can do it if that would be easier."

"No. I think it's better if it comes from me."

Keeping us a secret for a little while longer is not what I want, but if it's what she needs I can be patient. It's one thing to hide our relationship when we're locked away in one of our houses, but it gets a lot harder when we're out in public. Case in point, the way I couldn't keep my hands off Sierra at the baseball game today.

"The long weekend at Holden's place is coming up," I remind her, dreading the thought of having to pretend she's not mine for two entire days while we're away with our friends. "Do you think you'll tell him before we go?"

She nods. "I will."

I smile, reaching for her waist, pulling her into my lap. Her coconut scent invades my senses. "I'm going to miss sneaking around with you, sunshine. It's a lot of fun."

"Then we'll make the most of it for a little while longer," she whispers against my lips.

My hands fall to her thighs, then move slowly to her ass, gripping each cheek. "Starting now."

SIERRA

THE NEXT COUPLE of days are a whirlwind. Work is busy with a presentation I've been preparing for so I've had to stay late every night to get it all done. One night, Jules and I worked so late that Maya was already in bed when we finally wrapped things up, so we went for a quick bite and a glass of wine before calling it a night. Another night, I met Aubrey, Holden's girlfriend, at Dream Bean for coffee then we went for a walk along the beach.

But my mornings and nights are always spent with Grayson, hiding away at either his house or mine. We cook dinners together, curl up on the couch to watch movies, stay up way too late drinking wine outside on the porch.

I've been so busy that it hasn't been hard finding excuses not to talk to my brother. I know that I'm avoiding the inevitable, but I just keep wanting one more perfect day in the bubble Grayson and I have found ourselves in. We don't have to justify our feelings for one another or defend our relationship to anyone. And I don't have to see the look on Jake's face when I break the news to him that I'm falling for his best friend. I haven't even told Gray how strong my feelings for him are, but I know I like him a lot more than I should. It's a scary feeling.

But I can't put it off any longer. I invited Jake over for dinner tonight and I plan on sitting him down and telling him everything. Well, not *everything*, but as much as he needs to know. I can only hope that he'll understand and see how happy Grayson makes me.

I'm chopping vegetables for the salad when I get a text from Grayson.

> Grayson: Am I supposed to be this nervous? How are you feeling?

I smile as I read the message, imagining him pacing back and forth across his living room with his hand in his hair.

> Sierra: I'm a little anxious too.

> Grayson: Are you sure you don't want to tell him together? I can come over. Just say the word.

> Sierra: I think this needs to come from me, but thanks. That's sweet. ;)

> Grayson: I'm not going anywhere tonight. If you need me, I'm right next door.

> Sierra: Oh, is that where you live?

> Grayson: Smart-ass. I also love your ass. So much that I want it in the air when I have you on your hands and knees for me tonight.

My skin heats. Grayson is a master at sexting, and I love being on the receiving end of his spicy messages. I decide to have a little fun with him. I pull my shirt over my head and snap a picture of the lacy pink bra I'm wearing, the one that's so sheer you can faintly see my nipples through the material. I hit send with a caption that reads, "Bra on or off?"

> Grayson: Cancel your brother. I'm coming over.

> Sierra: I'll see you later, Gray. Kissing face emoji.

My body is still humming from Grayson's texts, when there's a knock at my door. My excitement immediately turns into panic. Shit is about to hit the fan.

I open the door, trying to stay calm. I've made up my mind. I just need to tell my brother the truth and then Gray and I can stop sneaking around. Jake smiles when he sees me, hanging his coat on the hook and following me into the kitchen.

"Something smells good. What's in the oven?"

"A lasagna. It's Mom's recipe. I know how much you like it."

My mom used to make lasagna every year for Jake's

birthday, it was always his favorite. I smile at the memory as I hand a glass of Coke to my brother.

"Kitchen's looking great." Jake's eyes sweep the space. "I can't believe you're doing this all by yourself."

I swallow, thinking about all the nights Grayson has been here helping me, painting, hanging the cupboard doors, screwing on the new hardware. My mind then drifts to how those nights usually end, wrapped up together in my bed.

"It's kept me busy," I say, banishing the picture from my head. "I wonder what Gran will think?"

"You're gonna know soon enough when she comes over in a few weeks. She told me that you invited her for dinner with me and the guys. I guess you forgot to give me the invitation?" Jake says from the table, grabbing a handful of potato chips.

"Shit. I'm sorry. I completely forgot to mention it to you guys. When I visited Gran the other day she was asking about Grayson, Holden and Tucker. It seemed like she's missing them. When I suggested having everyone over for dinner, her eyes lit up. Do you think you can make it?"

"I can make it." He nods, popping another chip in his mouth.

"Good. I'm going to make all Gran's favorites," I say, taking the tinfoil off the lasagna pan. "I was thinking we could all play cards after dinner. I know she'd like that."

"She's seemed good the last couple of times I visited. I think she's made a few friends," Jake says. "I saw her sitting by the fountain with some guy and it was weird. She looked all heart-eyed and seemed startled when I approached them. You don't think she could be—"

"Finish that sentence and I will stab you," I threaten, pointing a serrated knife at my brother.

"Geez," Jake snorts.

"I don't wanna hear about Gran and..." I shake my head, laughing. "Nope... that's gross. I'm changing the subject. The lasagna is ready. I hope you're hungry."

I cut two large squares of the spinach and ricotta bake, licking the sauce from my fingers. I sit down at the table across from my brother and slide one of the heaping plates in front of him. We're both quiet for a few moments as we take the first couple of bites.

Jake can drive me crazy at times, but it's so nice living in the same zip code again. It means a lot to me to be able to cook him dinner, to share our thoughts on Gran... and, apparently, her possible sex life at the nursing home. It makes my stomach twist in knots, knowing that I have to break the news to him about me and Grayson. But I can't put it off any longer. I need to just rip off the Band-Aid and tell him. As I sit gathering my courage, his phone buzzes with a message.

He picks it up, looking down at the phone. Then he frowns.

Jake stares at his phone for a moment before his fingers start flying across the screen. He's quiet, concentrating on the message before finally looking up at me. "I'm really sorry, Si. I have to go. Something's come up." He shovels the last couple of bites of lasagna into his mouth before pushing his chair away from the table and bringing his plate into the kitchen.

"Is everything okay?" I ask, setting down my fork.

"It will be," he answers. "It's nothing you need to worry about."

"Jake, does this have anything to do with the girl that you're seeing? And when will you introduce me to her? I feel like I'm in the dark, and I want to know what's happening in your life."

Fuck. Did I really just say that? Talk about the pot calling the kettle black.

"It's just... it's her daughter. She thinks she broke her arm. She's taking her to emergency, and I said I would meet her there," he says, scrubbing a hand across the back of his neck. "Sorry, Si, but are you okay if we wrap up tonight a little earlier than planned?"

"Of course," I say, following him to the door. "Will you let me know how she is?"

"I will. And I'm sorry. Dinner was incredible. Tasted just like Mom's. She'd probably get her feelings hurt if she knew how good you make it."

I smile. He's probably right. And then, because I just can't seem to help myself, I stick my nose back where it doesn't belong. "You know, I'm sure this girl means something to you, but if that's the case, shouldn't you be smiling more? Isn't that what's supposed to happen when you're in a new, exciting relationship? You've just seemed pretty distant lately, and I don't understand why."

He sighs and for the briefest of seconds I think I see hurt in his eyes. "She has a lot going on with her daughter," he begins, then pauses and starts over. "She's just been through a lot, and I'm trying to be patient and take things slow. That's it."

"Okay. I just want you to be happy. I worry about you."

"I'm happy. I promise." I follow him to the door, and he hugs me before walking to his car. "Thanks again for dinner."

I watch his truck pull out of my driveway. I had been nervous at the thought of telling Jake about Grayson and me tonight, but I was looking forward to at least feeling relief at having finally told him the truth. Now all I feel is frustrated.

Ten minutes later, I'm crossing the lawn to Grayson's house. He opens the door and greets me with a hesitant smile. "So, how did it go? Hopefully the fact that he didn't tear over here with a hacksaw is a good sign? Do I get to keep my legs or not?"

I shake my head with a sigh. "I didn't tell him."

SIXTEEN

SHOUT IT FROM THE ROOFTOPS, WHY DON'T YOU.

Sierra

I remove the petunias from the pot and place them in the soil, patting the loose dirt at the roots until there's no space around the plant. I'm up early today; Grayson left me in his bed when he went out for a bike ride this morning. He was quiet when he crawled out of bed, but when I rolled over and found he wasn't there, I couldn't fall back asleep. My mind too busy remembering last night's dinner with my brother, and the fact that Grayson and I are still a secret.

"Hey, Sierra," Tucker's voice calls from Grayson's lawn next door. "Whatcha planting?"

"Hey, Tucker. Good morning." I turn to look at him, a petunia plant still in one hand. He's eating one of the muffins I made Grayson yesterday, which means he probably stopped in at Gray's house and stole one from the counter before coming over here. He's used to just walking into Grayson's house without knocking and has a habit of going over there to scrounge for food. "Enjoying the muffin?"

"These are damn good. Did you make these? I sure as hell know it wasn't your boy —"

My eyes widen, and I glare. "Shout it from the rooftops, why don't you? Keep it down."

"Relax, Si," he says with a devilish wink. "Holden's at Aubrey's and there's no one around. Your steamy secret is safe with me."

I shake my head, shrugging him off.

"Flowers looks good," he says, scanning his eyes over the selection of flowers I bought at the nursery. "Are you going to add the geraniums? They plant well with petunias. Both sun worshippers. They can never get enough of the rays."

"And how would you know all that? I thought produce was your gardening specialty?"

"Ah, come on. I happen to know my way around a flower bed. Every good gardener should," he says with a grin. I don't know Tucker very well yet, but I can see why he's so loveable. He could charm the tail off a dog. "Let me help you."

He crouches down beside me, moving one of my other pots between his knees. I watch him assess the flowers that need to be planted before deciding on the pansies and zinnias I bought. He gets to work tipping them out of the plastic pots they came in, then planting them so they're standing perfectly upright before backfilling the soil and tamping it down all around the delicate roots.

"You're pretty good at that," I tell him.

"Did you ever doubt me?"

"Honest answer?" I ask. He nods. "I've never met a man in his twenties who likes to garden so yeah, I doubted you. But I stand corrected. What got you into it?"

He looks happy as he continues to plant more pansies.

His brown hair falls over his forehead as he works, his veiny forearms tan from the sun.

"My mom taught me. The garden is where she used to let her hair down. She was always covered in dirt— under her fingernails, all over her knees." He wipes his forehead with the back of his hand. "She spent summers outside in her garden and I used to help her. I guess I grew to love it."

"Aw, you're a momma's boy. I like that about you."

"Shucks, Si, you're gonna make me blush," Tucker jokes, dusting the soil from his hands.

We fall quiet for a while, working together in comfortable silence until every flower I purchased is planted. Finally, we stand up and survey the colorful pots. He lifts his hand for a high-five.

"We're a damn good team," he says. "Where do you want them?"

"Right over there," I tell him, pointing to the steps leading to my front door. "On either side of the walkway would be great."

"At your command," he says, hiking one of the pots into his arms and carting it towards the house. "You got a hose nearby? These beauties need a drink."

I grin at him. Tucker is a cool guy, and he seems like he'd make a good friend. "I do. I'll grab it for you."

Once he's thoroughly watered the pots, he bends forward and takes a drink from the spray. The water drips down his chin drenching the front of his T-shirt.

I watch him and laugh. "You look like a damn dog, Tuck."

"I think I'd make a very handsome dog, but what I think you're actually trying to say is that I look sexy."

I roll my eyes. "Oh yeah, like a hot fireman, Tucker. If

you keep this up, they'll give you your own month in the calendar."

"Watch out, or you're going to need this hose to cool down," he says, jokingly. "Your boyfriend is gonna be mad if he comes home and catches you enjoying the view."

"You're a good time, Tuck... I'm happy we're friends."

"I knew I'd win you over. And I'm glad that we're friends too, Si," he says with a carefree shrug. "I also think you make Gray really happy. Don't tell him I said it, but he's smitten with you."

I return his smile as he claps my shoulder before heading across the lawn. "Gotta get ready for a golf game. I'll see you soon, Si."

"Later, Tuck. Thanks for the help." I watch him walk away with mixed emotions. Asking Tucker to keep our secret has been wearing on me especially since he's been so sweet to me.

But it does feel good to have made one more friend in Reed Point.

FOR THE NEXT week I keep busy with work and the renos at the house. I see Grayson as often as I can, the two of us sneaking over to one another's houses just about every night. I've never slept better than I do when I'm in his arms. He seems to keep the nightmares at bay.

I haven't seen my brother, but we've talked on the phone. From what I can gather, he's been busy with the girl he's been seeing. Unfortunately, her daughter did end up breaking her arm from a fall off the monkey bars and Jake has been spending a lot of time with the two of them since. It hasn't felt right to talk to him about Grayson over the phone, especially when he seems to have so much on his mind.

But I can't help but wonder... what would have happened if I had told him that night over dinner, if he hadn't had to take off so quickly? Maybe Grayson and I would be a real couple right now, without all the sneaking around. Or maybe Jake would have completely freaked out and demanded we stop seeing each other all together. I'm not one to waste time on *what ifs*. For now, this is just how it is.

The trip to Holden's uncle's cabin in Cape May is finally here. I had hoped Grayson and I would find a way to drive up together, but it felt weird to insist on going with him when Beckett and Jules had room for me in their car. I'm worried that this whole weekend will be weird, sleeping alone while my boyfriend is in a room just steps away. Having to pretend Grayson is just a friend when really, he's so much more.

The drive to the Cape is around two and a half hours, but thanks to Beckett's killer country music playlist and plenty of snacks, the trip feels much quicker. We arrive to find Holden and Aubrey in the kitchen, already firing up the margarita machine. It's a beautiful home: two storeys with a gabled roof, white with black shutters and a thicket of ivy clinging to the exterior. It's homey and cozy and the perfect place for a weekend away with friends. There is plenty of room, a spacious kitchen, and a beautiful view of the coast from the patio.

Holden is a gracious host, passing out margaritas and then showing us to our rooms. I'm in the room next to Beckett and Jules, and I toss my bag on the chair and resist the urge to flop onto the double bed, suddenly tired from the drive up.

Instead, I head back downstairs, wanting to be there when Grayson arrives.

GRAYSON

"I FEEL LIKE A CONSOLATION PRIZE."

"A what? What the hell are you talking about?" I ask Tucker, who's sitting in the passenger seat beside me as we speed down the highway on the way to Cape May.

"You know, like some lame award they hand you when you don't get the one you really wanted."

I shake my head. "I have zero clue what you're talking about. Use your words, Tuck. Help a guy out."

"Do I need to spell everything out for you?" he says, shaking his head at me. "Sierra is the prize you wanted, and I'm the one you're stuck with. The *consolation prize*. Keep up, Gray. I know you'd rather have Sierra riding shotgun right now. Speaking of... this weekend is going to be awkward as hell with you two in full secret relationship mode. I thought you two would have talked to Jake by now. He's not stupid... he's going to figure it out."

I know he's right. The clock is ticking on how long we can keep this up. Jake has made it crystal clear that no one is to go near Sierra, and he's going to hate me when he finds out I've fallen for her. But he deserves to know the truth.

"For your sake, tell him soon," Tuck continues. "The longer you wait, the worse it's going to be for you. And if I were you, I'd do it in front of an audience. He's less likely to beat you to a pulp in front of witnesses. Maybe."

I don't bother to respond because I don't particularly want to think about the painful fate that awaits me. I'm

LILY MILLER

saved from any more of Tuck's advice when my phone rings, my mom's name appearing on the display. I hit accept to answer the call.

"Hi Mom," I say as I shoulder check before moving into the far-left lane. "You've got Tucker on the phone too. You're on speaker."

"Hey Mama Ford. How ya doing?" Tuck says with a smile on his face. Out of all my friends, Tuck probably knows my family drama the best thanks to late night drinks on my porch. Thankfully he's never judged me for it.

"I'm good, honey. You two excited to get away for the weekend?"

"We sure are if we ever get there. Gray has already stopped for a burger at In N Out and an espresso at Starbucks. The guy is high maintenance."

My mom laughs. "Oh, I'm aware. But I approve of the espresso if it keeps him awake and gets you to Cape May safely."

"Mom, I'm not driving across the country. It's like a two-hour drive. We'll be fine. What's up, did you need something or are you just calling to say hi?"

"I was just thinking about you," she says, but something in her voice makes me wonder if that's truly the only reason for her call.

"Is everything okay, Mom?"

I immediately wonder if something is going on with my dad. That's what it's like when your father is an addict. I'm always waiting for my mom's frantic call that he's passed out somewhere or has been missing for days. I hate it, but these are the cards we've been dealt, and I would never let my mom deal with him on her own.

"Everything is fine, Grayson. I promise. I only wanted to

say hi and tell you to enjoy your trip. Your dad said to say hi to you too."

When I'm silent for a moment, my mom adds gently, "He loves you, Grayson. I hope you know that. Now you boys have fun and drive safe. I'll see you when you get back."

"I'll see you when I get home, Mom. Thanks for checking in. Love you."

"Love you, Gray."

I adjust my Ray Bans and roll my head from side to side, trying to ease the tension that has suddenly settled into my shoulders. I know Tuck must feel the shift in my mood.

For years, my mom has put up with my dad's crap. His mood swings, his anger, the depression, and the pills. He's unpredictable, untrustworthy, unreliable. Unlike me, she's never given up on him. I wonder how she does it.

My sister, who is four years younger than me, was sheltered from a lot of the bullshit. My mom did her best to hide the lows from her by keeping her busy at dance classes or waiting until she went to bed to fall apart. But I heard the crying behind her closed bedroom door, I saw the blank expression on her face when she was wracked with worry.

I end the call, grateful to have at least one parent who has always been there for me.

By the time Tuck and I make it to the cabin, it's after dinner and we're ready for a few drinks. I'm hoping some liquid courage will also help to ease the awkwardness I will no doubt feel around Jake. "The fun can start. I'm here, y'all," I announce loudly as we enter the house.

I see Sierra as soon as I step into the kitchen. She's standing at the counter with a margarita in her hand and a big smile on her face that's directed right at me. My eyes lock on her and I have to physically restrain myself from running over to her and kissing the holy fuck out of her.

Instead, I settle for a quick hug in front of our friends. It feels fake and all wrong, but for the next two days this is how it has to be. I will just have to pretend that the woman I'm falling head over heels for isn't actually mine and do everything I can to keep my hands off of her.

I open the fridge and grab a cold beer, twisting the cap off, taking a long sip. This is going to be torture.

THE NIGHT STARTS off a little awkward. I can tell Sierra feels just as weird about this as I do, unsure how to act around me in a room full of people. But after an hour or so and a couple of drinks, we've loosened up and are having a good time with everyone outside on the patio.

I'm midway through an intense game of cornhole with Tuck and Holden when I steal a glance at my girlfriend. Sierra is sitting in a lawn chair talking to Aubrey and Jules under the glow of a string of Edison lights. I've kept tabs on her all night, itching to have my hands on her. Every few minutes our eyes lock and I have to remind myself to settle down.

Jules says something that makes Sierra laugh and the sound of it sends a shiver up my spine. I drink her in, from her long, loose waves to the leggings that hug her ass to the sweater that has slipped off one of her shoulders.

"Ford!"

I tear my eyes off Sierra, looking over to Tucker, Holden, and Beckett, who are all staring at me expectantly.

"What?"

"Take your shot," Beckett barks. "Jesus, earth to Grayson."

I take a long sip from my lime margarita, then toss a blue beanbag, landing it a solid foot from the hole.

"Better luck next time," Tucker says after sinking his beanbag and hitting 21 points, winning the game. "I mopped the floor with your asses."

I couldn't care less. If staring at Sierra means I lost the game, it was well worth it.

"Cornhole King... the ladies are going to be banging down your door to have a shot with you. Looks like your fuckboy days aren't behind you after all," I tease, raising my empty glass to him. "I'm going to refill."

I head straight inside, needing a mental reset from watching Sierra all night from across the yard. I sit alone at the kitchen island, scrolling my phone, hoping it will calm the pent-up frustration I feel from looking but not touching Sierra. Then I pour myself another drink.

I'm about to take my first sip when I hear the sliding glass door open. I turn to see my girl walk through the door towards me.

"Hi Gray," she murmurs.

The sound of my name on her lips is enough to send shivers over my entire body.

"Hi sunshine," I reply, feeling a rush of relief at finally being alone with her. I'm pretty sure Sierra senses it when she crosses the room and after a quick look to her left and right, slides her arms around my waist.

"Having fun?" she asks into my chest.

"I am now," I tell her, spreading my legs wide, pulling her body between them.

"How's my girl?"

"Better now," she says, tilting her head back to look up at me with a challenge in her eyes. "I'd be better if you kissed me."

I glance at the sliding door, then at the window with a view of the backyard. We're the only ones inside and no one is in sight, so I take advantage of the moment and lean in to kiss her. She melts into my arms.

I inhale the kiss, savoring the closeness of her lips, the scent of her skin, the feel of her body against mine. She tastes like lime and sugar, just like she did that first night together in Miami. Only now we've come full circle and she's all mine. *Mine.* I sigh against her mouth when she breaks the kiss.

"I was just getting started," I pout.

"I could tell, that's why I stopped you before you decided to push me up against the kitchen counter."

"Mmm... very good idea. My friend here agrees too," I say, pushing my hardening cock into her abdomen.

"You can never get enough, can you?" she asks with a laugh.

"Nope, not when it comes to you. I'm always starved for you."

She smiles, her eyes sparkling, and I feel the deep inhale she takes against my chest. "You can always have me," she murmurs, her voice soft.

My pulse whooshes under my skin. She said the words so easily, and God, I hope that she means them. It's starting to be hard to imagine my life without her.

She runs her fingertips under the cotton of my T-shirt and my skin erupts in goosebumps. My eyes drop to her lips, wanting—no, needing—to have them on mine again, but thankfully I remember where we are because suddenly the kitchen door slides open.

Sierra manages to take a step away from me, but then Holden is in the kitchen, his eyes moving from me to Sierra. He pauses, brows raised.

Sierra is quicker on her feet than me when she pretends that *thing* in my teeth is gone. But I'm not sure he's buying it. In fact, I know he's not. I've known him long enough to know he's suspicious. Thankfully, he doesn't press, and I feel like Sierra, and I have dodged a bullet.

But I can't help but wonder when our luck will finally run out.

SOMETIME AFTER MIDNIGHT, most of us call it a night. Holden couldn't wait to get Aubrey alone and Beckett and Jules were tired after an early morning with Maya. Sierra yawned and said goodnight and I lasted another 30 minutes before heading inside.

I crawl under the covers, my chest aching that she's not in my bed with me. I lie on my back and stare at the bunk above me. I can't sleep. I've gotten used to having Sierra's warm body cuddled up next to me. It's a strange realization because I've never liked sharing my bed.

Until Sierra.

My heart pounds. My palms sweat. I've fallen hard and fast for the girl.

Tucker is in the bed beside mine, and I check to make sure he's asleep before I slip out from under the covers and ease the door open, peering into the hallway. This is not a smart move. I know that. But there's nothing that can stop me—not the possibility of getting caught, not the potential consequences. I need to have Sierra in my arms.

I slip into the hall and walk towards her room as quietly as I can. I turn the knob and push her door open an inch. She's lying on her side, her back towards me. Her long blonde hair is splayed over the pillows. The room smells like her.

I close the door and lock it, slipping off my boxers before I peel back the covers and crawl underneath with her. I pull her back against my chest and breathe her in. My cock grows instantly hard when Sierra groans, wiggling her ass against it.

"I've been dying to get you naked, it's been way too long."

She quietly giggles when my mouth finds her neck. "It's been one day."

"One day too fucking long," I growl against her ear, pushing my erection between her ass cheeks. "You're going to realize very soon how much you missed me too, when you're wrapped around my cock."

The filthy things I'm going to do to her tonight.

I squeeze her ass cheek then move my hand up to cover her mouth. "Now you're going to show me what a dirty girl you can be."

We don't waste another second.

SEVENTEEN

HE'S PROBABLY PLANNING MY EULOGY.

Sierra

"Earth to Sierra."

I blink at the hand that's being waved in front of my face, drawing me back into the present. Jules gives me a knowing smirk before going back to spooning the red icing I made into a piping bag. Next to her, Aubrey is busy setting the dozen chocolate cupcakes we just baked on the counter while Jake watches us from the kitchen table. He's still in pajama pants, sporting a severe case of bed head as he sips from his cup of coffee.

"Sorry," I yawn. "I guess I didn't get enough sleep."

It isn't a lie, but it also isn't the entire truth, and I can tell that Jules sees right through me.

"Rough night, huh?" she asks, sounding innocent enough but giving me a knowing look.

I swear I am going to kill her. My brother is *right there*. I give her a very subtle shake of my head, turning my attention back to the dessert.

Grayson and I were up all night before he finally snuck out of my room and back into his bed just before dawn. My cheeks heat as I remember his mouth between my thighs, the two earth-shattering orgasms he delivered, the slow and sensual way he rocked into me as we tried to be as quiet as possible.

"Are you any good at this?" Jules asks, offering me the piping bag, once again snapping me back to reality.

"Yup. I can frost cupcakes. Do you want me to show you?"

"Ooh, yes, please. I have a feeling it will come in handy. I have years of kids' birthday parties ahead of me."

Tonight we're celebrating the last weekend of summer with a dock party and barbecue—and what's a summer party without cupcakes? Luckily, the girls and I found just about everything we needed to make them in the cabin kitchen. What I couldn't find, I was able to improvise.

Grabbing a cupcake, I squeeze the icing in a circle over the cupcake, round and round until the frosting looks like a rose.

"You *are* good at that." Aubrey says from over my shoulder. "Have you taken a class or something?"

I can feel my brother's eyes on me from across the room. He knows who taught me to bake. He also knows it's my dream to open a bakery in memory of our mom.

"I've been baking since I was a kid. I've had lots of practice," I say, giving Aubrey the easy answer.

My mom was a brilliant baker who taught me everything she knew. She made bread every Sunday and there was always freshly baked pie or cake when we had people over for dinner. At Christmas we would make sugar cookies, and Mom taught us to carefully roll out the dough and cut it into shapes. The four of us would watch episodes of *Survivor* while they baked, the heavenly smell filling the house. Icing the cookies was always my favorite part. It still is.

The days I baked with my mom in our kitchen are some of my fondest memories with her. I could always tell how happy she was when the two of us were together baking. I hope she knew I felt the same way too.

"Seriously, Sierra. If these things taste even half as good as they look you could sell them and make good money."

"Umm, nope," Jules says, swatting Aubrey's arm with a kitchen towel. "We like her at The Seaside, and we'd like to keep her there, so shut your mouth."

"Ow," Aubrey rubs her arm with a mock scowl on her face. "Never mind. Forget what I said."

I laugh at the two of them but stop when Grayson walks into the kitchen wearing nothing but swim trunks. He looks a little sleepy, but still gorgeous. His summer tan is the perfect golden brown.

He pours himself a cup of coffee before sitting down next to my brother at the kitchen table. He takes a sip, his eyes shooting up to meet mine.

A carousel of memories from last night flash through my mind: the feel of his hands skimming over my flesh, the labored sounds of his breath, his hand pressed over my mouth to muffle my moans.

Tucker follows seconds later, reaching around me to grab a handful of grapes from a bowl on the counter. "I trust you had a good night, Si," he says, quietly, so that only I can hear him. I can feel my cheeks turn red and when I turn and see his cocky grin it's clear he knows who was in my bed last night. He shakes his head, smiling like he knows something the rest of the room doesn't.

The blush deepens when I notice Grayson focused on us, the devilish smile on his lips not quite covered by the rim of his coffee mug. He shakes his head at Tucker and his antics.

LILY MILLER

I tear my gaze away from Grayson just in time to see Tucker trying to grab a cupcake from the counter. I smack his hand away. "Not so fast, cupcake criminal."

"It's only one," he pleads, pasting an innocent expression on his face.

"You're like a five-year-old," I tell him, pushing him away from the tray. "Maya behaves better than you and she's only one. Now, back away from the cupcakes."

"You heard the baker. Out of her kitchen," Grayson pipes up. "Those cupcakes are really impressive, Sierra. You have mad skills."

I'm embarrassed at how good his words make me feel, his compliment sending a rush of happiness through me. My love of baking is all tied up with memories of my mom, so Grayson's kind words mean a lot to me.

Grayson means a lot to me.

I'm beginning to realize this is so much more than a crush, or even lust. This is something I've never felt before. Grayson makes me think about my future—a future I can see with *him*. And that's not something I've ever allowed myself to dream about.

It might be terrifying, but I need to admit to myself...

I'm falling in love with Grayson Ford.

GRAYSON

I'VE SEEN every inch of Sierra's body, so seeing her in a bikini should have zero effect on me. That's what I told myself as we all got ready to head down to the beach. Turns out I was dead wrong.

She walks down to join us at the dock, and she looks

fucking delicious, like every fantasy I've ever dreamed up in my pervy brain.

I have to bite my lip as I take her in. The fuchsia pink bikini has strings that are tied in bows at her hips and a triangle top that makes her tits look fantastic. God, she is a work of art. I want to drag her upstairs, pin her to the bed and devour her, leave marks on her skin that won't disappear. Ever. Except, of course, I can't touch her.

She watches me as my eyes follow the curves of her body, curves I'm dying to run my tongue over. I can't tear my eyes away from her... until I remember her brother is sitting in the chair directly across from me. When I force my eyes off Sierra, I look in Jake's direction to see he's staring right at me with a look that says, *get your eyes off my fucking sister*. The smile I was wearing slips from my face.

Oh, shit.

I need to do a better job of hiding my feelings for Sierra. And I need to do it fast.

Luckily for my ass, Holden pulls Jake's attention away, asking him if he is ready to fire up the boat.

"I'm ready. You driving?" Jake asks.

"You cool to drive for a bit?" Holden asks, lifting the cooler from the beach.

Jake stands from his chair, pulling his T-shirt over his head, "Fuck, yeah. Who's coming?"

We all pile into Holden's uncle's ski boat and Tucker unties the rope, pushing us off the dock before hopping in. Once we're far enough away from shore, Holden is first up at wake surfing.

"How much you wanna bet he goes down in under a minute?" Tuck says, watching Holden lying in the water with his feet flexed on the board, rope in his grasp, ready to go.

"You really think you can last longer?" I ask him, taking a bottle of water from the cooler.

"I'll be up twice as long as all of you," Tucker shoots back with a wry grin.

"Wanna bet?"

Tuck snorts at that. "Only if you want to lose."

I shrug. "I like easy money. You're on."

An hour later, I've easily won the bet. I surfed Jake's wake so long I finally had to quit, but not before landing a perfect tail grab followed by a flashy dive into the cool lake water.

It's Sierra's turn next, and although she's only tried wake surfing once, she's game to go. Jake drives the boat while I talk her through the steps, getting her stance just right on the board so it flips up under her feet.

Then Jake kicks the boat in gear and accelerates so that the tow rope Sierra is holding tightens. I holler at her to draw her knees to her chest and dig in her heels, and she does as I say until she's standing, riding the wake.

"You did it!" I holler at her over the noise of the engine. "You're killing it. Now toss the rope to me."

She takes a few seconds to gather her confidence, then tosses the rope in my direction. Leading with her left foot forward, she looks happy and sexy as hell as she surfs the waves. Her toned legs shimmer under the sun's rays, the sliver of abs just visible below her lifejacket making my cock take notice.

I can't take my eyes off her, I'm so damn proud of her. I continue to cheer her on until she loses her balance and falls into the water.

I look over my shoulder at Jake to make sure he knows she's off the board and when I do my smile immediately disappears. Jake's jaw is clenched tightly, an angry expression on his face. He looks away from me without a word, turning the boat around to go back and get Sierra.

I keep my distance from Sierra for the rest of the ride, but I can feel her presence from where she sits on the bow of the boat like an electrical current flowing through my veins. I watch her when Jake isn't looking, the way her blonde hair whips around in the breeze, her profile serene as she looks out to the horizon. She's so beautiful it fucking hurts.

Jake is quiet on the boat ride back to the cabin and I give him space, reading his cues. When we get back to the dock, everyone piles out of the boat to get ready for dinner, but I stay back to clean out the boat with Holden. When he gets a call, I wave him off, assuring him I can finish up on my own.

I'm just about finished when I hear my name. "Ford." I look up to find Jake standing on the dock.

"Fuck, man. I didn't hear you coming," I say, startled. "What's up?"

I lift the cooler and pass it over the side of the boat to Jake, who looks annoyed. His lips are pressed together in a straight line, and I swear I see a pulse point in his neck beating. I swallow, trying to stay calm. He's probably planning my eulogy.

"Is there something I need to know?" he asks me point blank.

Shit. There's *a lot* he needs to know, but getting into it with him here at the cabin in front of everyone is not the way I want to die. "I don't know what you're talking about, man."

"I'm talking about Sierra," he says, his eyes drilling into me. "I've seen the way she's been looking at you this weekend. I think she has a thing for you."

"Okay, and—"

"And..." he says. "You know how I feel about this. I don't want my sister dating any of you guys. She's too good for you. She doesn't really know you, the way you avoid anything resembling a relationship. So, don't lead her on. Just leave her alone."

His words are like a blow to the gut. I want to tell him that he's wrong about me. I want to tell him that she *is* into me and that I'm into her too and that this thing between us is real. It's the best thing that has ever happened to me. I want him to know she means everything to me.

"I'd never hurt your sister, Jake," I tell him, keeping my voice level. "I wouldn't do that to her, and I wouldn't do that to you. I mean it."

"What are you saying, Gray? Is there something—"

I hate this. I can't keep lying to my best friend. I'm seconds away from coming clean and confessing everything when Tucker walks down the dock, interrupting us. "The girls are hungry. They want burgers but I can't find the patties. Do you remember where you put them?"

"I'm pretty fucking sure they'd be in the fridge," I joke, a lame attempt at easing the tension in the air. "Did you look there?"

"Geez," he says, putting his hands up. "Fiery. You must be hangry too."

"Dick," I snap back. "I'm not hangry. It's just fucking logic that you keep raw meat in a refrigerator. I'll come and take a look."

I grab onto the excuse to make a quick exit, heading back towards the cabin before Jake has a chance to say anything else. Ten minutes later, I'm grilling burgers on the barbecue when Tucker sidles up next to me with two IPAs in his hands. He cracks one and hands it to me.

"Dude, you owe me big time. You were about 10 seconds

away from getting your ass kicked when I showed up and saved you from Jake's fists. You really need to do a better job of not eye fucking your girl in front of him. Jake is on to you two."

Tucker is right. Sierra and I are walking a fine line, and I'm pretty sure we're going to get caught soon.

We need to tell Jake the truth before he gets even more suspicious. I feel like shit lying to him, sneaking around with Sierra behind his back. I know he's not going to be happy, but prolonging this will only make it worse. But I don't want to do it here, in front of a crowd. Sierra and I just need to stay away from each other until we're back at Haven Harbor in our own secret bubble and away from Jake's constant watch.

EIGHTEEN

THAT'S NOT THE HOLE I WAS HOPING FOR.

Grayson

I wipe the sweat that's trickling down my neck with the hem of my shirt, ignoring my tired muscles as I finish my Saturday morning run. I left Sierra in my bed with her laptop. She needed 20 more minutes to wrap up some work, then she promised me she'd be mine for the day. It's been almost a week since we got back from Cape May, and Sierra and I are still living in our little bubble. I haven't seen Jake since the weekend, and Sierra and I have found ways to avoid the topic, neither of us wanting to drop a bomb on this perfect routine we've fallen into together.

I'm walking up the driveway, out of breath, when I spot her. She's standing in my doorway, fresh from a shower, hair damp and tied up, no makeup on. She's a fucking vision. I slowly make my way to her. She's wearing my T-shirt, which lands just above her knees, and her long, bronze legs and bare feet make my dick twitch. There is nothing sexier than Sierra wearing my T-shirt. Not lingerie. Not a black slinky dress. Not even close.

I'm a sweaty mess when I walk the three steps to her,

noting the smirk on her face. She doesn't flinch when I pull her by her hips into my sweat-soaked shirt.

"Miss me?" I ask, one of my warm hands reaching around to palm her perfect heart-shaped ass, smoothing my fingers over her flesh. I swallow. "No panties, sunshine?"

"I just got out of the shower."

"A shame," I whisper in her ear.

"Why is that?" Her eyes are on mine, and I see the challenge in them.

I squeeze the apple of her ass. "You're about to need another."

"Not before I feed you," she says, slipping out of my embrace and grabbing my hand, pulling me into the house. I shut the door behind us and trail her into the kitchen, following her instruction to take a seat at the counter while she finishes up breakfast.

My kitchen has become her kitchen and I love seeing her baking and cooking here with her music on and a smile on her face. I've been assigned as her sous chef, preparing whatever she needs, only too happy to be bossed around by this blonde-haired beauty who has all but moved in with me. I wouldn't have it any other way.

"Did you work up an appetite?"

"I'm starved," I admit, eyeing the eggs and loaf of bread she has on the counter.

"Well, you're in luck. I am making you eggs-in-a-hole."

I laugh into my coffee cup. "Excuse me. Eggs in a what?"

"Egg-in-a-hole," she answers.

I can't help but laugh at the joke that's just begging to be made. I can't help myself, it's like low-hanging fruit.

"That's not the hole I was hoping for this morning." I say as Sierra slides a fresh cup of coffee over the counter to me. My hand reaches for her wrist before she has time to return to the stove, and I pull her across the counter for a chaste kiss.

"Stop it right now!" She pulls away, covering her ears with her hands. "Do not sexualize Gran's favourite breakfast. She used to make this for Jake and me all the time. I have memories attached to it that I'd like to keep PG-13."

She shakes her head and gets started on breakfast. I watch her take a drinking glass, flip it upside down and press the rim into a piece of bread. Then she places the bread into a frying pan with melted butter and cracks an egg into the hole. Once she's sprinkled the egg with salt and pepper, she flips the whole thing over. When she's happy with how it looks, she flips it onto a plate with a spatula, adds a spoonful of hash browns from another pan on the stove and some fresh fruit, then slides the plate in front of me.

She leans against the counter, crossing her arms over her chest, watching as I take my first bite.

I groan. How is this so damn good? "You have many talents, Sierra Matthews. This is delicious."

"Don't act so surprised," she says, taking her plate and sliding onto the stool beside me.

"Everything you make is unreal. Usually a person is either a cook or a baker, but you're both. I'm not sure which you're better at."

Sierra smiles a little at that. "I'm definitely a better baker," she says, taking a sip of her tea. "I enjoy it more too."

"That so?" I say, before taking another bite.

She clears her throat. "I've actually had this dream of opening a bakery ever since I was a little girl."

"That long, huh?"

A smile creeps over her face. "That long," she says, moving her fork through the egg that's left on her plate. "I specifically used to dream about my mom and I opening a bakery together. We used to talk about it a lot. We even had a name for it. We were going to call it Buttercup Bakery, after her nickname for me."

I still, looking over at her. I wasn't expecting Sierra to be so vulnerable. Her admission has my heart cracked wide open. "Your mom called you Buttercup? How come?"

Sierra's smile softens a little. "I would always beg her to make lemon buttercups. They were these little treats she used to make, and I absolutely loved them—a flower-shaped pastry filled with a cream cheese and lemon filling. They are a lot of work, but she made them because she knew they were my favorite. She used to say that if I ate too many I would turn into a buttercup, and I guess the nickname sort of stuck from there."

"You two were close," I say, a statement rather than a question. "For what it's worth, I think you would have knocked it out of the park if you had gotten your wish and opened up that bakery with your mom."

Her eyes turn glassy. "I know it sounds silly—"

"Nothing about your dream sounds silly," I tell her, hopping off my barstool, taking our empty plates to the sink. "Come on, let's go get dressed."

Her curious eyes connect with mine from across the kitchen. "Why are you in such a rush?"

"I have somewhere I want to take you. Come on, sunshine. It will be fun."

She eyes me like she doesn't quite believe me. "Grayson, where are you taking me?"

"You'll see," I say, reaching out my hand to her.

She shakes her head but slips off her barstool and takes my hand.

But when I drag her into the shower with me, peeling

my wet T-shirt off her body as she stands under the spray of hot water, I know my surprise is going to have to wait. An hour—and two orgasms—later, we're finally in my truck.

Sierra

AFTER DRIVING FOR 30 MINUTES, Grayson's truck pulls off the highway. He still hasn't told me where he's taking me.

We drive another five miles before he pulls his truck to a stop in front of Sweet Dreams, the most adorable bakery with a pink-and-white striped awning, windows trimmed in pink and a sandwich board that reads, *Enjoy life, Eat cake.*

"How did you know about this place?" I ask when he takes my hand in his, bringing our joined hands to his lips.

"I've been here once, on my way to The Cape. I had an espresso and the best slice of lemon pie and it always kind of stuck with me. I thought you might like it here too. Maybe inspire you a little."

I'm so touched that he thought to bring me here, that he seems to believe in my bakery dreams, no matter how unrealistic they may seem.

"I love it, Gray, really. But I'm not sure my childhood dream will ever be anything more than that."

If I had any doubts about the kind of guy Grayson Ford is, the next words out of his mouth remind me.

"Dreams can come true, sunshine," he winks. I melt. "Come on, let's check this place out."

When we walk inside, my eyes go wide. It's like walking into cake heaven. Cupcakes, pies and cakes line the display cases. Shelves are stacked with oven mitts branded with the bakery's logo, cookie cutters and homemade chocolate sauces wrapped in pretty pink ribbons. There are cloches lined up in rows on top of the glass cases filled with pastel-coloured macarons and mini-Bundt cakes decorated with frosting and sprinkles. My mouth waters. I want two of everything.

"It's impossible to decide," I tell Grayson, peering into the glass case.

"Who said you need to? We can try it all," he says, like he means it. And he probably does. I'm learning there isn't much he won't do to put a smile on my face.

"I doubt we could walk out of here if we did, but maybe we share a few things?"

"Whatever you want, babe. You choose. I'm just here to look good next to you."

I roll my eyes at him, secretly loving his cocksure attitude. On any other guy it would be a turn-off, but Grayson somehow manages to make it seem charming. It's not arrogance, it's confidence. He's also sweet and kind and funny and thoughtful. And he has my heart in the palm of his hands.

We end up settling on a slice of strawberry champagne cake with fluffy pink icing and one perfectly red raspberry placed on top, and a slice of Limoncello cake because the woman behind the counter recommended it. We add an espresso for Grayson and a cup of Earl Grey tea for me and then take a seat at the bench seat in front of the window that's stacked full of blush pink pillows.

"Did I just die and go to bakery heaven?" I ask, swooning a little.

Grayson sits across from me, laughing. He's wearing a plain white T that is stretched across his impressive frame, his muscular arms taunting me like arm porn—all smooth, corded, and lean. For a moment, I just stare at him and wonder how he's mine.

"I had a feeling you'd like it here," he says as a waitress delivers us our order. She sets the cakes and hot drinks down in front of us, then whisks away to help a couple at the counter. "Tell me what *your* bakery looks like," Grayson says, digging his fork into the Limoncello cake first.

I sigh, happily transporting to the place I've imagined so many times. "Well, if I were to design one it would probably be similar to this. Something small and quaint with vintage pieces, antique mirrors... you know... a space that feels welcoming and cozy."

"If you could do anything in the world, would opening a bakery be it?"

I shrug. "I don't know. I have a good job at The Seaside. I love the people I work with. The Bennetts treat me like family and pay me very generously and I'd miss Jules if I didn't get to work alongside her every day. So, I'd say I have it pretty good."

"But is it your dream job?"

I pause a long moment before answering him truthfully. Working at The Seaside checks my boxes—I make good money, I get to travel, and my boss and the people I work with genuinely care about me. It's challenging, but am I fulfilled? Not really.

It *is* my dream to open a bakery, but that isn't easy for me to admit. Sure, I've been saving, but opening a business costs a lot of money and requires a ton of work. I'm embarrassed to tell anyone about my dream in case it never comes true. But I trust Grayson enough to share it with him.

I know what brings me the most happiness. I know what makes me feel inspired. I love creating recipes, getting a buttercream just right, designing cakes and cupcakes and

ONE GOOD MOVE

other treats that not only taste good but make people smile. I love baking for people, and I would love to make a career out of my passion.

But right now, it's a pipe dream. It probably always will be.

"I'm not sure," I finally answer, giving Grayson the short answer. "It's complicated."

"It's okay, sunshine." He shrugs. "It's very okay to not know right now. You're young and have lots of time to figure it out. Hell, you can make a career change at any age."

I nod, then take a bite of the strawberry cake, "God, this tastes so good. The frosting actually tastes like pink champagne."

"It's definitely good, but it has nothing on your apple pie."

I blush. "You're just saying that."

Grayson sets down his fork. "You really have no idea how incredible your baking is, do you?" Grayson says, as his warm brown eyes pierce mine. "Sierra, I'm not just saying it because you're my girl." *My girl.* "You have what it takes. I believe that."

His words spark something in me. And I wonder if maybe Grayson is right.

NINETEEN

COUNT THAT AS A WIN.

Sierra

Later that night, while Grayson and I are in his bed watching TV, he gets a text from his mom. He goes silent when he picks up his phone to read the message, running his hand over the scruff on his face.

His jaw is clenched as he stares at the screen. He looks stressed. He is definitely annoyed.

We've had such a perfect day. Breakfast, the surprise date, takeout sushi for dinner and now we're cuddling in bed together. But it seems like it's about to take a turn. And not in a good way.

I sit up in bed cross-legged and turn to face him, placing a hand on his cheek so he looks at me.

"Is everything okay?"

He pinches the bridge of his nose. "It's my mom. She invited me for dinner."

I exhale a breath, thankful that it's nothing serious. "Okay. From the look on your face, I thought it might be bad news. Why do you seem anxious about it?"

Grayson sits up, his back against the headboard. He

stares out the bedroom window before shaking his head. "I hardly ever go home because I hate it. I hate being around my dad."

I find his calf underneath the bed sheet and squeeze. Grayson had told me that he and his dad weren't close, and I knew about the accident, but I didn't realize things between them were this bad. There has to be more to the story, but I'm not sure Grayson will open up and tell me. "I'm sorry, Gray. Do you want to talk about it?"

He doesn't answer right away, but I can see from his expression that he's okay with me asking about it.

"Do you think you and your dad will ever have a better relationship?"

He sighs. "Good question. I'm not sure. He's a tough person to love. He has his struggles."

"What kind of struggles?" I ask carefully, my hand still on his leg. "It's okay if you don't wanna talk about it."

His chest deflates. "No, it's fine. I should probably fill you in," he says, inhaling then exhaling a sharp breath. "My dad is an addict… pain pills and alcohol. It started after the accident that crushed his leg. Doctors were able to put his leg back together through several surgeries, but the pain never went away. And I guess… he started abusing his meds, drinking a lot. He lost control. On top of it all, he was angry all the time. And if he wasn't angry, he was high —too high to go to work some days, or even to get out of bed."

I listen quietly while he tells me about his childhood, about growing up with an unstable dad and a mom who was often exhausted. It's clear how much Gray loves his mom. Even though she was distracted by her husband's addiction, he says she never missed a game or practice, and she tucked him and his sister in every night. I listen, filled with compassion and also with hurt, for the worry and disappointment Grayson has been through.

"He missed a lot of work, and the garage was struggling, so my mom had to pick up extra hours at the grocery store where she worked. And I started to help out at the garage so that my mom wasn't the only one carrying the financial burden."

"Grayson, my God. You were just a kid. That shouldn't have been your responsibility."

"My mom took on most of it. She was a saint through all of it. Still is."

"She's lucky to have you. Your dad is too."

Grayson gives me a sad smile. "I wish you had your parents when you were growing up. It's not fair."

My heart shoots up to my throat. That familiar pang of sadness grabs hold, threatens to take me under.

"I often wonder how different my life would have been if that night never happened." I admit shakily. "But it is what it is. I can't go back and change things. I can't bring them back."

"If I had one wish it would be to bring them back to you."

My eyes flood with tears, "Gray—"

"Come here," he says, reaching for me, hauling me into his chest. "I'm glad you didn't let their deaths defeat you."

I breathe him in, soaking in his woodsy scent. "For a while I think I did, but at some point, I stopped feeling that crushing weight of sadness and started finding happiness in little things every day. It took some time, but with the help of my grandparents and Jake I cried a little less every day. Sometimes I still have bad days where I struggle to understand why them, or what we could have done differently."

"There's nothing you could have done differently, Sierra."

"I know."

"You know you can talk to me anytime. Even when you have a nightmare."

I nod against his warm skin, wondering if he knows just how much that means to me. I want more than anything for him to be the person I can turn to when I'm hit hard with those terrifying memories.

I snuggle into his chest, suddenly tired from the day. "If it makes it easier, I can go with you to your parents. If you're okay with that."

"You would do that?"

"Of course, I would," I say with a yawn.

Grayson kisses the side of my head and shifts us so we're lying down again. "Sleep, my sunshine girl," he murmurs into my hair, flicking off the TV. "You must be tired."

"I don't want to," I protest sleepily.

He laughs, tightening the hold he has around my waist, my back tucked perfectly against his chest. "I won't let go. I promise. All night."

"Gray?" I whisper as I'm on the brink of sleep. "I'm sorry it isn't easy with your dad. And I'm sorry it isn't easy with me either."

"You're worth it, Sierra. And it won't be like this forever."

"Promise?"

"Promise."

I slip into sleep, and at least for tonight I forget about everything else.

GRAYSON IS CLEARLY anxious on the way to his parents' house for dinner. I've never seen him like this—fidgeting with his hair, tapping the steering wheel with his thumb, hyper-focused on the road. It breaks my heart a little.

"You okay, babe?" I ask him. "Wanna talk about it?"

He glances at me for a brief moment before turning his focus back to the road. "Nah, I'm fine."

He's definitely far from fine.

"It's okay if you're not fine, you know," I say, resting a hand on his thigh. "I'm not going to judge you if you aren't. I have *not fine* days sometimes too."

He glances my way again with a half-smile on his face, but it doesn't reach his eyes. There's no mistaking it when Grayson smiles at you— you feel it deep within your chest. That smile felt all wrong.

"You're so good at never letting the tough stuff get you down," he says quietly. "You never let life get to you. I don't know how you do it."

I'm not sure what to say to that, knowing it isn't true. I have bad days like everyone else. But I choose to ignore it, not wanting to talk about me. This dinner isn't going to be easy on Gray and I want to do what I can to be there for him.

Ten minutes later, Grayson parks in front of a yellow two-storey home. It's small but well-kept, with a row of gorgeous white rhododendrons underneath the front window and a large oak tree in the yard.

"You ready for this?" he says, putting the car into park.

I run my palm over the stubble of his jaw. "I am. I'm here, Gray, because I want to meet your mom. I also really want to meet your sister, and your dad too." I smile. "I want to see where you came from, the people who loved you first. I'm here because I want to be here, for you, and hopefully to make tonight easier."

He smiles at me, and this time it's a real one. It makes my heart race in my chest. "I don't know what I did to deserve you but I'm not going to question it, sunshine. My mom is going to love you."

And all of a sudden, it's me who's nervous. But I'm not going to let it show. If it means Grayson gets through this night unscathed, I'll gladly take on some of the anxiety.

GRAYSON

MY MOM IS GOING out of her way to make everyone feel at ease, talking a mile a minute and buzzing around the kitchen putting dinner together. I know she's trying to impress Sierra, the first girl I've brought home since Layla. That was six years ago. My mom is obviously excited, and I can't blame her. She's been waiting a long time for me to have someone special in my life.

My dad on the other hand is quiet, which works for me. The less he says, the more likely it is that he doesn't embarrass me. I've glanced in his direction more than a few times to check that he's sober. It's usually a roll of the dice whether he's lucid or whether he's high as a damn kite, stoned and nodding off from the painkillers.

Today he looks presentable in a button-down shirt, his face cleanly shaven and his hair freshly trimmed. If I had to place a bet, I'd say he's clean, but I've bet wrong in the past. Thankfully he isn't being obnoxious like I've seen him so many times before. My mom and my little sister Kyla are more than making up for his silence, asking Sierra a million questions, smothering her with kindness.

LILY MILLER

"Grayson said you love to bake," my mom says, once we've sat down for dinner. "Do you have a specialty?"

Sierra is in the seat beside me and I squeeze her thigh under the table, where my hand is firmly placed on the fabric of her dress.

"Actually, I love to bake almost anything," Sierra answers. "But if you ask Grayson, he'd probably say my specialty are my pies."

"Oh, so we are in luck," Mom says with a smile on her face to match my own. I'm damn proud of all the incredible desserts Sierra makes, including the apple pie she made this morning to bring to dinner. "I can't wait to try it."

"Well, I hope you like it," Sierra says, accepting the green beans my mom passes her.

"I can guarantee it will be the best apple pie you've ever had," I insist, watching Sierra's cheeks turn that perfect shade of pink that they do when she blushes.

"Are you from Reed Point?" Kyla asks.

"I've lived here since I was a kid, but I moved to Virginia Beach for four years for work. I actually just moved back into town recently."

"Happy to be back?" Mom asks. "It's so beautiful on Haven Harbour. It's one of my favorite pockets of Reed Point."

"I *am* happy to be back," Sierra answers. "I have a brother that I'm very close to and a grandma who keeps me on my toes. It's good to be closer to them."

I notice a crease form between my mother's brows and I'm pretty sure she's wondering where Sierra's parents are in all of this. I shoot her a look that says *don't ask*, and thankfully she changes the subject.

"Are you still working for The Seaside?" Mom asks. "I've

never met the Bennetts, but I've heard they are a lovely family."

"I am. I love my job there and yes, they are honestly one of the kindest families you will ever meet. I consider myself very lucky to work for them."

"I've actually dealt with one of the sons at my shop. I think his name was Parker if I'm remembering correctly. He seemed like a good guy," my dad says, looking a little cautious at joining the conversation. It isn't like him—he typically says exactly what's on his mind whether it's appropriate or not—and it throws me off a little.

"What about Miles Bennett?" Kyla jumps into the conversation. "It's crazy that he's from Reed Point. He is so gorgeous. Have you met him?"

Jules's family is practically Reed Point royalty. She has three brothers: Parker, who also works for The Seaside, Liam, who is a well-respected lawyer in town, and Miles, who is an A-list Hollywood actor. His face is regularly splashed across tabloid covers. But Jules insists that the stories about him are usually at least half made-up.

"I have met Miles," Sierra says. "And he's just as nice as you would hope. His wife Rylee is a sweetheart too."

Kyla's eyes are wide, and her mouth hangs open. Women go crazy over Miles Bennett and apparently my sister is no exception.

Kyla and Sierra talk for a little while longer, eventually moving from the topic of Miles Bennett to some show called *Temptation Island* that they both watch. My sister asks her a million more questions because she's nosey like that. I should jump in and save Sierra from the interrogation, but she seems to be handling it just fine on her own.

"So, son," my dad says and my skin prickles. "How are things at the hotel?"

That's the last thing I want to talk about tonight. Things were shit the last time I was at work. I go out of my way to avoid Blair, but it's hard when we work together. I still haven't filled Beckett in on our history. Looking back now, if I could undo that night I spent with Blair, I would. Then there's that damn gala. There is no way I'm getting into all of that at the dinner table in front of Sierra. "Things are good. Business as usual," I answer simply.

"I guess it must be interesting working for rival hotel companies," my dad says, looking from me to Sierra. He's trying, I'll give him that, but it still feels weird having normal conversations when he knows next to nothing about my work or my life. My guard is up, like it has been since I was 15 years old. There have been too many times when my dad would relapse and turn everything to shit. Like when he stumbled into a parent-teacher meeting or when he fell asleep at the dinner table when I had friends over. It all took its toll on me, and eventually I decided I didn't want to feel that way any longer. So I put as much distance between my dad and me as I could.

After dinner, Sierra's pie is served and as expected, my family goes crazy over it. Sierra even offers to come over one day and go through the recipe with my mom. When we're saying our goodbyes at the end of the night, my mom pulls me aside with a smile the size of the moon.

"She is amazing, Grayson. Thank you for bringing her here tonight. Your father and I were so happy to meet her."

"Thanks, Mom," I say, feeling a little awkward, but also happy that Sierra made such a good impression on her. I had no doubt that she would. "I like her a lot."

"I know you do, sweetheart. It's obvious. And it's obvious she feels the same way about you."

I smile as I watch Sierra give all three of them a hug

goodbye. My dad seems genuinely happy, and for a minute I let myself think that maybe he's finally changed. But I've been here before, and I remember what it feels like to be sorely disappointed.

But tonight went much better than I could have imagined, and I'm going to count that as a win.

TWENTY

WERE WE REALLY THAT OBVIOUS?

Sierra

We've all been looking forward to having Gran over for dinner. The guys have been particularly excited, which has been cute to see. Tucker even pulled me aside to make sure it's okay if they play a few hands of poker when she's here. I told her it's fine by me as long as he doesn't mind giving her his money.

Jake has gone out to the assisted living home to pick her up, and in the meantime Grayson, Tucker and Holden are helping me get things ready for dinner. Tucker set the table, Grayson tossed the salad and Holden is busy setting up the card table. You'd think Gran was a long-lost friend by the way they're fussing. I guess in a way she is.

"I hear you're nervous to show your grandma what you've done with the place," Holden says from the living room, where he's stacking chips into neat little piles.

"A little," I admit, wiping my hands on a dish towel as I join him in the living room. "I'm just worried she's going to think I hated the way she kept things."

"You're worrying for nothing," Tucker chimes in with a

beer in his hand. "I still can't believe what you did with the place, and all on your own. It's really impressive, Si. You should be proud."

Grayson winks at me from across the room. Everywhere I look, I'm reminded of the times he and I spent together working on the house. Like the time I painted a stripe down his old T-shirt when we were painting the kitchen and he promptly got me back by running his paint-dipped fingertips up and down my arms. Or the time he caged me into the counter from behind as I was screwing in a door handle and one thing led to another and before we knew it, we were naked on the kitchen floor.

This house already holds so many memories for me, and right now I am about to make more.

Even though Gran and Grayson have known each other for years, it still feels like I'll be introducing them to each other for the first time because this time is different. This time he's mine, even though we're still a secret. It makes my heart swell to know that Gran knows and loves the man who has become my boyfriend.

The timer goes off on the stove, and I remember I still have to finish up dinner. I'm pulling the roast potatoes from the oven when I hear the front door open and Gran's sweet voice filling the space.

I walk towards the front entrance in time to see Grayson wrap up Gran in a big, adoring hug. My heart melts inside my chest as Gray takes her arm and walks her to the couch, grabbing an extra pillow for her back. He sits next to her and immediately starts asking her questions about how she's feeling, how she likes her new place. Gran soaks up the attention, while I try and process the emotions flowing through me. I can see how much he cares for her. I can see it in the way he talks to her, the way he listens to her so intently. It's just one more reason that I'm falling for him.

"Hi, Gran," I say, slipping off the apron I'm wearing, as I walk into the living room, and give her a hug.

"My baby," Gran says against my neck. "I can't believe what you've done with the place. It looks beautiful. I hope you had some help from these boys."

I chuckle, taking a seat on the couch. "Oh Gran, the boys have better things to do than help me strip wallpaper. But I did get some help. I'm glad you like it. To be honest, I was worried you wouldn't."

"She was," Tucker adds, nodding his head.

"How could I not? The place needed a makeover. I'm glad you got rid of all the owls," she says, looking around the room. "Honest to goodness, the place was starting to look like a sanctuary... I just didn't have the heart to get rid of them."

Jake almost spits out his beer. "Gran! We thought you liked owls. That's why Sierra and I kept buying them for you."

Gran snickers. "I did wonder about that," she admits. "How many owls does an old lady really need? But they came from you two, so I loved them. Now... who's ready for a game of poker?"

"You don't waste a beat," Tuck laughs. "What do you say, Si? Do we have time for a quick game?"

I sigh, getting up from the couch. "You have time for a few hands. Dinner is almost ready."

While I finish up dinner in the kitchen, the boys and Gran play poker in the living room. I can hear their conversation—mostly a lot of trash talk about who has the worst poker face or who doesn't know a flush from a full house from a hole in the wall. I laugh as I listen in, pouring each of them a glass of lemonade. The five of them are adorable together. Anyone looking in would think all four of the guys were her grandsons.

"Have you ever even won a hand?" Jake asks Tucker, sliding a stack of chips towards his chest.

"I've won plenty. Right, Gran?" Tucker says as he shuffles the deck.

"Maybe when you've been doing this as long as I have, you'll get the hang of it," she says matter-of-factly as she stacks her pile of chips on the table in front of her.

"Listen, you're lucky we even let you sit at the table with us," Grayson teases Tucker. "Watch and learn from this woman right here. She's the GOAT of poker. She could teach you a few things."

Gran winks at Gray as I walk into the living room with their drinks. My insides turn to mush at the sight of them—Gran and my boyfriend. I love that she makes him laugh. I also love how sweet he is to her, how he treats her as if she's his favorite person in the world.

"Thanks, Sierra, but you didn't have to do that. We could have sent Tucker in to get us drinks. He'll need something to do once he loses this hand," Gray jokes, taking the lemonade from my hand and then pushing his chair back. "I'm sitting the next one out. Let me help you with dinner."

I can feel Jake watching us and it makes me uneasy, so I try to brush off Grayson's offer. "It's okay, Grayson, I've got it. Just about done now anyways."

"Let the man help you, Sierra," Gran says, catching my eye. "It's not every day you get a man who looks like that offering to help you in the kitchen."

The legs of Jake's chair screech across the wood floor. "You know what? I'll help my sister—"

"Sit down, Jake. I'd like to play some poker with my grandson."

He returns to his chair reluctantly, and I can't get to the kitchen fast enough. Grayson shoots me an apologetic smile when we're alone, tucking his hands into his pockets. I'm glad he doesn't try to touch me right now, because I'm feeling so on edge with my brother on high alert in the next room. As happy as I am to have Gran here, I'll be happy if we survive this evening in one piece.

I put Grayson to work, cautious to steer clear of him as we work together in the kitchen. Ten minutes later, Grayson has gotten everyone to take their seats and dinner is on the table. Grayson and I end up sitting beside each other, with Gran and Tucker across from us and Holden and Jake taking seats at each end of the table.

The conversation is easy and enjoyable, but it's hard to miss the fact that Jake eats his dinner in almost complete silence. The longer it goes on, the more obvious the tension between us becomes.

He doesn't say more than two words when I bring out dessert—a strawberry rhubarb pie that has always been his and Gran's favorite. But Tucker, Grayson, Holden, and Gran make up for it when they go on and on about how delicious it is.

Once dinner is over and Gran needs to get back to the nursing home to make curfew, we all say our goodbyes.

"I'm so happy you could come tonight, Gran. Looks like you had fun obliterating the boys in poker," I add with a laugh.

"They're good sports," she says, turning her attention to the boys. "One day I might let one of you win."

The guys hug her goodbye at the door while Jake hops in his car. I hold Gran by the elbow and walk down the steps to the driveway. She pauses before we reach the car, turning to face me.

"He's a keeper, Sierra. You found a good one."

My jaw drops, and I'm pretty sure my heart bottoms out of my chest. Is Gran referring to Grayson? Were we really that obvious? I look down at my feet, trying to hide the shocked expression on my face.

"Gran..."

"Don't you bother trying to pretend there's nothing going on with you two. You don't have to hide it from me. I may be old, but I'm not blind," she says, hooking a wrinkled finger under my chin until our eyes meet. "That boy loves you and you love him. I can feel it."

I sigh. "It's complicated."

"Does this have something to do with Jake?" she asks. "Your brother only wants you to be happy, you know. I promise you, baby, he'll understand."

"I don't think he will," I sigh. "You know how overprotective he is with me. And he specifically told Grayson not to come near me."

"That's not his call to make. It's okay to follow your heart, honey... and so what if he's upset with you for a little while? Your brother will get over it. And if he needs a kick in the butt, then I'll be the one to give it to him. Now, go tell your brother and stop hiding your feelings from the world. You deserve love, Sierra."

I force a smile, then kiss her cheek. I wish it was that easy. Jake is a private person. He doesn't just let anyone in, but he trusts Grayson. I would never want to come in between their friendship.

But I know Gran is right. I need to be honest with Jake, and I just have to have faith that he'll understand.

No more hiding.

LILY MILLER

I'll tell my brother tomorrow.

JAKE DRIVES Gran back to her nursing home while the guys and I finish cleaning up. Once the table has been cleared and most of the dishes are done, Holden and Tucker pack up the poker table and head home. Finally alone, Grayson and I flop onto the couch and flick on the TV. Sinking deeper into the cushions, I lift my legs into Grayson's lap.

"So, Gran knows about us," I announce as Gray flicks through channels.

He's been massaging my foot with one hand, but he suddenly freezes, looking over at me. "She does? How?"

"She said she could see it in our eyes. She told me I picked a good one."

Grayson smiles. "I always knew she was a smart woman. She knows a good catch when she sees one. The feeling is mutual, you know. I love Gran."

"Pretty positive she loves you too," I tell him, letting my eyes drift shut as he returns his attention to my tired feet.

"We need to tell your brother, sunshine," Grayson says softly. "We need to tell him soon."

My heart hurts from the pain in his voice; it's the same pain that has been gnawing at me too. This secret feels heavier with each passing day.

"I know," I sigh. "I'm going to tell him tomorrow. I just hope I'm not too late."

"I hope so too. It felt like he was on edge tonight. Was it just me or did you catch that vibe too? It's the first time I've seen him since the long weekend. If he was suspicious then, it only seems to have gotten worse since."

"Yeah, I felt it too. I think I'm just trying to pretend that I didn't."

"Come here," he says, reaching his hand across the couch to me.

He pulls me into his lap, and I wrap my legs around him. His hands slide to my ass, pinning me to his hips. He rocks his pelvis into me, kissing my neck. I shudder. We're fully clothed, but if we weren't he'd be inside of me. It doesn't matter. I still feel so close to him.

His mouth moves to my lips, capturing my mouth in a demanding kiss, one that leaves me breathless and desperate for more. How is he able to make me feel like this with just a kiss? Desire crashes through me like a tidal wave, threatening to pull me under.

Every inch of me is vibrating. Every inch of me wants more.

My pulse picks up when his fingers move to my throat, applying the slightest pressure there. I still, not moving, waiting for his hand to tighten around the column of my neck. Wanting it. I can barely stand the anticipation, the thrill of being dominated by Grayson.

Grayson squeezes lightly, but then releases his grip on my neck. As soon as he does, I'm aching for him, kissing him, begging him to overpower me again.

"My sexy fucking girl likes it when I'm rough with her."

I try to respond, but all that comes out is a moan. I whimper as his hand slides lower, reaching underneath the hem of my top, fingers teasing the underwire of my bra.

I'm aching for more.

Shamelessly, I arch my back into his hand, silently pleading with him to touch me where I want him most. He finally gives me what I've been craving, slipping his warm hand under the wire of my bra, palming my breast, pinching my nipple between his fingers. My head falls back at the feel of his thumb rolling over the sensitive peak. I shiver, a blanket of goosebumps covering my skin.

"You want more, sunshine?"

I want to rip my shirt and my bra over my head. I want to push his mouth into my chest until he's sucking my nipple into his wet mouth. I want it all. Instead, I rock my pelvis in small circles over the ridge in his shorts, so he knows exactly what it is that I want.

"I want you to fuck me."

He smirks. That fucking Grayson smirk. "Happily."

He stands from the couch, taking me with him, his hands gripping my ass. My legs wrap around his waist as he carries me towards my bedroom, his mouth still sealed to mine.

When he pauses to adjust his hold on me, I decide that I have other plans. I lower my feet to the ground so that I'm on my tiptoes then pull his face down to meet mine for a punishing kiss.

That's when I hear the front door open and the sound of footsteps on the hardwood floor.

I tear my mouth from Grayson's and turn to find Jake standing in the entryway, eyes glued to us, hands fisted at his sides.

The expression on my brother's face makes me want to hide, but I'm rooted to the floor, frozen in place. I've seen him angry before, but not like this, and never directed at me. He looks at me and Grayson like he physically can't stand the sight of us.

"How long has this been going on?" he seethes, and I can practically feel the rage vibrating off him. "How long have you both been lying to me?"

It's been eight weeks. *Eight weeks* and in that time I

found a hundred different excuses not to talk to Jake about this. I had been so wrapped up with Grayson that I stalled, I put it off, I ignored every instinct that told me I needed to talk to my brother.

"Jake. I'm so sorry," I breathe, feeling a bolt of pain shoot through me. The expression on his face is twisted, cruel. It's so unlike Jake that it tears me apart knowing that I'm the one who caused him this much hurt. "Jake, I was... we were ... going to tell you. We wanted to. I swear."

Words tumble out of me, but it's not what I want to say to him. I need to find the right words, to make this better.

"But you didn't," he says, voice flat. "Instead, you made me look like an idiot, lying to my face, sneaking around behind my back. Well, fuck you guys."

I blink back the tears that are streaming down my cheeks. This isn't him talking. I *know* Jake. I know him by heart, like my favorite recipes, like a book I've read over and over again. The Jake I know would never say those words to me.

"Jake, you don't mean that," I say, lips trembling. "You're angry, but I know you don't really mean that."

Jake shakes his head in disgust before turning to Grayson next, and the look he gives him wrecks me. I brace myself for what he's going to say to his best friend. The one guy in the world who I knew was off limits.

The silence drags on as Jake just glares at Grayson and it's torture waiting for what will come next.

"Dammit, Gray!" he finally shouts. "I trusted you. I fucking trusted you. I told you not to touch my sister and what did you fucking do?"

"Jake—"

"And you," he yells, cutting off Grayson and turning back to me. He's so angry, but his eyes soften when he looks at me this time. "Don't you understand, Si? He never sticks around. He's going to leave. And then where does that leave me? Out a best friend and left trying to put back the pieces of your broken heart."

"Jake... you're wrong," Grayson tells him. "I would never hurt her. I told you that at the cabin and I meant it."

"You expect me to believe that?" Jake spits back. "Save the bullshit. I know your track record, man. I've watched it happen so many times I've lost count."

"I don't expect you to believe anything. But I'm telling you I'm not that guy anymore, and I mean it. I'm not going anywhere. And I'm really sorry that we didn't handle this better, but I'm not going to stop seeing your sister because you don't like it." Grayson's eyes snap to mine, clear with intent. "I love her. I love her, man. So, whether you like it or not, I'm not going anywhere."

He loves me. He just said he loves me.

Jake looks at Grayson, and he seems stunned by his admission. He turns his gaze to me briefly before saying, "I have to go."

"Jake, don't," I beg.

He turns for the door, leaving me with tears staining my cheeks and a hole in my heart. He walks out the door, slamming it shut behind him, and I let him leave.

There isn't any other choice.

I have to let him go.

I CAN STILL HEAR the echoes of the door slamming when Grayson crosses the room and takes me into his arms. I lean into him, letting him hold me up. Without a word, he guides me to my bedroom. He finds one of his T-shirts in my closet and then takes off my clothes, pulling the T-shirt over my head. He pulls back the covers and tucks me into bed, kissing the crown of my head and telling me he'll be right back. Ten minutes later he returns with a cup of tea, which he sets on the bedside table before stripping off his T-shirt and joining me in bed. He pulls me between his legs, and I rest my head against his chest. Once I'm in his arms I feel like I can breathe again.

"He'll come around... I promise. He just needs some time." Grayson murmurs, running his fingers through the strands of my hair.

"I hope so."

"Give him time," he says into my hair. "He loves you too much not to."

I have to believe that, but I also know how stubborn Jake can be. And I saw how hurt he was. It feels like there is a ton of bricks sitting on my chest. I stare at the ceiling and try to concentrate on Grayson's fingers in my hair but all I can think about is my brother and the look on his face when he saw the two of us together. I squeeze my eyes shut. I can't just lie here.

Flipping off the covers, I pick up the mug of still-hot tea and stand up.

"Where are you going?" he asks.

"I need to bake. I'll feel better if I can get my mind off my brother."

Grayson flips the covers off and shifts so he's sitting on the edge of the bed. "Then I'll bake with you."

I nod, knowing he's feeling just as terrible as me. How could he not be? I take his hand in mine and tug him towards the kitchen.

I get to work gathering everything I need—butter, flour,

eggs, vanilla— while Gray plugs in the mixer on the counter.

"What are we going to make?"

"Crinkle cookies," I say, reaching for a bowl. "Do you mind turning on the oven for me? 350 degrees."

"Got it," he says, patting my ass on his way to the stove.

I swat at him with a kitchen towel. "If you want to bake with me, you're going to need to behave."

Grayson leans against the stove, crossing his arms over his sculpted chest with a sigh. "I'm having a hard time focusing with you wearing that."

He thinks he's having a hard time concentrating. Grayson Ford, shirtless, is enough to make any grown woman forget her first name.

But I manage to tear my eyes away, returning my attention to the task at hand. I cut the butter into the mixer, then add the sugar. I ask Grayson to turn it on, which he does, flicking the switch immediately to high and sending an explosion of sugar right out of the bowl.

"First time baking?" I ask through a giggle, dusting off my apron.

Grayson is laughing too as he sweeps the sugar from the counter with his hand. "Do I look like a guy who bakes a lot? Yeah, it's my first time."

I guide him through the rest of the recipe, showing him how to crack eggs, shape the dough into balls and spread them evenly out over a parchment-lined cookie sheet.

We fall into a quiet routine as we work side-by-side. I know that his heart is broken, just like mine, but we are getting through it together.

It turns out Grayson is a quick learner and soon he doesn't need my help. I step aside and let him at it, unable to take my eyes off his hands as he works. The way he rolls the dough in his palm like I showed him, his long, perfectly manicured fingers pinching and rolling. *Lord, help me.* The man makes manipulating dough look like hand porn. I'm wet I'm so turned on.

I had hoped baking would distract me, but I didn't expect it to happen in quite this way.

When the dough has all been rolled, Grayson looks up at me with a grin. "Not bad for a guy's first time, right?"

"Not bad at all," I agree.

"Better test it, just to be sure." He reaches for my hand and sucks the sticky dough from my fingers, moaning.

And so it begins.

He sucks one more finger clean before leaning over to kiss me, tasting like sugar and chocolate, and soon my hands are all over him. They work their way up to either side of his jaw, while his hands fist the T-shirt that I'm wearing.

"This shirt is going to be destroyed," he says against my mouth, wiping what is left of the cookie dough over the front of my shirt.

"Mmm," I murmur, wiping chocolate from his chin. "So are you."

"Fuck, sunshine," he curses, lifting me in his arms and carrying me to a kitchen chair. "I'll sit on the chair so you can sit on my cock."

He lowers himself down, legs spread wide, and I straddle his hips.

"Hands up," he commands with darkening eyes, looking at me like I'm his prey. My arms reach over my head as he pulls the fabric off me and lets it drop to the floor. I'm left completely naked in his lap.

"No panties, you naughty girl." He palms one of my

breasts while the other dips down between my legs, teasing my opening.

He moans when he feels how wet I am, pushing one wide finger inside of me, then another. My fingernails make moon shaped marks in his shoulders as I hang on for dear life, riding his hand, seeking out that glorious feeling that sends me over the edge and makes me see stars.

Then he withdraws his hand from me and lifts me from his lap, quickly removing his own clothes.

He sits back down on the chair, bringing me with him so that I'm sitting on his lap, his hard cock wedged in between us. He holds my hips firmly in his hands as he kisses me roughly, our tongues lashing together.

"Sit on my cock, baby," he says, reaching down taking hold of his erection in his hand, guiding it to my entrance, filling me in one fast thrust.

"Fucking hell, Sierra," he moans when I'm all the way seated. Then his pelvis begins to rock up into me in a dizzying pace. "You were made for me. You were meant to be fucked my cock and my cock only."

We're both needy, desperate to forget, kissing and breathing hard as we fuck with reckless abandon. It feels like this might be our last time together, like the clock is running out on us. I close my eyes, forcing the thought from my mind.

His hands squeeze the globes of my ass while I rock up and down on his lap, taking everything from him. He stretches me, fills me, over and over until I forget about the secrets and the agony, as if we can fuck it all out of us.

And then we're both coming—coming hard—our orgasms hitting us both fast and furious as we cry out. My head flies back and his mouth finds my neck, mouth open, trying to catch his breath.

I feel him spill into me, his cock buried so deep as I ride the aftershocks, jolt after jolt. I've never felt this way before. It's never felt like this. I've had Grayson almost every day for months, and every time somehow feels better than the last. But this was different. This wasn't just fucking. This felt like love.

My heart races behind my rib cage while Grayson holds me tightly in his arms, like he's afraid to let me go. And we stay like this for what seems like hours. We hold each other without saying a word until he softens inside of me and needs to pull out.

Everything feels extra sensitive when he slips out of me, and when we're no longer joined, I feel tears well in my eyes. I pull him back to me, nuzzling my face into his neck until I can compose myself enough to stop the tears from falling.

One thing is clear... I love Grayson. And I will never be okay saying goodbye to him.

For tonight, Grayson and I can try to forget everything else. About Jake, about how much we hurt him and the way he looked at us when he found out the truth. But when we wake up in the morning, we're going to have to face reality.

And the reality is, Jake is my family and family will always come first.

So where does that leave Grayson?

TWENTY-ONE

I DON'T REGRET A THING.

Grayson

Tucker, Holden and Beckett are on the trail in front of me, wearing full face helmets and cruising down the mountain with their feet on the brakes to control their speed. The sky is blue and there's a slight breeze in the air. It's a perfect day and I'm in my favorite place with my best friends.

And I'm miserable.

Usually, the mountain is where I go to decompress, to clear my head and get that rush of adrenaline that downhill riding always gives me. But today all I can think of is Sierra. She's heartbroken, and I'm partly to blame for that.

I should have backed off. If I had, we wouldn't be in this mess and Sierra would still have her brother.

But I followed my heart instead of my head. I was so infatuated with Sierra that she was all I could think about. I should have been thinking about Jake and his feelings too.

Despite everything, if I'm honest, I don't regret a thing.

Sierra is worth it.

Now if I could only get her brother to understand that he has nothing to worry about. That I love her.

I haven't spoken to Jake in almost a week. The last time I saw him he was storming out of Sierra's place. I've lost count of how many times I've tried to call him, how many messages I've left. Worse than that is the fact that he's ghosting Sierra as well.

She's heartbroken. She's gone from sad to angry to... empty. It kills me every time I look at her and see that vacant, lost look in her eyes.

I haven't seen much of Sierra in the past few days, which has me tied up in knots. She's been sleeping at her own house, making up excuses as to why I can't stay with her. I've gotten so used to having her in my bed that now I can't sleep without her there. I hate it.

I've tried to convince myself that this will pass, that I just need to give it time. I go through the motions of the day, dragging my ass to work. I've done a good enough job that most of my team hasn't seemed to notice—with the exception of Beckett, who's been walking on eggshells around me, watching me like I may lose my shit at any given moment.

Deep down, my biggest fear is that Sierra will decide that we're not worth it. And how could I blame her? Her brother and her grandma are the only family she has left. What kind of an asshole would I be if I make her choose between me and Jake?

Every day, I wonder if this is the day when Jake will show up. And if he does, will he be ready to forgive me? Or will he take a swing at me for lying to him for the past couple of months? Maybe he'll never forgive me. All I know for sure is that he's still hellbent on avoiding me.

I can tell that the guys feel bad for me. When I finally told them that Sierra and I are together, they weren't surprised. "Yeah, I've known for weeks," Holden said. "How stupid do you think I am?" Beckett was all too happy to rub it in my face. "Did you learn absolutely nothing from me?"

Of course, they wanted to know how it started, and how long we've been sneaking around. But they never asked *why* we kept our relationship a secret. I think they understand. They know that Jake would have blown a gasket.

Holden and Tucker both tried to reassure me, saying that Jake will come around. Here's hoping they're right.

When I catch up to the guys at the bottom of the hill, my helmet isn't even off before they're giving me the gears.

"We were scared we were going to have to ride back up and help you down," Tucker says, sweat dripping from his neck. "We thought you got lost or someone kidnapped you. We were just about to draw straws to see which one of us had to go rescue your ass. What the fuck took you so long?"

I rest my helmet on my lap, shaking my sweat-soaked hair like a dog. The rush of adrenaline I always feel when I barrel down a mountain is missing. I had hoped a ride would take my mind off everything for a little while, but instead I feel numb.

"You guys are assholes. I'm just having a shit morning," I say, unzipping my pocket and digging out my phone. I swipe the screen, hoping to see a missed call from Sierra. *Nothing*. "I'm gonna skip lunch today and help my dad at the garage."

"You sure?" Beckett asks. "We can make it a quick one."

"Yeah, he needs a little help."

"Okay, man," Beckett says after a moment. "If you need anything, you know where we are."

I nod, put my helmet back on and ride towards my car. I'm done talking about this mess. I just want to get this shit day over with.

ONE GOOD MOVE

MY HEAD IS under the hood of an old Chevy when a familiar voice startles me from behind. I blink, looking up to see my dad. I narrow my eyes at him, trying to gauge how he's doing. He looks okay. His eyes are clear, and his skin looks normal, not greyish and washed out. The blank stare that I grew so used to seeing is gone too. I can tell he has most of his weight on his good leg, but his shoulders are square and pushed back. It's been a long time since I've seen him look this good.

I wipe the grease from my hands with a rag and take the bottle of water he extends to me. "Thanks," I say, before bringing it to my lips and taking a long swig.

He nods, looking at me like I'm a riddle he doesn't know how to solve. "You've been here all day, son. Any plans of going home?"

I blow out a heavy breath. "Not at the moment."

"No plans with Sierra tonight?"

"I highly doubt it."

My dad looks at me for a moment longer, and I can tell he's trying to carefully choose his words. I get the feeling that he's scared to say the wrong thing.

"Son, I know I'm not the guy you want to talk to about this stuff, but I'm here and I can be a good listener, believe it or not. So, if you have something on your mind, I'm here to listen. Or you can just go back to beating the hell out of that oil filter."

I think on it for a moment. Do I want to talk to my dad? He's put me through so much shit over the years, but truth be told I'm getting tired of hating the man. And I can tell that he's actually trying.

"I'm not sure where Sierra and I stand at the moment."

Dad swallows, nodding. "Well, that explains why you've been here all day. Is it something you can fix?"

"I'm not sure."

I surprise myself by telling him everything that has happened until now, from the way I pursued Sierra relentlessly even though I knew I shouldn't, right through to Jake walking in on us and our secret imploding.

It wasn't my plan to spill my guts, but once I started talking about it it was like a dam broke. Before I knew it, I had shared the entire story.

"I didn't want to hurt Jake," I say with a heavy sigh. "I fucked up and now Sierra is heartbroken. She may have lost her brother and I may have lost her."

"You really love her, don't you, Gray?"

I nod, feeling surer about that than about anything else in my life.

"You wanna know what I think?" he asks, one eyebrow raised.

I nod, surprised to realize that I actually do want his opinion.

"I think what you *all* need is time. Jake will come around, he'll stop being so stubborn, and he'll forgive you. You're just going to have to be patient. And that includes being patient with Sierra."

His words make me pause—two words, to be exact. Be patient.

Be patient.

I haven't been very good at being patient with the man standing across from me.

But I can do better.

I can be better.

Now seems like a good time to start.

TWENTY-TWO

PIGS WILL FLY.

Sierra

Numb.

Everything in me feels numb.

Grayson and I are lying on the couch watching *White Lotus*, his arm around me, his hand drawing feather-light circles on my hip. I stare at the screen but can't seem to focus on the show.

I've felt like this for days. My mind keeps wandering to when Jake and I were kids. The nights he would lie beside me when I was crippled by my nightmares, the days he took me to the beach with him and his friends, so that I wasn't alone at Gran's. For my entire life, he has supported me, protected me, made me feel safe and cared for. We both lost our parents the night of the fire, but he saw through his own pain to make sure I was okay. He got me through the worst days of my life, and I have always been grateful to him. So how did I have it in me to lie to him for months?

"What's on your mind?" Grayson asks gently.

"Nothing."

"I don't believe you," he says, slipping his arm from

around my back so I'm forced to shift and sit up. "You've been so quiet. I don't blame you, but it's killing me slowly to see you like this. And I hate that you're shutting me out."

I hate it too.

I know that I've been distant from Gray, but how can I let myself be happy without first mending things with my brother? I feel like I can't just carry on with Grayson when I know that we don't have Jake's blessing. He has always put me first. How can I not do the same for him now? I hate it all. But there's a chance that my brother will never see how happy Grayson makes me. And if that's the case, my instinct is to protect my heart. Old habits die hard, and kicking into survival mode is what I've always done.

I need things to be right with my brother before I can give my entire heart to Gray.

"I'm sorry." I squeeze my eyes shut.

"I know."

Tears blur my vision. This is exactly why I've never wanted a relationship, why I've never wanted to let myself love another person again. It hurts too much to lose them.

"We haven't really talked about this, but Sierra, I meant what I said to your brother when he walked in on us," Grayson says, eyes glassy. "I love you. I love you so fucking much and I'm not going anywhere. I want this with you."

I feel my heartbeat in my chest like a thousand wild horses. *I want him too.*

"You were made for me," he continues. "And your brother is going to come around and see how good we are together. I promise you."

Grayson reaches for my hand, lacing our fingers together. "I've been patient, and I'll continue to be, but I don't think this is going to get better if we just keep avoiding it. I'm not waiting this out anymore. I'm going to talk to him."

"And what if he doesn't come around?" My voice trembles, and I hate how it sounds. "What if he can't forgive us?"

"I've known Jake long enough to know that the man is stubborn and he doesn't like change. He's protective of you —maybe a little too protective—but after what you guys went through, it's easy to understand why. Your brother wants you to be happy and if being with me makes you happy, he'll support us. I'm sure of it."

I sigh. "I've never seen him that upset, Gray. It broke my heart."

"I know. I hated it too," he says, softly tucking a strand of my hair behind my ear. "But trust me, sunshine, he'll come around. He has to, because I'm not willing to lose you."

I've never felt this way about anyone, Grayson says, his eyes on mine. "I'm not giving up on us. I won't. You're the one I want... you know that, right?"

I love him with every fibre of my being, but I can't bring myself to say it out loud. Not now. I'm numb, going through the motions. Nothing will feel right until I have my brother back.

"Sierra, baby," he says, reaching for me and pulling me across his lap. His worried eyes are still the most beautiful shade of brown I've ever seen. "I need you to trust me when I tell you that we're worth it. We're going to get through this. I promise."

I know how much he needs me. Needs us. I hear it in his voice, I see it in the way he's looking at me. And although I can't give him my whole heart, I can give him every other part of me.

He kisses me hard, like he's afraid to lose me. Neither of

us know what the future holds, and the kiss feels desperate, charged with emotion.

As the evening slips into night and darkness washes over the room, Grayson undresses me slowly, lying me down on the couch before stripping out of his own clothes and lowering himself over me. He kisses me again before pulling back, his eyes searching mine.

"You've buried yourself so deep into my soul, sunshine. I never want to know what it feels like to lose you."

Tears prick the corners of my eyes, feeling the emotion in his voice in every inch of my body. The three words I've never said to any man sit heavily on my tongue. I wish I could tell him that I love him. That I never want to be with anyone else ever again.

But instead, I kiss him, and his mouth captures the words that stay on the tip of my tongue.

And I feel a little less numb.

GRAYSON

MY BLOOD PRESSURE rises as I type out an annoyed response to an email from Blair. It's the third one in the past week asking me to meet her in her office for some ridiculous reason or another. This time she wants to discuss a strategy I worked on to maximize sales efforts— something that can definitely wait until tomorrow morning. It's past 6 p.m. and I'm itching to get out of the office.

I hit send. Pigs will fly before I waste my time in a bogus meeting with that woman. It's bad enough that I have to attend this stupid work event with her tomorrow night. I had been on the fence about it, but my mind was made up for me when I received an email from Blair stating that my attendance was mandatory now that Max Collins was going to be there. Beck's orders. *Just fucking great.* Working with Blair is testing my patience and remaining professional around her is getting harder and harder every day.

For now, I'm doing my best to just stay away from her.

Sort of like Sierra is doing to me.

The two of us seem to be on pause. She hasn't come out and said she wants to put space between us, but she doesn't have to. It's clear in her actions.

Three nights ago, I was buried deep inside of her on her couch. Since then, I have seen her once, and that was only because I showed up at her door with takeout, pushing her to have dinner with me. I ended up staying the night, but when we woke up the next morning she was off again, quiet and distracted. My heart deflated like a balloon in my chest as I watched her leave for work. After spending every waking minute with her for months, the distance between us is feeling like some form of torture.

I miss Sierra. I miss her so much, my bones ache. We're not us. It feels shitty and I want things back to the way they were, back before I was afraid every day that I'm going to lose her.

I scrub a hand over my jaw. I can't stand this. Why am I holding back when everything in me is telling me to fight for her? Fight for us.

Suddenly I'm flying out of my office, and into my car, on the way back to Haven Harbor.

I slam my truck into park in front of my house, noticing Sierra's car parked in her driveway. I try her front door, but it's locked, so I knock and wait, but there's no answer.

"She's not home."

I whirl around at the sound of Tucker's voice.

"Where is she? I need to talk to her."

He points to the beach, and I see Sierra about 10 feet from shore paddling towards the purple and pink horizon.

She's standing on her board, her golden skin shimmering under the late summer sun.

I'm about to grab my paddle board from the garage and make a run for the beach when Tucker stops me with a hand on my forearm.

As if sensing my presence, Sierra turns at the same time, her eyes locking with mine over her shoulder. My pulse races like it always does when she looks at me.

"Let her paddle," Tuck says gently. "She needs to clear her head."

As I watch her, a million things I want to say to her hang in the air between us. *I need you. I love you. I'll love you through it all.* But I let her go. I'm back to being… *patient.*

Does she have this constant ache in her chest that never goes away, the same way I do? It's devastating.

"You really miss her, huh?"

"Like you wouldn't believe. I thought it would get a little easier but every day that goes by, I only miss her more. Fucked up, right? I was never that guy. I barely recognize myself anymore."

"It's okay to fall in love, Gray," he says quietly. "I'm not surprised you did. You have a heart bigger than any of us. You're the guy who has always loved his friends, his mom, his sister fiercely. You're a big old sappy mush, destined to fall for the girl. So no, I'm not surprised."

I breathe out a laugh. "I fell hard," I shake my head. "And then I fucked it all up."

Tuck sighs. "Sierra is one of the best people I know. She's kind and empathetic and she sees the best in people. She's been through a lot—more than any of us—and she's been through some majorly tough moments with Jake. It's killing her that he won't speak to her. But I know Jake, he just needs some time to cool off. He'll let her in again. And when he does, she'll come back to you."

I swallow the lump in my throat. I never planned on finding love but somehow, I found it with Sierra. "I'm so fucking scared she won't."

"It's okay to be scared," Tucker says. "Tell her how you feel and when she's ready, you'll be waiting for her."

I feel like a heartsick teenager, missing her so much even though she's only 100 feet away.

Because it doesn't matter that she's not here with me, she's always wherever I am.

My eyes are still on her as she paddles towards a cotton candy sky taking my heart with her.

BLAIR GREETS me as I walk into the ballroom of the hotel. She's wearing a fitted black dress that ends above her knees, her hair swept up in a twist on top of her head. Her lips are painted a bright red. She looks much happier to see me than I am to see her. I'm sure my face conveys my foul mood. I hate that I have to be here with Blair instead of anywhere at all with Sierra.

If only she answered her phone.

I called her this morning, but her phone sent me straight to voicemail. A few hours later I texted her asking her to call me. I wanted to tell her where I'd be tonight, but she messaged back saying she was visiting her gran and we could talk later.

"Grayson, you're here. And you clean up nice," Blair purrs, making my skin crawl. I'm putting in exactly two hours and then I'm out of here. And I can guarantee it will be the longest two hours of my life. "Come on, let's get a drink."

I reluctantly follow her to the bar, where I order myself a scotch on the rocks and knock it back. The liquor burns its way down my throat, and I can feel the tension in my body start to unravel itself. I'll need another one of those if I'm going to make it through the next couple of hours with the woman who's been making my professional life hell.

Let's get this night the fuck over with.

We sit for a presentation then mingle with the who's who of the hotel industry, stopping for a few photos. Noticeably missing in the well-dressed crowd is Max Collins—and his presence is the reason I am here in the first place. Blair seems unfazed by it. She hasn't left my side all night, making me uncomfortable as hell. She laughs when I say just about anything and finds any excuse to squeeze my arm. I overhear someone asking her if we're dating—I'm not surprised, considering the way she's been hanging all over me. What *does* surprise me is that she doesn't say no. It took everything in me not to set the other woman straight. After being here for exactly two hours on the dot, I'm ready to get the hell out of here.

"Where are you going?" Blair asks, her voice low and flirty after a couple of drinks.

I not so subtly glance at the door. "I'm leaving. Get home safe, Blair. See you at the office."

Her expression turns pouty. "Come on, Grayson, it's still early. I have a room here at the hotel, we could go there and get away from this crowd. Catch up."

My body stiffens. I. Am. Done. "I did what was asked of me and now I'm going home. If you have a problem with that, you can take it up with our boss."

At this point, I've had all that I can take. She can tell Beckett about our one-night stand. I don't give a fuck. She can tell him I was a complete dick to her tonight too for all I care.

As far as I'm concerned, this conversation is over, so I ignore the anger I see in her eyes and head for the door.

TWENTY-THREE

HE IS WAY BETTER THAN THAT TOY YOU KEEP IN YOUR DRAWER.

Sierra

"I'm here with coffee," Jules says, holding two to-go cups in her hands when I open my front door.

I take one of the cups, noticing it's from Dream Bean, my favorite coffee shop on the planet. I don't really feel up for company, but my craving for the liquid drug wins out. I push the door open further, welcoming Jules in.

It's Sunday afternoon and I was supposed to be out for lunch with the girls. Not in the mood to be social, I opted to stay home and sulk. Besides dragging myself to work every morning, eating three almost-meals a day and showering, moping around my house is all that I seem able to accomplish these days. I don't even have it in me to bake. Ever since that night Grayson and I made cookies together in my kitchen, the thought of baking alone in the same space feels too lonely.

Jules brushes past me into my living room. I notice my reflection in the mirror on the wall and I cringe. My hair is a tangled nest, my eyes are smeared with yesterday's eyeliner and I'm wearing an old T-shirt of Grayson's that has an ice cream stain on my boob. I'm officially a hot mess—minus the "hot" part.

Jules flops down on the couch while I take the armchair next to her, pulling a blanket over myself to cover the dirty shirt.

"You know you can't hide your wallowing from me," she says, her eyes meeting mine. "I know something's going on. I'm assuming Jake found out about you and Grayson?"

I'm surprised by her question. I haven't been able to talk about the mess I've made to anyone. "How did you know?"

Jules shrugs. "I didn't," she says, pulling her legs up underneath her. "You haven't been yourself in days and neither has Grayson—Beck said that he's been a bear to be around at work. As for your brother, he's been MIA, which Beckett says usually means he's in a mood. So I put two and two together."

"Good work, detective," I say with a small smile.

She looks up from her coffee with compassion in her eyes. "Ahh babe, I'm sorry. It really is a mess, isn't it?"

"It is."

"Can I give you my two cents?"

I shrug. "I feel like you're going to whether I say yes or not."

"I know what you're doing—even if you might not realize it," she says. "You feel bad because you lied to your brother about falling for his best friend. And now you're punishing yourself by pushing Grayson away. I get it, but it's stupid."

I haven't intentionally pushed him away. I've just been so overwhelmed and filled with guilt. I know I haven't been myself, but I've been buried so deep, I haven't really been noticing what has been going on around me. All I can think about is repairing my relationship with Jake.

"I don't think that's what—"

Jules shoots me a side-eye, cutting me off. "I get that you feel bad about hiding it from your brother, but is what you and Grayson did really that terrible? You followed your heart. Sometimes love is messy. But life goes on and one day you're going to need to stop moping. And stop pushing away the guy you're so obviously falling in love with."

I take another sip of my coffee, using the moment to absorb everything she's said.

"Besides, you must be missing all those orgasms."

"Stop it." I cover my entire face with the blanket.

"Admit it."

I shake my head from side to side, my face still covered.

"What? You're going to tell me you're not? I saw your blissed out face at the cabin the morning after Grayson snuck into your room. You looked like you had the kind of sex that makes you grip the sheets."

I peek with one eye out from behind the blanket. "You're not going to give up, are you?"

She winks. "Nope. Not until you admit he is way better than that toy you keep in your drawer."

I rip the blanket off my face entirely giving her a major dose of side-eye. "I don't have a toy in my drawer."

Another wink. "Okay, Si."

"Jules," I shake my head. "I'm not talking about this with you."

"Prude," she says with a mischievous smirk. "I have to pick up Maya from my Mom's, but I'll see you at work tomorrow. I'm taking you out for lunch, and you can't say no to me. I'll even promise not to order a lobster roll if that will make you happy."

I smile—a real smile—for the first time in days as she gets up to leave.

"Thanks for the coffee... and the chat. You're a good friend, Jules."

"You're welcome. I love you," she says, pausing at the door she's already swung open. "And you really are being stupid." She gives me a grin as I watch her walk out the door.

GRAYSON

BECKETT IS in my office first thing Monday morning with a concerned look on his face.

I had been going over a contract when he sat down in the chair across from me, but I set it aside and look across the desk at him. If the look on his face is any indication, he's about to drop some news.

"Were you at the Travel Forward Gala on Saturday night with Blair?"

I sit up straighter in my chair. "Yeah, of course I was. Why?"

He gestures to my computer. "I'm assuming you haven't seen the photo yet?"

"What photo?" I ask, but I already know. My suspicions are confirmed when I google my name. A photo pops up of Blair and I making me want to throw my computer against the wall. Blair has her hand on my shoulder and we both look like we're having the time of our lives. I'm smiling directly at the camera while Blair's gaze is ardently looking at me. From the photo you would almost think we are a couple in love, when in reality my skin was crawling from just having to stand next to her.

And then it gets worse. The caption underneath the

photo reads, *Grayson Ford and Blair Winters of The Liberty are couple goals.*

"You've got to be fucking kidding me." I close the search window and push out of my chair, pacing towards the window. "You know, you're partly to blame for this, Beck. Collins wasn't even at the damn event!"

"*Max* Collins? What the hell are you talking about? And why did you even go to that thing with Blair Winters? I didn't realize you were such a sucker for a gala," Beckett says, laughing.

I whirl around to face him. "Because *you* told her I had to be there."

He stares back at me with a look on his face that tells me everything I need to know. He had nothing to do with this. It was all Blair. She lied and manipulated me into thinking I had to be at that event. Then hit on me the entire night while I continuously told her I wasn't interested. I feel like a fucking fool.

"I had nothing to do with it, Gray. I had no intensions of sending anyone from The Liberty because Travel Forward focuses on larger hotel groups. When Blair told me she had an extra ticket, I told her as much."

"Fuuuuuuck," I groan, dropping my face to my hands. "I can't believe I fell for it."

"I don't get why Blair would go to all of this trouble," Beck says. "What's the angle? She barely even knows you."

I wince. I could have probably avoided all of this if I'd just sucked it up and told Beck about my history with Blair that first day she showed up at the office. Instead, I was embarrassed and uncomfortable and hoped I could just avoid it. And her.

The shit with Jake already taught me that complete

honesty is always the best policy. This just hammers that lesson home. Message received. I get it.

I take a deep breath and fill Beckett in, minus a few of the sordid details. I apologize for not having told him about it sooner. When I'm done, he just shakes his head and then turns to leave the room.

"Where are you going?" I ask, even though I think I have an idea.

Without stopping, he says in a perfectly calm voice, "You and I will talk more about this later. But right now, I'm going to talk to Blair."

I DIDN'T SPEAK to anyone at the office for the rest of the day, my mood so sour I was afraid of what I might say if anyone brought up the photo.

I worked in my office like a caged animal, rage boiling in my veins at Blair's manipulation. I tried to set that aside, instead focusing on how I was going to explain that photo to Sierra. She already has me at an arm's length, and I doubt this will help.

She didn't pick up either of my calls today, but I know she was busy at The Seaside with a presentation so I tried not to read too much into it. Sierra and I are already in the middle of one giant mess, how is she going to react when I tell her about a second one?

My heart is in my throat when I climb the three steps to Sierra's front door after work. I don't knock, we haven't done that for weeks. I find her in the kitchen, pulling a tray of frozen chicken tenders from the oven. Her long hair is pulled back with a headband and she's wearing a summer dress. When her eyes find mine, I can see they're tired and veiled.

"What smells so good?" I ask, standing in the doorway of the kitchen.

"Nothing fancy. I didn't feel like cooking."

I watch her dig a pair of tongs from a drawer, and I flash back to the night we painted these cabinets together. That particular drawer kept sticking, we couldn't for the life of us get it to line up straight. We were deliriously tired from working all day and after a half hour of failed attempts I ended up tossing the drawer out the door onto her front yard in frustration. We collapsed on the floor in a fit of laughter. The next morning, Sierra managed to get the drawer in with no problem. What I wouldn't give to go back to that day.

"How did the presentation go?" I ask her, my thoughts returning to the present.

"It went just fine," she says, transferring the chicken tenders she baked one by one to a plate, not looking in my direction once. The tension in the room is so thick you can cut it with a knife. I hate it. And the worst part is that I know it may only get worse when I tell her about the photo.

And it does.

"I saw the photo, Grayson. Is that why you're here? To try to explain why you were on a date with... who is she, anyways?"

My breath catches in my throat. Someone must have shown her the article because it's not the type of photo you just stumble upon. "Her name is Blair. She works with me."

"She's beautiful."

"She's—"

"Look, Gray, I'm exhausted." Sierra finally turns around and looks at me, her back against the counter, her expression pained. "I'm tired of being sad. I'm tired of not talking to my brother. And then I see a photo of a beautiful woman on your arm—a woman who is clearly into you, judging from the way she's looking at you—and "couple goals," and well... I don't know what to think. What I *do* know is that I just don't have the energy to deal with this right now."

"I want to explain, Sierra," I say, moving to stand in front of her. "It was a work event. I only went with her because she lied to me and told me that Beckett wanted the two of us to be there to represent The Liberty. She lied to me, but I'm the idiot who believed her. I only have myself to blame."

"Why would she do that?"

I exhale, looking down at the floor. I have no choice but to tell her about Blair and me, about our history. Technically, I haven't done anything wrong, but I *did* hook up with a woman I now work with, and even though I feel nothing for Blair, Sierra deserves to know that.

So, for the second time today I find myself telling the story of how I met Blair at the bar and about the day I found out that Beckett had hired her at The Liberty. I tell her everything, including how Blair had been flirting with me and even asked me up to her hotel room.

My heart pounds inside of my chest. I feel relieved that everything is finally out in the open. Now all I can do is hope that she believes me.

"She sounds awful," Sierra says. She sounds tired, but the edge that was in her voice earlier is gone.

"She is."

I tentatively reach for her hand, and she lets me take it. "I swear to you, Sierra... I never wanted anything to do with her."

"I know."

I squeeze her tiny hand in mine. All day I've been so

worried about the damn photo, about how Sierra might react. Thinking that she might not believe me was the scariest feeling in the world. Now I can put those fears to rest, but something still isn't right between us. The distance that I've felt for days feels like it's only growing wider.

"Tell me we're okay, Sierra. Why does it feel like I'm losing you?"

She looks up at the ceiling before pulling her hand from mine. "We're okay, Gray." I exhale. She closes her eyes for a split second until they're back on me. "I believe you about the photo. I never doubted you. But it's more than that. I'm *this* close to losing my brother. I've already lost so much, Grayson. He and Gran are the only family I have left. I can't lose him."

"So, what are you saying? That's it? You're just going to give up on us?" I ask as she turns her back to me, staring out her kitchen window. "Because I sure as hell am not going to give up on you. I couldn't if I tried. I want a relationship with you, you're it for me. Forever, Sierra. I want everyone in Reed Point to know that you're mine. And I know that you want the same things too, I've seen it in your eyes."

I watch her head fall forward into her hands and her shoulders slump in defeat. Seeing her like this, so hopeless and distant, is painful in the most heartbreaking way.

My world is empty without Sierra's happiness.

"I'm sorry, Grayson. I'm tired. I'm not giving up on us, but I can't do this right now. Please, I just need a little more time."

And I just need you.

TWENTY-FOUR

YOU'RE PREACHING TO THE CHOIR, BIRTHDAY GIRL.

Sierra

Gran and I sit across from each other in McDonald's, her favorite restaurant. We're eating McChicken meals, just like we do every year on her birthday. Usually Jake would be with us, but this year it's just the two of us. I'm trying not to dwell on his absence. As long as Gran has a good day, that's all that matters.

She looks adorable, happily sipping her Coke while wearing the button that was attached to the birthday card I gave her that says, *Happy Birthday to the Queen of Grandmas.*

"Nothing beats a McDonald's Coke," she says, before moving on to her fries.

"You're preaching to the choir, birthday girl," I say, raising my cup to her in cheers.

Gran's a one-trick pony when it comes to her birthday. It always has to be McDonalds. I think she would eat here every day if she could.

Her eyes narrow, looking at me. "So, still nothing with your brother?"

I sigh, looking down at my meal, unable to look her in

the eye. It must break her heart to have her only two grandchildren not speaking to one another.

"He's still not speaking to Grayson or me," I admit.

"I figured as much when I talked to him this morning," Gran mutters. "What is wrong with that boy? Would he rather you date some idiot who treats you like dirt and can't stand your family? He has always been so darn protective of you." She shakes her head before popping a French fry into her mouth. "Now, where is that handsome boyfriend of yours and why isn't he here? I know he wouldn't miss my birthday on purpose."

I wipe my eyes before the tears can roll down my cheeks. "It's not his fault, Gran. I didn't tell him it's your birthday. I didn't even tell him I'm having lunch with you today."

"And why the heck not? Just because your brother is being a giant pain in the ass doesn't mean you need to take it out on Grayson."

I inhale a sharp breath. "I know."

"No, you don't know. If you knew, he'd be here with you," she says, shaking a fry at me. "Don't push that boy away, Sierra. It's not fair to him or you. Anyone can see that you love each other, and love should never be wasted."

Something clicks into place. I've been struggling to do the right thing, but Gran's right. I made a mistake with Jake, but it won't be fixed by making another one with Grayson. I *have* pushed him away, and I've done it because I'm afraid. Afraid to hurt my brother even more, but also afraid that if I let myself really love him and my heart gets broken, I'll never be able to recover. But Gray has proven over and over again that he's steady and reliable. I need to trust that not everyone I love will leave.

And then there's my brother... I love Jake, but I am a grown woman who should be able to decide for herself who

ONE GOOD MOVE

she loves. It shouldn't matter what my big brother has to say about it. It should be about who makes me happy. And that's Grayson Ford.

Grayson is sweet and thoughtful. He supports me and my dreams. He loves me for me.

And I'm madly in love with *him*.

So why have I been trying so hard to push him away?

Suddenly I know what I need to do. I just hope it's not too late.

GRAYSON

BOUQUET OF FLOWERS IN HAND, I lean against the doorway to Gran's room and watch as Sierra adds birthday candles to a bright yellow cake. It's decorated with tiny white daisies and nicer than any store-bought cake I've ever seen. I shake my head, suppressing a laugh. Gran obviously had ulterior motives when she called me this morning and asked if I would visit her for her birthday.

I rap my knuckles gently on her door, more nervous than I've ever felt in my whole life. My lips part, wanting to say something but then I pause listening to the three hundred thoughts fighting for space in my brain. *Will she be happy to see me? Will she even want me here?*

My heart is racing when Sierra turns and sees me, her face lights up. She flashes one of those perfect, knock-the-breath-out-of-you smiles, and my skin reacts with a shiver. She looks like sunshine.

Sierra is the most beautiful sight I've ever seen, her hair falling around her shoulders in loose waves and her pale-yellow sundress showing off her summer tan. But it's the sparkle in her eyes that takes my breath away. I haven't seen that for a while.

My heart feels like it's beating out of my chest as I wait to see what happens next. It doesn't take long.

She stops what she's doing, letting the candles in her hand fall to the table, and makes a beeline for me. I scoop her up in my arms as she nestles her face in my neck, her legs wrapping around my waist.

"I've missed you, Gray. I've missed you so damn much," she whispers into my neck. My hand cradles the back of her head as she starts to cry. With Sierra back in my arms—back where she belongs—I feel like I can finally exhale the breath I've been holding for days. I squeeze her tightly to me, trying not to crush the flowers I bought for Gran. "I'm sorry, baby. I've been an idiot. I know I pushed you away."

I can feel her heartbeat against my chest. "It's okay, sunshine. I'm not mad. I understand."

Still in my arms, she pulls back, her brown eyes locked with mine. "You're not upset with me?" she asks.

"No. I could never be." And this is the last time there will ever be space between us. I'll make sure of that.

Her hands cradle my jaw, and she smiles. "I'm so happy to see you."

"I am so happy to see you too. We can thank your grandma for this." I wink at Gran, who's watching us from across the room. "But we can talk about everything later." I find her eyes with mine and kiss her. "Okay?"

"Okay." She smiles, kissing me, her arms wrapped tight around my neck.

I lower her down to her feet before kissing her chastely again because I can't get enough, and then I take her hand and walk towards Gran who's smiling back at us.

"There's the birthday girl," I say, smirking at Gran

when she winks at me. "You've been busy today," I joke, pulling her into a hug. "Thank you," I whisper against her ear.

She gives my cheek a gentle squeeze. "Oh, is it ever good to see you. Perfect timing."

I don't know what she said to Sierra, but she obviously played a part in her change of heart. And for that, I am forever grateful. I hand her the flowers, watching her dip her face to inhale their scent.

"These are beautiful, Grayson," she says, admiring the purple and pink flowers I picked up from Bloom, a local flower shop owned by Jules' sisters-in-law. "Sierra, do you mind putting them in a vase for me? I think there's one in the cabinet over there."

I help her get a vase down from the shelf and then sit with Gran while Sierra goes to the bathroom to arrange the bouquet. I'm happy to see that her suite is more spacious than I imagined—there's even a patio area with a table and two chairs and a few pots bursting with flowers. The sliding glass door is wide open, letting fresh air into the homey space.

"You love her, don't you?"

I nod. "More than I've ever loved anything before."

"My granddaughter loves you too, you know."

Heat rolls down my spine, and I smile. "I'm not sure if you're right, but it's only a matter of time before she does. I'm pretty irresistible." I wink.

Gran laughs, squeezing my knee. "I practically raised that girl and I know her better than anyone. She loves you... she's just too afraid to tell you. She'll get there, Grayson, I know it. Just be patient."

Patient. I can be patient.

I swallow the lump that sits in my throat. As long as I

have Sierra, I *can* be patient and wait for her to say those three important words.

Sierra returns, setting the vase on the living room table. I stand up to give her the seat next to Gran when a familiar profile catches my eye in the hallway. Before I can say a word, Jake is walking into the room. He pauses when he sees Sierra, then stops dead in his tracks when he sees me. He looks tired, his hair scruffy and his beard longer than I've ever seen it.

Last week, I would have been intimidated by his broody presence, but this week I am not. I'm not losing Sierra this time. I refuse to let her go, whether he likes it or not.

I flash him a small smile and nod. To my surprise, he nods back and then crosses the room to give Gran a hug.

"I guess we all got the same call from Gran," he says, easing some of the tension in the room as he releases her.

"Well, when you're all being impossible, what do you expect?" Miss Millie has always been direct and to the point. After the past week, I think it's exactly what we all need right now.

Sierra hasn't said a thing, but I can tell by the tension in her neck and shoulders that she's anxious.

I'm about to get up and go to her when Jake pulls a chair in from the patio inside and sits down next to me.

My heart hammers in my chest when I flick my gaze to Sierra, who's looking at her brother with a worried expression on her face.

I watch her open her mouth to speak, but before she can get a word out, Jake clears his throat. I square my shoulders, ready for what he has to say. Maybe it isn't the best time to hash this out, but if an argument right here and now in front of Sierra and Gran is what it takes to get us all talking again, then I'm prepared to do it.

I brace myself for the worst, but instead Jake stretches out his hand towards me. I shake it, and I'm sure shock is written all over my face.

"You can relax, I'm not going to hit you," he says. "I'm sorry, man. I was a dick. Oops, sorry, Gran," he adds, apologizing for his language.

"It's all right, Jake, you were one," she answers without cracking a smile. She pats his knee. "Now, go on. Say what you need to say. It's about time."

Jake huffs out a laugh before carrying on. "I shouldn't have said the things I did... if you really do love my sister like you say you do, then we're cool."

That's good enough for me, but I still very much owe him an apology. I blow out a long breath. "I do. We're cool. We've always been cool. And I'm sorry for lying to you," I say, pulling him in for a bro hug. "I've missed you, man."

"I've missed you too."

Jake turns to Sierra next, a pained expression on his face.

"Jake," she begins, then stops. Her eyes brimming with tears.

"Fuck, I'm sorry, Si. You know how much I love you... and I ... I'm sorry, I'm not good at this stuff," he mutters, pinching the bridge of his nose. "I was an asshole. I know I shouldn't have freaked out when I caught you with Gray, but you've got to be able to see it from my point of view." He swallows. "I just didn't want you to get hurt. Grayson had never wanted to be in a relationship, that's just the truth. But I see it now, how much he loves you. It's so damn obvious and I don't know why I didn't see it then, but I do now. And I want you to be happy. That's all I want."

"I'm so sorry too, Jake," she sobs. "I swear we never meant to hurt you. We shouldn't have lied to you. We both felt so terrible."

Jake stands up and pulls her into a hug as she swipes at her eyes. "Let's forget about the whole thing, Si. I've missed my sister."

She nods, smiling. "I'd like that."

Jake lets her go, taking a step back. "Besides, Gray knows that if he ever were to hurt you, even a little, nobody would ever find his body. Right, buddy?" he adds with a smirk.

"Right," I nod, laughing. "But you've got nothing to worry about."

"Good," Jake says. "Then let's just get back to normal."

Then Sierra sits on my lap, squeezing my neck, a smile on her face that's prettier than a sunset. My God, how I love this woman. I want forever with her. I want to wake up to her smile every morning, watch her bake in our kitchen in nothing but one of my old T-shirts, sit on our porch swing with her in the middle of the night.

I wipe a tear from her cheek with my thumb. "No more crying."

A giggle bursts from her when I pull her into me, so damn happy to be back to the way we used to be. "They're happy tears, Gray. No more sneaking around."

Then she takes my face in her hands, sealing her lips to mine.

And as much as I want to deepen the kiss, to slip my tongue past her lips, and wrap her legs around my waist, I keep it chaste, swallowing a groan.

"Just because I said I was cool with the two of you dating doesn't mean I want to see it," Jake says, shaking his head. "Can we do cake before I lose my appetite?"

Sierra scrunches up her nose and laughs, slipping off my knee. Before she can walk away, I stand, grab her wrist, and pull her back to me. I whisper into her ear, "I'm going to fuck you so good tonight you won't be able to walk tomorrow."

"I hope so." She winks at me, beaming.

We sing "Happy Birthday" as Miss Millie blows out her candles, then dig into the delicious cake that Sierra baked.

And as good as it feels to be back on good terms with Jake and celebrating with Sierra's family, I'm counting down the minutes until I can take her home and into my bed and show her with my mouth how much I've missed her.

TWENTY-FIVE

I'VE BEEN STARVING FOR YOU.

Sierra

"Come here, baby. I wanna kiss you," Grayson says into my neck, and a giggle escapes my throat as he picks me up from behind and twirls me around.

When he lowers me down to my tiptoes on my driveway, he turns me in his arms and kisses the mile-wide smile off my face. The one I haven't been able to erase since earlier today at Gran's party. His lips crash into mine, his arms wrapping tightly around my waist. I cling to him as he dips me backwards in an over-the-top display of affection.

I know exactly what he's doing. I can already read him like a book. Grayson wants to officially kiss me in public. He wants all of Haven Harbor, and soon all of Reed Point, to know that I am his.

When my head falls back, his lips find my neck and he sucks hard, latching onto my sensitive skin.

"Grayson, you're going to give me a hickey!"

He groans. "Damn right, I am," he says when he unseals his lips from my skin. "And I'm just getting started. Just wait until I get you inside and strip you out of everything you're wearing. There will be 20 more."

Grayson lifts me in his arms and throws me over his shoulder. I laugh, smacking his ass as he hauls me through my front door. My pulse races at the thought of having marks all over my body from Grayson—knowing they would be there, under my clothes.

He takes my keys from me and unlocks my front door, slamming it shut behind us and carrying me straight to my bedroom. He lowers me onto my bed and makes quick work of our clothes. He leaves me lying there as he rounds the bed, flicking on the lamp on my nightstand. My eyes soak him in—his pecs, smooth and hard, his abs, the lean V-shaped muscle that points toward a thatch of light blond hair and his erection, already hard and proud and jutting straight ahead. When he turns, my mouth waters at the sight of his perfectly smooth, round ass.

He's the most beautiful man in the world.

Every inch of him is toned, golden brown and hard like granite, and he's crawling up my body with the naughtiest look in his eyes.

"We're not a secret anymore," he says, nuzzling his nose into my neck. My back arches and my chin tips to the ceiling to grant him better access. I bite my bottom lip to keep from moaning when he plants open-mouthed kisses down the side of my neck. "But that doesn't mean I'm not willing to lock you in this bedroom for the next 48 hours and keep you my dirty little secret for a little while longer." He drags his nose up to my ear and sucks the flesh into his mouth.

I shiver against him, groaning my approval. I'm not going to argue. I'm just not sure 48 hours will be enough.

"I'm sorry I pushed you away," I say, playing with the short blond strands at the base of his neck. "I just needed to sort things through in my head, but I... want you, Gray. I want you more than I've ever wanted anyone."

He pulls back, runs his hand over the edge of my jaw, then across my bottom lip. The motion is slow and soft, but it's enough to light my whole body on fire.

"Then tell me you're mine." He dips his head down to my neck again, kissing my throat, then down the center of my chest while his fingers run a path to my hip.

My eyes flutter closed, desire taking over my entire body as my hands drift over his shoulders, down his arms to his back, my spine arched as my pelvis seeks out the hardness between his legs.

"Yours," I breathe when his mouth latches around my nipple, sucking and teasing, licking, and pinching the stiff, rosy peak between his fingers. "I'm yours, Gray."

My fingers grip his hair from the pleasure he's giving me, and when he's done teasing my nipple, his mouth finds mine again in a slow, lingering kiss.

He takes his time, and when he finally pulls back and looks down at me, I place my finger over his lips. He stills. I know I can't wait another second longer.

As he waits for what I'm about to say, his body relaxes on top of mine, where I like him the most, our bare skin pressed together.

"I love you, Gray. I loved you yesterday and the day before that and I think I'm pretty sure I loved you the night you showed up on my doorstep and convinced me to go paddle boarding. I've been insane for you ever since." His smile is so big it's contagious, and I have to pause so that I can contain my own. "I will be happy every day for the rest of my life if you're in my bed at night. If I wake up to your brown eyes looking at me every morning and have your big, beautiful heart loving me."

He swallows, threading his fingers through my hair. "I'm going to marry you one day, sunshine. Sierra Ford has a nice ring to it, don't you think?"

I grin. "Who said I would take your last name?"

His eyes widen. "I'd never make you...I know it's your parents' last name, and I would never want—"

"Gray, I'm kidding. I'd take your last name in a heartbeat. Nothing would make me happier."

"Really?"

My chest tightens, threatening to crack wide open as I feel my heart expand yet again. Gray is cocky and confident, and I love that about him, but my boyfriend can be so vulnerable at times and it's in these moments I fall even deeper in love with him.

"Of course," I murmur. "I'll always be my parents' daughter. Taking your last name will never change that. I refuse to live in the past, Gray, when I have such an exciting future to look forward to with you."

"My God," Grayson breathes. "I love you."

I have to catch my breath every time he says those three words to me.

"And I plan on showing you just how much," he says, lowering his lips to mine. The way he opens his heart to me brings me to tears and when he kisses me it tastes salty. His palm slides up and over my hip to my ribcage until his hand palms my breast, his fingers moving to pinch my nipple. "Starting with these perfect tits that fit in my hands just right."

"And what else?" I ask, licking my lips, watching as he inches his way down my body.

"And this part of you right here," he says as his fingers roam down my body to my stomach while my fingers sink into his hair. "When you wear those fucking shirts, and they show off this sexy-as-hell band of skin, it kills me. Abso-fucking-lutely destroys me."

Like he's destroying me right now.

He kisses a trail from my belly button down to my pelvis. "And this part of your body right here," he murmurs between my thighs, as I spread my legs wide for him. "I love how you are always drenched for me, and you hug my cock so tight."

He runs two fingers along my seam, soaking them, making me tremble. When he sinks them inside of me, my back arches and I swear I see stars.

My pelvis grinds down on his fingers, rolling, begging, chasing that feeling he's so good at finding, as he works his fingers in and out. My hips lift off the bed when he crooks his fingers inside of me, finding that place that makes my legs shake and my eyes roll back in my head.

"Fuck, I need to taste you," he says, bringing his fingers to his mouth, licking them clean. "You better grip the sheets in your tiny little hands and hold on. I've been starving for you."

"I... yes..." I swallow as his arms hook around my hips. I'm already bracing myself for what's to come because Grayson knows how to use his tongue.

"I'm going to show you how much I've been dying to eat you, baby." Then, without further warning, his tongue licks a slow path up the center of me, brown eyes watching me as I writhe and moan, crying out his name. One lick of his tongue is all it takes for him to show me how badly he's needed me, starved like a man who hasn't eaten in days.

"Gray... baby... more," I plead in desperation, needing the relief. This man eats me like a god. "I want more. Your tongue is the best fucking thing I've ever felt in my life."

"And it's yours whenever you want it. I'll gladly go down on you every day for the rest of my life."

I come alive at his words, rocking against his warm, slippery mouth while his tongue devours me, eating me like I'm his last meal. I plow one hand through his blond hair while I grind myself against his face, working to chase that feeling, tossing my head back against the pillow.

I'm moaning and panting, and he's licking and sucking, while his hands grip my hips, tugging my opening against his face. And when his lips seal over the bundle of nerves between my legs, I come undone, clenching like a vise around his tongue.

"Fucking hell," he curses. "You're soaking for me. So fucking perfect. I could slide into you right now and fill you up with every inch of me," he says, sitting up on his knees, dragging his hand across his mouth, stroking his hard-as-granite dick once, then twice.

He holds my gaze, crawling up the bed to me with a smile that could set the world on fire. "Tell me you love me again." He smirks against my mouth, pinning me underneath him. "I want to hear you say it again."

The stubble on his jaw tickles my skin, and I giggle as his hand tickles my side.

"Don't make me beg," he says in a low growl, his mouth buried against my neck. He knows I love it when he kisses me there.

He's found my spot—the one that makes me squirm and laugh. "Okay, okay... I love you, Gray."

He stops, pulling his face away from my jaw and catching my gaze, "I love you so goddamn much. And I'll never get tired of hearing you say it. For the record, you can tell me you love me as often as you want."

I giggle, pulling his lips down hard to mine, stealing a kiss. This man melts me into a puddle without even trying.

I'm catching my breath when he goes onto his knees between my spread legs, his hard cock eager and glistening at the tip. "You ready for me, sunshine?"

I'm already dizzy for him. "So ready."

"Good, because I'm not going to fuck you this time, I'm going to take my time, worship you, because you're all mine and there's no one else for me. Now spread those legs wide for me. Let me see how wet you are before I make love to my sunshine."

My knees drop open, and I watch his eyes drink me in. He groans, pumping his hard cock in his fist, and I can do nothing but lie here and feel the heat of his stare sear into me.

"You're so dam perfect," he murmurs, his hand fisted at the base of his dick like he's already trying to stop himself from coming. "Gorgeous."

My breath hitches when he guides himself to my entrance, pressing his arousal against me, slowly easing himself inside of me. I can't count how many times he's fucked me, but this time feels special like the first time he told me he loved me. I know I'm going to remember this night for the rest of my life.

I lift my hips, needing to feel him as deep as I can as he plunges forward until he's buried inside of me.

"You're squeezed so tight around me... you're such a good girl... you take me so good, baby." Grayson's abs flex with every rock, his hips snapping back and forth as he picks up his pace and I match him with every thrust. He groans, pulling all the way out before driving back in. Then he pulls all the way out again.

I pout, needing him back inside of me. "Gray... don't stop."

I wasn't prepared for how good it was going to be tonight—the time apart made me feral for him and I'm pretty sure he's feeling the same way.

He dips his face down to my mouth and he kisses me, his fingers gripping the column of my neck. "I will never again hide the way I feel about you, Sierra. You. Are. Mine. All fucking mine, and you will always be," he says, tightening his grip just a fraction on my neck. "My hands will be the only ones that touch you again. My name will be the only one you scream. And my cock will be the last one to make you see stars. Ever. You are mine. You belong to me forever."

"Forever." I brush my lips to his as I reach between us, gripping him in my hand, stroking him up and down until he moans my name. Then I'm lining him up with my entrance, wanting him back inside of me.

"Ohhh, God," I cry when he slides into me, not stopping until he's balls deep inside of me.

"My beautiful sunshine girl." He hikes one of my legs over his shoulder and rocks into me in short, strong thrusts. "How does it feel?"

"So good, Gray. I'm going to come."

My legs shake, my skin slick with sweat and I'm seconds away from the release I'm craving when his thumb reaches down to where we're joined together, rubbing tiny circles where I need him the most.

"Look at me, baby. I wanna watch you come all over my dick."

"My God, Grayson," I breathe as I explode all around him. "So... I... yes..."

He smirks that Grayson Ford smirk as he continues to

thrust deeper and harder inside of me until, his eyes squeeze shut, and he lets go.

His muscles tremble in pleasure as he spills inside me. When he's finished riding out his climax, he lifts his head, and his eyes find mine and he tells me again that he loves me. He doesn't even need to say the words, I can see them in his eyes, and my heart inflates. *It's Love*. I see love so perfectly in his eyes and it feels so wonderfully good.

We connected tonight like we've never done before, laying our hearts wide open for each other to see. It was hot as hell, because it's always that way with Gray, but tonight we gave one another everything.

"I'm never going to give you space again, Sierra. I can't, because if I don't have you, I have nothing." He pauses, resting his forehead against mine. "I'm going to love you forever."

Forever.

And with a tilt of his chin, his lips meet mine, and my heart soars from my body as high as the sky.

TWENTY-SIX

A LITTLE PRIVACY WOULD BE NICE.

THREE WEEKS LATER.

Grayson

"What do you put in these things, Si? These are like crack," Tuck says, unwrapping his second cranberry-lemon muffin.

I rip it from his hand before he has time to stuff it in his mouth. "I will *crack* your arm in two if you steal another. Sierra baked these for Gran and her friends, not for you to sit here and inhale them."

"Geez," he mutters, frowning at Jake. "Someone woke up on the wrong side of the bed."

"I came downstairs in my underwear to you two clowns," I grumble, looking between Tucker and Holden. "And then this guy shows up." I glower at Jake. "For some reason you fuckwads think my kitchen is an all-you-can-eat buffet."

Sierra giggles as she carefully places each muffin into a basket, out of Tuck's reach. Gran has been raving to everyone at her nursing home about Sierra's baking. She went so far as to bet the woman down the hall—who just happens to drive her *up* the wall—that Sierra's baking is better than her granddaughter's. Sierra thinks it's ridiculous,

THREE WEEKS LATER.

but she will do anything for the people she loves. Thus, this morning's batch of muffins—which will demolish the competition, in my biased opinion.

I'm not sure why I was so surprised to see Tuck and Holden here when I came downstairs this morning to grab a cup of coffee. It's not like it's the first time they've been here uninvited, looking for food. It's turned into a pretty regular routine on the weekend. They're here all the fucking time.

It's not that I don't like their company—I do—but when you have a girlfriend as hot as Sierra, there's no telling when and where I decide I need to strip her naked. And if it so happens that I want to bang her on my kitchen table on a Sunday morning, a little privacy would be nice.

Holden pours himself a cup of coffee then gives Sierra's ponytail a tug as he returns to the table. "Sierra doesn't mind feeding us. Do you, Si?"

"It's not the point," I sigh. "Maybe I would like to enjoy breakfast alone with my girlfriend."

"Ahh, I get what you're trying to say," Tucker says, waggling his brows. "You and Sierra like to get it on in the morning."

Jake's face turns the shade of a tomato. "Tuck, I will rearrange your face if you say shit like that again."

"Do you really think they're not..." Tucker makes an obscene gesture with his hands —think finger-in-hole. "They're in that honeymoon phase, when all you want to do is—"

"Fucking hell, man," Jake seethes, pushing himself up from his chair, swatting a hand at Tuck's head.

"What? I didn't *say* it. I mean, I could have said it, because we all know they go at it like rabbits." He rubs his head where Jake got him. "It was funny, though. Right?"

Sierra laughs while I shake my head, scrubbing my hand

CHAPTER TWENTY-SIX

through my hair. Luckily, I threw on a pair of shorts before finding the guys sitting in my kitchen, but apart from that I'm shirtless, sockless and could use a shower.

"Not funny to Jake, apparently," Holden murmurs under his breath, reaching for the bowl of fresh fruit that Sierra puts in front of them.

"Don't keep feeding them," I tell her, moving behind her to press a kiss to her neck. "You're just encouraging them."

"He doesn't know what he's talking about, Si. Keep it coming," Holden says with a wink. "So, what are we doing today?"

"*We* aren't doing anything today," I say as I pour milk into my coffee. "And don't you have a girlfriend? Why aren't you at her house eating *her* food?"

"Because she can't bake like Sierra can," he says. "No one can. Besides, she eats some weird shit for breakfast... chunks of avocado on toast and Kefir. I don't even know what Kefir is."

"Does anybody?" Jake mumbles.

"Holden, you can break in anytime and eat my treats."

I wrap my arms around Sierra, pulling her back into my chest. "I'm the only guy in this room who gets to eat your treats," I say, looking directly at Jake, not able to help myself. I like riling him up.

"Motherfucker," Jake fumes as I tilt my head back in laughter.

Tucker pops a blueberry into his mouth. He shakes his head at me, clearly enjoying this exchange. "You're a brave man saying shit like that."

"Ignore Gray, that wasn't a euphemism for anything," Sierra says with a tilt of her head, eyes aimed at me. "I like having you guys here."

"And I don't," I add.

THREE WEEKS LATER.

Sierra presses a kiss to my temple, patting my bare chest. "He doesn't mean it, boys," she says. "Gray, be nice to our guests."

"Yeah, Gray. Be a nice boy and pass me another muffin, will you?" Tuck says with a grin.

The room erupts in laughter. And even though it's at my expense, I laugh along with them, because the four people in my kitchen right now are my family. They mean the world to me. And when you find the people who make your life better, you hang on to them with everything you have.

"You'll miss me, Ford, if I stop bringing this pretty face over here for you to stare at," Tuck says with a stupid grin.

I snort, smacking Sierra's ass with my palm as she walks to the stove. "Not when I have this brown-eyed blonde to stare at."

"We've been replaced, Tuck. Face it," Holden chimes in, flipping his napkin onto his empty plate.

Tucker frowns. "I never thought the day would come."

I shake my head and make a mental note to change the locks on my door.

Tucker and Holden are still cracking jokes at the table when I look over at Sierra leaning against the counter with a steaming cup of tea in her hand. I watch her until I catch her eye, then blow her a kiss.

She laughs, rolling her eyes. She loves it when I do cheesy shit like that, even though she'll never admit it.

"We better get going," Tucker says, getting up from his seat and taking his plate and coffee cup to the sink. "Grayson's got *the look* in his eye. He wants to take Sierra to the bone zone."

"I hate all of you motherfuckers," Jake grumbles. "I don't know why I ever said this guy could date my sister."

"It wouldn't have mattered if you didn't. I've got it bad for

CHAPTER TWENTY-SIX

your sister. I would have dated her anyways whether you liked it or not. Nothing could have stopped me."

"You're just lucky I let you live. Remember that." Jake side-eyes me as he passes me on his way to the sink with his dishes.

"Noted," I say, tapping my skull like a cheeky fucker.

Jake follows Tucker and Holden to the door with me hot on their heels, itching to get them out of here and get my girlfriend alone.

"We're brothers now," I tell Jake, clapping him on the shoulder before he's out the door. "One big happy family. I know you love me."

"You need to marry my sister before that can happen and even then, I'll never agree to it."

"Aw, come on, big guy," I say with a grin, and I swear I can see his pulse tick behind his temple.

"Don't make me hurt you."

The three of them finally leave, and I can't shut the door behind them fast enough.

I FIND Sierra in the bathroom, turning on the shower. She's naked and she looks like a dream. She always does, whether she's in shorts and an old T-shirt covered in paint, a fitted black skirt and four-inch heels or tights and an oversized sweater. But right now, seeing her naked with her golden hair spilling over her shoulders, I'm having a hard time keeping my hands to myself.

It's been three weeks since our relationship has been public knowledge. We were forced out of our little bubble, but we picked up right where we left off, except now it's so much better.

THREE WEEKS LATER.

We go back and forth between both of our houses. Some mornings I wake her up with a cup of peppermint tea, and other mornings she brings me freshly baked muffins, or my new favorite breakfast, egg-in-a-hole. And if I'm really lucky, she wakes me up with her face between my legs and her pouty lips wrapped around my cock.

She has become my whole world, and never in my wildest dreams would I have thought that it was possible to be this happy.

"We should probably shower together," I suggest, pressing my lips to Sierra's bare shoulder, my fingers tracing every groove of her spine.

Sierra opens the shower door and slips under the hot spray of water. "You should know by now that I'm expecting you to follow," she says over her shoulder.

I stifle a groan. "I will follow you wherever you go, for the rest of your life." I tear my T-shirt over my head and peel off my shorts and briefs, then follow her into the shower.

My eyes drift over her perfect round ass, landing on the two dimples right above it that I want to kiss every time I strip her naked. "You're fucking gorgeous."

"Mmm," she moans, pushing her ass into my hardening cock that's already aching to be inside of her. But he'll have to wait. I'm taking my time this morning.

My hands slide slowly up her back to her shoulders then drift to her hair, gripping a handful in my fist.

Her chin tips up to the ceiling when I jerk the fistful of her hair back towards the floor, and I watch the stream of water pour down over her exposed neck to her tits. With my cheek on her shoulder, I breathe in her scent, the smell of coconuts and summer, kissing my way up her neck.

I take a minute to admire her: ample tits, nipples a dusty

rose, flat stomach, long legs. Then I reach for her body wash and soap her up, head to toe.

When I'm done, Sierra turns to face me and lets her eyes sweep over me in a slow, heated gaze as I rub the body wash over my own wet skin.

"I want to fuck you in this shower so if you could please put your hands on the wall and stick out that ass of yours?"

"Only because you said please." She smirks, turning to face the wall.

Her hands move to the tile on either side of her face as she rises to her toes, tipping her ass up as high as it can go. *Fuck me.*

This girl is mine. She's all mine and I never plan on letting her go. My skin tingles in anticipation, my dick screaming, knowing how good it feels to be seven inches deep inside of this woman. I want this feeling with her to last forever, and I tell her that as I sink inside of her.

And then I fuck her so good she doesn't remember her own name.

SIERRA

JAKE, Grayson and I walk into the multipurpose room where Gran is sitting at a table with five of her friends. She looks happy and maybe a little smug. Jake elbows me in my side and mumbles under his breath, "You better take this chick down with those muffins, Si. Gran is here to win."

"She looks like she's Rocky Balboa in that scene where he finally knocks out the Russian guy, Drago," Grayson adds in a low voice.

THREE WEEKS LATER.

"Oh shit, that was good. I rewound that part at least 15 times."

My boyfriend and my brother have officially lost their minds.

Grayson waltzes down the narrow hall to the right of me, his stride confident, his shoulders square, sucking up all the oxygen in the room. The silver-haired ladies take notice—how could they not? They're ogling him shamelessly. He's already worked his magic on them too. Grayson Ford is sex on a stick.

"You ladies ready to taste the best damn muffins in the world?" Grayson asks when we reach Gran and her friends. Gran beams while the other women stare wide-eyed at Grayson and Jake, jaws slack.

Grayson may be slightly biased, but it turns out he was right. The vote an hour later is unanimous when they declare my baking the winner.

Once Gran is finished rubbing my win into the other woman's face— I finally had to stop her—she invites us up to her suite.

"I have something for the two of you," she says to Jake and me, motioning for us to take a seat on the little patio. Grayson hangs back in the living room, sensing that Gran wants a moment with her grandchildren.

"I wanted to give this to you both today, and not when I'm gone." She hands us each an envelope. "You two have been the greatest gifts in the world, besides your mother. She was something special, my dream come true," she sniffs as her eyes turn glassy. I swallow the knot in my throat. "But the two of you saved me when I had no hope. Without you both, I'm not sure how I would have been able to go on."

"Gran, don't say that. We love you," I tell her, as Jake moves to rest a hand on her shoulder.

CHAPTER TWENTY-SIX

"Go on and open them," she says with a nod and a gentle smile.

Wiping my eyes, I tear the envelope open, curious as to what could possibly be inside. And when I see a cheque made out in my name for $50,000, I freeze.

I stare at the piece of paper in my hand in total disbelief.

"The money is yours. Do what you want with it. I know whatever you use it for, you'll make me proud. Both of you always have."

"Gran..." I whisper. Tears blur my vision. "I can't... this is too much."

"I want you both to have it. It's not up for negotiation. You both deserve it." She nods, as if to say it's settled. "I love you, kids."

"I don't know what to say," Jake gasps, standing to give Gran a long hug, thanking her for the years she had to put up with him, for the years she loved him back to himself.

The emotion in Jake's voice sends the first tear down my cheek. Watching my stoic, always-in-control, six-foot-something brother barely keeping it together hits me like ton of bricks.

I give Gran's hand a squeeze, "You are the best thing to ever happen to Jake and me. You took us in without question. You raised us like your own. We will always love you for that."

There is so much more I want to say to her, but I know I won't be able to get the words out without sobbing like a baby. Instead, I make a promise to myself to do something with the money that will make her proud.

I think I have a good idea.

TWENTY-SEVEN

THE SECRET CRUSH WHO SHALL REMAIN NAMELESS.

Grayson

It's Sunday morning, which means mountain biking with the boys.

Jake is leading the way down the hill, with Beckett, Tucker and I close behind him and Holden at the back. Our cheeks are flush from the cooler fall weather.

I'm fucking happy. I snuck out of the house with Sierra asleep in my bed and when I'm finished with the ride, I'm picking her up and taking her out to Catch 21, Reed Point's nicest restaurant, because I'm still not done showing her off.

"Damn, that felt good," Tucker says, whipping off his helmet when we all reach the bottom of the mountain. "Gray even kept up this time. I guess getting his dick wet on the reg is good for his mojo."

"What the actual fuck?" Jake punches him in the arm.

"What the fuck *is* a mojo anyways?" Holden asks. "I knew a cat named Mojo once."

We all stare at him. "We're not talking about a fucking cat, dumbo," I groan. "Mojo is what attracts people to you.

Your charm, your power, your magic. Look it up in the dictionary and you'll see a picture of me."

"You're an idiot, Ford. I have no idea how you landed Sierra." Holden shakes his head.

"It's because I know how to make her feel good with my wonder dick." I say, ready to get punched in the nuts.

I glance at Jake, who missed the fucking joke, dammit. He has his phone propped up against his handlebars, furiously typing.

"You talking to the girl?" I ask. "The secret crush who shall remain nameless?"

"She has a name," Jake grumbles.

"Not one that you've bothered to share with us."

"Her name is Everly. Happy now?"

"Delighted," I deadpan.

"Maybe Jake is the next to settle down," Beckett adds. "We're dropping like flies. First me, now Gray. Love is in the air in Reed Point, boys."

"And on that note, I'm out," Tuck says, "Great ride."

"I think we're all out," Beckett adds with a nod, cycling towards his car.

Before Jake gets his foot on his pedal, I stop him. "Can I talk to you for a sec?"

He frowns. "Am I going to want to hear what you have to say?"

"I guess we're about to find out." I reply. "This could go one of two ways."

He follows me to where we've parked and after loading our bikes in the back and stripping off our jackets, he meets me behind my truck.

I inhale a breath. "I normally would be asking your dad this question, but since I can't, I'm asking you." I swallow, hoping like hell this goes okay. "I'm asking you because you're the guy who's been there for Sierra, all of her life, and done a damn good job of taking care of her."

Jake's eyes sweep to the gravel under his feet, and he scuffs the toe of his runner through the crushed-up rocks. "What are you asking, Gray?"

"I'm asking," I grin. "I want to marry your sister. I want her mine in every way possible."

He scrubs his hand through his sweat-soaked hair. "Man, you're really sure about this, aren't you?"

"I've never been more sure about anything else in my life." I shrug. "I don't want to wait. I don't see the point. Why postpone the inevitable?"

He takes a moment before reaching out his hand to me. "You've got my blessing, Gray. I know how happy you make her."

I shake his hand and he pulls me in for a hug, slapping my shoulder. "I'm happy for you. Just don't make this moment all cheesy like you do with your *we're family now* crap. You know I hate that shit."

A deep laugh tilts my head back. I'm smiling so hard my cheeks ache. "But we *are* going to be family now, bro. Admit it, it's pretty fucking cool."

"Whatever," he mutters, rolling his eyes as he heads for his truck.

SIERRA

THE ONLY THING better than sleeping in on a Sunday is waking up to Grayson—all six-foot-one of him, his warm, naked body wrapped around me like a blanket.

I raise my head from where it's resting on Grayson's pec

to check the time on the clock on the nightstand. Nine-thirty in the morning. I could slip out of his arms and tip toe down to the kitchen to make breakfast or I could stay here for a little while longer. I nestle into his chest, deciding he feels too good.

He blinks awake a few minutes later. "Morning," he whispers, his voice raspy with sleep.

"Morning," I say, sitting up and slipping out of his hold when he stretches his arms towards the headboard.

"Where are you going?" he says, snagging my wrist in his hand.

"I'm going to make you breakfast. How do you feel about strawberry crepes?"

"Not today, my beautiful girl. I have other plans for you."

He kisses the tip of my nose and slips out of bed, finding his boxer briefs on the floor.

"Where are you going?" I ask, watching him step into his underwear, not missing a second of this. Gray is always a feast for the eyes.

"To run you a bath."

My brows scrunch together, but I smile as I listen to him humming as he turns on the bathtub faucet. I pad across the hall, leaning against the door frame as I watch Grayson pour my favourite lavender bath salts into the hot water. When he turns around and sees me standing there, a secretive look flashes in his eyes.

"Come here. Lift up your arms."

I do as he says, walking towards him, raising my arms to the ceiling as he gently lifts my tank top over my head. His thumbs hook under the band of my thong next, slipping it to the floor. He orders me into the tub, and I follow his instructions. I love it when Grayson is bossy.

"Relax. Take your time and when you're dressed come find me," he says before bending down for a lingering kiss.

I relax deeper into the hot water, closing my eyes. A blissful half hour passes before I step out of the tub, towel off and get dressed. I wander through the quiet house to the kitchen but Gray's not there. I call his name, moving from room to room, but he's nowhere to be found.

Opening the front door, I check for his truck, which is still parked behind mine. *Weird.*

But then I notice him on the beach, the ocean behind him like a painting. An unexpected burst of emotion hits me. This little street is my home, the ocean the picture-perfect backdrop. And the man I love more than anything else in the world is standing in front of me, 50 feet away.

Grayson waits patiently with his hands stuffed in his jean pockets as I walk to meet him, the hem of his jeans rolled up to his ankles, a hoodie keeping him warm. I breathe in the salt air, enjoy the now-familiar feeling of the morning ocean breeze against my skin. The smell of salt and fall air fills my nostrils.

"Hi," I say when I reach him, noticing for the first time the blanket and picnic basket at his feet. "Breakfast on the beach?" I can see the neck of a champagne bottle sticking out of the basket.

"Something like that," he says, and when I turn to look at him my eyes go wide, and I press a hand over my mouth.

Grayson is down on one knee.

Is this for real?

Oh my God. I think this is happening.

"Gray, baby. What are you doing?" He reaches for my hand which is trembling like a leaf. "Are you really... Oh my gosh, this is really it."

He laughs, ignoring my blabbering, and smiles back up at me. "Sunshine girl…"

His beautiful face blurs before me as tears pool in my eyes. He gazes down at me with his deep brown eyes.

"You are mine," he begins, and already my heart is racing, my pulse hammering under my skin. It's almost more than I can bear.

He drops my hand and reaches into his pocket to pull out a tiny velvet box. He snaps open the top, revealing an oval shape diamond on a dainty platinum band. It's the most beautiful thing I've ever seen. I'm speechless.

"I've known I've wanted to spend all my days and nights with you since the first day I saw you. The rhythm of my heart changed that weekend we met in Miami. Every time you smile my heart beats triple time in my chest. When you laugh, my heart hammers against my ribs. And when your big brown eyes find mine, I swear it stops beating all together. I tried to stay away from you. Hell, I tried to forget you all together after that night in Miami. But I couldn't forget your smile, the way you made me feel. I've always been powerless when it comes to you."

He squeezes my hand. "I never saw you coming, Sierra, but I've never been the same since meeting you. Let me take care of you for the rest of your life because I promise you, sunshine, no one will do it better than me."

"Gray—"

"I want all of you. All of your Friday nights and every one of your Sunday mornings. I want babies, a dog, I want it all." He pauses, a frown crossing his face. His dark eyes pierce mine, holding me captive. "Why have we never talked about this? You want babies, right?"

"We can start trying tonight," I answer quickly with tears streaming down my cheeks.

He laughs, then closes his eyes for a moment and takes a deep breath. "What we have is fate. You're the girl I want to love for the rest of my life. You are my every dream come true. And God, how I wish I could have asked your dad for his blessing to marry his daughter, but instead I asked Jake. So... marry me, Sierra. Make me the happiest man on the planet."

My eyes blur with unshed tears. He's on his knee, gazing up at me with those eyes and asking me for forever.

"Yes," I blurt out. "Yes, of course I'll marry you." He slips the ring on my finger, and it fits like it was made just for me. I lean over, kissing him, falling into his lap. "I love you so much, Gray."

With gentle hands, his thumbs wipe the tears from my stained cheeks. "I love you more."

This is it. I've found the one.

I've found my forever.

I'm going to be Grayson Ford's wife.

I could die of happiness right here on this beach. Warmth fills my chest and that feeling that I get whenever I'm in Grayson's arms unravels me.

It turns out coming back home was one good move.

I can't wait to see what happens next.

EPILOGUE

BUTTERCUP DREAMS. SIX MONTHS LATER.

S ierra

"Why is it a bazillion degrees in here?" I ask Gray, as I fan my face with my hand.

"The air conditioning is blasting, baby. It's not that hot."

I think it's just nerves.

I blow out a breath, checking the clock on the wall for the 100th time, smoothing my dress over my hips. Guests are arriving in 10 minutes. *Breathe, Sierra. Inhale. Exhale. Everything looks perfect.*

Today has been a whirlwind, coordinating party rentals, and flower deliveries and making sure everything is just perfect. Not to mention staying up all hours for the past couple of nights, frantically making sure there are enough treats for everyone to eat. It's not every day a dream you've had since you were nine years old comes true. Today needs to be one for the books.

I move the three-tier cake I made a little to the left because...well... I don't know... then I fiddle with the balloons because... again, I don't know. I need to keep myself busy, so I don't lose my mind. Just as I'm about to start poking at the flowers from Bloom that were delivered today, Grayson sweeps me into his side with a knowing smile.

"Come here, sunshine. It's going to be great. Don't worry about a thing." He pulls me into his chest, pressing a kiss to my temple.

"I love you."

"I know. I love you too."

Tonight, I open the doors of Buttercup Bakery to friends and family, and tomorrow its doors will open to the rest of Reed Point. I can hardly believe it's really happening.

Grayson talked me into a grand opening party and I'm so glad he did. Sharing this milestone with the people who have supported me and helped to get my little bakery up and running makes it even more meaningful to me. Every one of the guys—Jake, Tucker, Holden, and Beckett—have been here helping me out as often as they can. And decorating the space? I have Jules to thank for that.

It looks *perfect*. The walls are painted the faintest shade of pink, the counter white with glass shelves to display my cupcakes, cookies and other treats. On the wall at the back of the shop is a neon sign that reads *Buttercup Dreams*.

Not long after Gran gave me the money, I made an appointment at the bank and it turned out that with her gift and my own savings, starting a small business was within my reach. I started looking for bakery locations right away. As luck would have it, Grayson found a small space up for lease. It was a coffee shop with a small industrial kitchen just down the street from Bloom, the flower shop owned by Olivia and Ellie, Jules' sisters-in-law. As soon as we had the keys in hand, we got to work painting and decorating, transforming the 1,700-square-foot space into the bakery of my

ONE GOOD MOVE

dreams. I named my business-baby Buttercup Bakery, in honor of my mom.

A lump forms in my throat when I think of how proud my parents would be. It's days like today that I miss them so much it physically hurts. Thank goodness for Jake. Having my brother here to share this moment means everything to me. And of course, Gray has been by my side every step of the way. Between helping out with my house renovations for months and now the bakery, I'm pretty sure he is qualified to be a professional painter at this point. But he hasn't complained once. I know that my parents would have absolutely adored him.

My eyes rake over my fiancé. *Damn, he looks good.* Gray is wearing perfectly tailored grey dress pants with a crisp white button-up, the sleeves rolled up to his elbows. The top two buttons are unbuttoned, and his blond hair is freshly cut and styled, the day or two of stubble on his jaw just the way I like it.

My God, he's beautiful.

My breath hitches in my throat.

A lot has happened in the six months since Grayson proposed to me. I moved in with him two weeks later and we really haven't been apart since. I've always heard that the first year of living together is the hardest, but we developed a rhythm quickly and things just seemed to fall into place.

It's probably because neither one of us can stand to be away from one another. It's just the way we are—happiest together.

I blink when the bell on the door chimes and Grayson's mom and dad walk in, his sister Kyla on their heels.

Grayson moves to greet them, pulling his sister and his mom in for hugs and then shaking his dad's hand. He and his father have really been working on their relationship.

Yeah, it's not always easy, but for the first time in a long time, Grayson feels like he has his father in his life again. His dad has been clean now for almost two years, and he has apologized for the years of being absent and promised that this time it will be different. For Gray's sake, I'm hoping that turns out to be true. We make sure to go over and visit them once a week for dinner, and even though anxiety will sometimes still eat at Grayson on our drive over, it's an emotion that he's learned to deal with.

"Wow. The place looks unreal, Si," Tucker says a second after walking inside, kissing my cheek.

"I owe you, Tuck. You know I couldn't have done it without you and the guys," I say, squeezing his bicep.

"Anything for our favorite baker. Besides, you can pay me back in food," he says with a wink, snagging a cupcake from the platter on the counter. "This one has my name written all over it."

Jules finds me next, throwing her arms around me as soon as she walks through the door. "It's happening, Si! I'm beyond proud. You made your dreams come true."

Hugging her back, I squeeze my eyes shut. "I know. I can't believe it. I just wish my mom and dad were here to see it."

"I know, babe," Jules whispers into my hair. "But I know they're up there watching you with the biggest smiles on their faces."

As Jules pulls back from the embrace, I take a step behind the counter and survey the room with happy tears in my eyes. All around me, the bakery is full of family and friends here to celebrate me. Holden and Aubrey are chatting with Tuck and Gran. Gray is with his sister, laughing at whatever story Beck is telling. And then there's Jake, who is standing next to a beautiful brunette and listening with rapt attention to the sweetest little girl with strawberry blonde pigtails. Her name is Birdie, and I am crazy about her. Today she is wearing a cat ear headband and a pair of glittering fairy wings. Grayson has already had to tear me away from her twice.

"Your brother looks like a natural," Jules says, leaning against the counter and looking over at the little girl licking pink buttercream icing off her cupcake.

"It's funny, but it's true. He really does," I say, absent-mindedly twirling my engagement ring around on my finger. The minute my brother asked if he could bring two guests to the party, I knew who he meant. I didn't bother hiding my excitement either when he told me he was bringing Everly and her daughter. I'm pretty sure I screamed.

"Maybe she's the one," I say to Jules. "You never know. It's funny how life works."

"You and I know that better than anyone," she agrees as Grayson arrives with two flutes of champagne, passing one to each of us.

Grayson clears his throat and then gently clinks a knife against the champagne glass he's holding, gathering the crowd's attention.

"We're all here today to celebrate this gorgeous woman beside me," he starts. Someone whistles. Tucker calls out, "I love you, Si." The whole room erupts in laughter.

Grayson clears his throat. "Sierra is incredible. She was born to bake," he says, reaching for my hand, locking his eyes with mine. "You work tirelessly. You've taught all of us here today that you can achieve anything you want if you put your mind to it. For the past six months, I've watched you chase your dream and I'm so proud to be standing here next to you to watch you achieve it."

He smiles at me. I drink him in. He has forever in his eyes. Mine say *I'm yours.*

"Sierra, you're an inspiration. Smart, resilient, and bright like the sun." He continues as I blush, soaking in his compliments while noticing that many of the ladies in the room are looking on with lovesick expressions. God, Gray really could charm birds out of trees.

"And I'm going to marry the hell out of you now that Buttercup Bakery is officially open."

The crowd cheers. He smirks, always cocky, happy in the spotlight. My stomach does a cartwheel. Cocky Grayson turns me all the way on. If I look at him for five more seconds, there's a chance I'll get pregnant.

But first things first. Grayson has asked me to set a date for the wedding every week since proposing and now that the bakery is up and running—almost—I know I'm ready to become Mrs. Ford. He is mine until the day I die.

I can't help but smile thinking about where Grayson and I started and where we are now. Three years ago, we met in Miami. It was a chance encounter that I ran from, knowing that if I stayed a minute longer, I would never want to let him go. And now here we are, starting a life together that is better than either of us could ever have dreamed of.

I lean into him a little closer, exhaling a breath as Grayson pulls me close to his side. I'm this man's girl forever and I will spend the rest of my life showing him how much I love him.

GRAYSON

. . .

ONE GOOD MOVE

"LEAVE some for the rest of us, fuckstick," Holden says, watching Tuck stuff a mini cupcake into his mouth.

"Waat," Tuck shrugs, his mouth full of cake.

"Leave some for the rest of Si's guests," Holden says again, shoving a napkin at Tucker's chest. "And tomorrow morning, when you can't ride worth shit because your stomach hates you, I'm not going to be the one towing your ass up the mountain."

Tucker smirks, then snatches another vanilla cupcake from the table before saying, "Man, you talk like we're 60 years old. I'm not even 30. I'm at the literal peak of physical health. Look at me, I'm fucking unstoppable."

He shoves the whole cupcake into his mouth, staring at Holden the entire time. I can't help but laugh.

"Yeah, right," Beckett says with a laugh, rolling his eyes. "We're definitely towing this guy tomorrow."

My eyes drift over to Sierra. I've barely been able to look at anything else all evening.

Her dress is ridiculously sexy: Emerald green and backless, with two thin, criss-crossed straps, a long, flowy skirt that dusts the floor. Her hair cascades down her back in loose waves, and she looks like a damn supermodel. She blows my mind.

Being here today, celebrating Sierra with our family and friends, is surreal. Never in a million years could I have imagined being engaged to the woman of my dreams. Sierra is beautiful and talented and so far out of my league it isn't even funny. I don't deserve her, but I'm not going to be the one to point that out to her. I'm going to just stay right where I am, sipping champagne while Sierra effortlessly works the room. I'm so fucking proud of her.

I watch as she crosses the room to where my parents are standing, making sure they are feeling welcome and comfortable. It means a lot to me that they're here tonight. It's important to Sierra too; she has adopted my mom as her own over the past six months. Sometimes it feels like it's me against the two of them; they both love to give me the gears. And that's just fine with me, because my mom has become someone who Sierra can talk to. When Sierra finally told her that her parents had died in a fire, my mom held her hand and listened with tears in her eyes. She told Sierra she was family now and that she'd be there for her whenever she needed anything.

My dad has been clean now for almost two years. His addictions took a toll on me for a very long time. Those years were dark. I was angry, scared, and resentful, never knowing what to expect. My heart felt closed off to him, but we are on much more solid ground now. We've worked hard at our relationship. I won't let my past upset my future, not when I'm this happy with my dream girl by my side.

Sierra quit her job at The Seaside to focus on Buttercup Bakery. There were tears and a big farewell party at Catch 21. As for me, work is as busy as ever with The Liberty still sitting *just* behind The Seaside. Hopefully not for long, though. I still have hope I'll be sipping those Aperol Spritzes with Beckett in Italy someday soon. As for Blair? She won't be invited. Beckett had her transferred out of state, and she's never showed her face again.

Jake claps me on the shoulder, bringing me pack to the present.

"She's cute as hell, man," I tell him, nodding towards Birdie, who is showing Jules and Sierra her cat purse.

"She's a good kid," Jake says fondly. "Somehow I'm already attached."

"Things seem serious," I say, careful not to push.

He rubs the back of his neck, his shoulders sagging.

"There's a whole lot more involved than just me and her mom liking each other. What do I know about dating someone with a kid? We've only known each other for 8 months. I'm sure I'll fuck it up."

"You won't fuck anything up," I say, glancing at Everly and Birdie. "Just follow your heart, bro."

"Not this again," Jake says, elbowing me in my side. "For fuck's sake, cut the brother crap."

There's no time for a cheeky comeback because my gaze finds Sierra crossing the room towards me, a sexy sway in her hips. She's smiling from ear to ear, but behind that smile I can see the exhaustion in her eyes.

She did it. She has had this dream since she was a little girl, and now it's a reality. I hug her tightly, emotion getting the best of me as I realize yet again just how far gone I am for her. This girl hung the damn moon. A love like hers is once in a lifetime.

I brush my lips against her hair.

She's my world.

And she's mine to keep.

I pull her into my chest. "Today was incredible. You're incredible. But I can't wait to take you home and run you a bath."

Sierra rises on her toes, pressing a kiss to my mouth, and I taste the champagne she's been sipping on all day. She drags the kiss out until she's nibbling on my bottom lip while I fight to remain in control, so my dick doesn't get hard. I'm already sporting a semi. "I like the sound of that. My feet are aching."

I kiss her again and give her a squeeze before letting her go. "We need to take a picture."

"Gray, we've taken a thousand already."

"Then what's one more?" I shrug with a smile. The night

is almost over, the party has emptied out now—with the exception of our friends, who have stuck around to help Sierra with the clean-up.

"Hey everyone, let's take a group shot before we lock up for the night," I call to them. "Everyone in front of the counter."

Tucker crowds in next to Holden and Aubrey, while Jake, Everly and Birdie move to stand on the other side of them. Jules and Beckett squeeze in and everyone makes a little room for Sierra to stand in the center. I hold my phone up high in front of me and snap a bunch of photos.

It's only fitting to capture this special night with the people who have been with Sierra and I every step of the way. I scroll through the pictures, my eyes settling on Sierra in the middle of all our friends. The love I have for this girl is never-ending, and the life I have with her is worlds away from my life before I met her, but with every passing day I feel even more certain that it's the life I'm meant to live. With Sierra.

When the bakery is spotless, our friends say goodbye and head home. Sierra turns off the lights in her brand-new bakery and locks the door behind us.

We walk to my truck together and I open the door for her. With one foot on the running board, I pull her back into my chest before she can slide into the passenger seat. "You did it, sunshine. You made your dream come true. I'm proud of you."

She's looking at me like she's mine, and damn rights she is. She will be until the day I die. I fold her into my arms, and I count my lucky stars.

"I love you."

"I love you too," I say, my lips brushing hers. "After your bath do you wanna fuck like wild animals tonight?"

She laughs against my lips. "You have a way with words, Gray," she says, her pillowy lips stealing another kiss. "And the answer is always yes. I never stand a chance when it comes to you."

THE END

CURIOUS ABOUT JAKE? You should be... broody, possessive with the filthiest mouth. He's up next! Read his reverse age gap, single mom, extra spicy HEA NOW! Play For Keeps

AND FOR BOOK news and for where you can find Lily, follow her here and make sure to sign up for her newsletter:

WWW.AUTHORLILYMILLER.COM

ACKNOWLEDGMENTS

The list is long, but I'll do my best to keep things short and extra sweet.

To my readers—those who have been with me from the beginning and those who have just discovered my love of small-town steam—thank you for picking up my books. Thank you for supporting my dream of writing happily-ever-afters. Your continued excitement and passion for my books inspires me to keep dreaming up spicy stories. I hope you know how much I love you all.

To my editor and friend of over 20 years, Carolyn, for bringing my stories to life. There is no one on this planet I'd rather do this with. Your wit and humor and eye for detail turn my stories into so much more. I love you and don't plan on letting you go. Ever. We're doing this together forever.

To my ARC readers and the many bookstagrammers who I've fallen in friendship-love with, I will always be grateful for every post, mention, comment and reel. I hope you know how much you all mean to me. I couldn't get my books out to the world without you. A special shout-out to my girl gang Indie Author Love on Insta for having my back, shouting my name from the rooftops and giving me honest feedback when I need it the most.

To my cover designer Kim Wilson, for knocking my covers out of the park every time. You are patient and kind, and you don't stop until I'm screaming on the other end of the call hysterically that this is it! I'm the luckiest to work with you.

To Rebecca Crawford of Bare Moments Photography for answering my email after I stalked her Pinterest page. The image you captured for my couple cover is beyond beautiful and I'm not sure what I would have done if you had said no. You are not only an incredible photographer, but you are sweet and kind and your enthusiasm over this cover made the process so much fun.

To Sami and Alex, thank you for allowing me to use your image for my cover photo. That green dress, the way Alex is kissing you and the embrace are chef's kiss. Congratulations on your own happily-ever-after!

To Ellie of Love Notes PR, for introducing *One Good Move* to the world! So thankful for the book hype.

To Emily Silver, Alexandra Hale, Nicole Dixon and Mickey Miller for keeping me sane during the writing process, keeping me on track and keeping me motivated—you are the best hype-squad a girl could ask for.

To my girls, my other hype squad, who had to listen to me go on and on about Grayson and Sierra for months. Brandee, Erin, Carmen, Leah and Mary, you are among my favorite people in the world, my chosen sisters, and if it wasn't for you, I'm not sure I'd be sane. I love you all infinitely.

To my family, thank you for allowing me the space I need to tell stories. For *hardly* complaining when I lock myself away to write or forget to feed you because I'm lost in Reed Point. You mean everything to me, and I could never do all of this without your support. I love you more than a lifetime.

Lily xo

ALSO BY LILY MILLER

THE BENNETT FAMILY SERIES

Always Been You

Had to Be You

Heart Set on You

Crazy Over You

Printed in Great Britain
by Amazon